"This isn't Deathlands! Where in nukin' hell are we?"

J.B. stared up at the wall-to-wall buildings as if he'd never seen the like.

Ryan didn't seem to notice the Armorer's distress. He took stock of their surroundings, realizing that the companions had been there before, in the future, amid ashes and ruin. He focused his attention on the traffic, looking from one license plate to another.

"What year is this?" he asked Veronica.

"It's 2001."

Doc groaned. "We have jumped back in time."

"You're from the future?"

Ryan ignored her question. "What month is it? What day?"

"It's January 19," Veronica replied. "Why, do you have somewhere more important to be?"

"Any place but here and now would be just fine," Ryan told her. "The world ends tomorrow at noon."

Other titles in the Deathlands saga:

JAMES AXLER
DEATHLANDS®
END DAY

A GOLD EAGLE BOOK FROM
W❂RLDWIDE®

TORONTO • NEW YORK • LONDON
AMSTERDAM • PARIS • SYDNEY • HAMBURG
STOCKHOLM • ATHENS • TOKYO • MILAN
MADRID • WARSAW • BUDAPEST • AUCKLAND

Recycling programs
for this product may
not exist in your area.

First edition March 2015

ISBN-13: 978-0-373-62631-1

Special thanks and acknowledgment to
Alan Philipson for his contribution to this work.

End Day

The time is out of joint—O cursèd spite,
That ever I was born to set it right!
—William Shakespeare,
Hamlet

THE DEATHLANDS SAGA

This world is their legacy, a world born in the violent nuclear spasm of 2001 that was the bitter outcome of a struggle for global dominance.

There is no real escape from this shockscape where life always hangs in the balance, vulnerable to newly demonic nature, barbarism, lawlessness.

But they are the warrior survivalists, and they endure—in the way of the lion, the hawk and the tiger, true to nature's heart despite its ruination.

Ryan Cawdor: The privileged son of an East Coast baron. Acquainted with betrayal from a tender age, he is a master of the hard realities.

Krysty Wroth: Harmony ville's own Titian-haired beauty, a woman with the strength of tempered steel. Her premonitions and Gaia powers have been fostered by her Mother Sonja.

J. B. Dix, the Armorer: Weapons master and Ryan's close ally, he, too, honed his skills traversing the Deathlands with the legendary Trader.

Doctor Theophilus Tanner: Torn from his family and a gentler life in 1896, Doc has been thrown into a future he couldn't have imagined.

Dr. Mildred Wyeth: Her father was killed by the Ku Klux Klan, but her fate is not much lighter. Restored from pre-dark cryogenic suspension, she brings twentieth-century healing skills to a nightmare.

Jak Lauren: A true child of the wastelands, reared on adversity, loss and danger, the albino teenager is a fierce fighter and loyal friend.

Dean Cawdor: Ryan's young son by Sharona accepts the only world he knows, and yet he is the seedling bearing the promise of tomorrow.

In a world where all was lost, they are humanity's last hope…

Prologue

Ryan Cawdor peered through the 2.5x telescopic sight of his Steyr Scout Tactical, index finger resting against the longblaster's trigger guard. Behind the scope's center post, through the heat shimmer rising off the desert floor, he tracked the five-wag convoy rattling over dirt the color of rust, down a string-straight track between clumps of dry sagebrush and scattered sentinels of saguaro.

At his side J. B. Dix said, "Got a shot on the nukin' bucket of bolts?"

Ryan didn't answer. The two wags in the lead, a camouflage-painted SUV and a three-quarter-ton, black-primered pickup, sporting a cabover-mounted machine blaster, raised billowing clouds of dust. If the patterns of the past held, Magus was lounging in the third wag—a big, steel-plate-armored Winnie. The half-human, half-machine monster liked to ride in style, with room to keep spare parts and unspeakable experiments close to hand. Although the drop-down, bulletproof metal shutters on the side windows were raised, a coating of orange dust obscured the view through the glass.

Even if he'd had a target, Ryan wouldn't have fired. With the Winnie in motion and bouncing over rough terrain, the odds of scoring a hit, let alone a clean kill, were too long. And to open fire would have revealed the companions' presence to an enemy force they had reckoned was at least thirty-five to their seven.

The issue was more than just superior numbers.

Steel Eyes's enforcers, which looked like bipedal crosses between carnivorous dinosaurs and bulls, weren't actually blasterproof but, thanks to a horny, knobby hide two inches thick and bone like reinforced concrete, the squat three-hundred-pounders came damn close to it; in fact, none of the companions had ever seen one downed by a bullet—or a dozen bullets. In a previous encounter, on Magus's remote gladiator island, they had learned the only way to chill the enforcers was by fire. When the temperature of their copious sweat—a potent secretion that smelled like a combination of ammonia, ether and acetone—was raised to ignition point, they turned into living candles, or more accurately, living blowtorches.

The empty socket under Ryan's eye patch itched, but he didn't scratch it. With the sun baking his shoulders and back through his worn black T-shirt, he watched the convoy rumble across the plain, heading for the barren mountains in the eastern distance. When he found himself looking at the rear of the last wag in line, he pulled back from the notch between sandstone boulders, stood up, and slung the Steyr.

"What now, lover?" Krysty Wroth asked.

A layer of desert dust had dulled her usually radiant red prehensile hair; her clothes and high boots were coated with grime. Perspiration mixed with rusty dirt smeared her forehead. The other companions were likewise tinted orange. Doc, Jak, Mildred, Ricky and

J.B. looked as if they had just risen from shallow desert graves.

Ryan knew there would be no graves for any of them if they lost the battle ahead; and the dying when it came would be triple hard. Gutted, disemboweled and torn limb from limb, their remains would be scattered across the hardpan, fought over by mutie coyotes, buzzards and pincer-jawed scagworms.

"We follow the convoy at a safe distance until the bastards stop to make camp," he said. "Wait until they're all settled in, nice and cozy, then we use frag grens to disable the wags, stun the enforcers and chill any sec men. Mop up the enforcers with the incendies."

They'd found the cache of AN-M14 TH3 grens among the corpses of a band of coldheart scavengers after a disagreement turned into a gun battle in the hills of New Mex. The nine scavengers wanted to trade some of their predark treasures for a no-holds-barred, romantic overnight with Krysty and Mildred. When they wouldn't take no for an answer, they took a crisp volley of lead instead. The incendie grens didn't explode, but when ignited, they burned for thirty to forty-five seconds at 4,330 degrees Fahrenheit—twice the temperature needed to melt steel. The moment Ryan and the companions had laid eyes on the red canisters, they'd all had the same thought: they'd come in handy at some point, especially if they happened to cross paths with Magus and his nasty, sweating playmates again.

Fate had granted them that favor—thanks to the mile-a-minute prattle of a jolt-stoned gaudy-house slut.

"We don't have enough gas and water left to follow

the convoy for another day," Ryan went on. "We have to make our move tonight. It's been a hard and bloody road, but this is going to be Magus's last sunset."

"Justice finally delivered," Doc Tanner intoned. "Without mercy or restraint, swords buried to the hilt."

Even though Doc was the only one who carried a sword—a rapier, actually, which lay concealed inside his silver-handled, ebony walking stick—there were grim-faced nods of agreement all around. After so many years of wandering the hellscape together, the nineteenth-century time traveler's archaic metaphors rolled off the companions like water off a duck's back.

Gathering up their longblasters and backpacks, they remounted the dirt bikes they'd acquired from the mountainside ville some eight thousand feet above the desert plain. Krysty took a seat behind Ryan. J.B. and Mildred, and Doc and Ricky were riding double, too. Only Jak Lauren, the albino, was riding solo.

J.B. hawked and sent a gob of rust-colored spit flying over the handlebars and into the dirt. Then he thumbed his spectacles back up the bridge of his nose and screwed down his fedora. The Armorer was ready to roll.

So was Dr. Mildred Wyeth. Having settled in on the seat behind J.B., the African American freezie clapped a steadying hand on his shoulder, which raised a sizable puff of dust.

To Ryan it looked like orange smoke.

"Remember to stay clear of the road," he said. "Spread out and keep the speed down. If they bother to look back, they'll think we're a dust devil. They won't be able to hear our bike engines over their own racket. Jak, take point. Get as close as you can without showing your hand. When they stop to make camp, turn back at once and catch us up."

"Yeah," Jak said, kick-starting the dirt bike and revving the engine. His shoulder-length white hair was streaked with orange, as were his front teeth and dead-pale face. With his ruby-red eyes and the .357 Magnum Colt Python strapped on his hip, he looked like a nightmare clown.

Bristling with their own armament, kerchiefs pulled up over their noses and mouths, Ryan and the others followed Jak down the steep, rocky trail to the valley floor. Without another word the albino zoomed off after the convoy, white hair flying behind him as he jumped the ruts in the crude road.

Ryan waved for his companions to fan out, and they began to advance in a thin skirmish line on either side of the track. Krysty's arms wrapped around his waist as he zigzagged around sagebrush and cactus, avoiding exposed rocks and navigating flash-flood gullies. Because he was moving so slowly over the soft, loose terrain, he had to keep planting his boot soles to make the bike stay upright. It was hard, sweaty work but necessary: for them to have the best chance of success, they had to catch this enemy by surprise.

As he plowed forward, fighting the drag of the sand, images of what he'd seen high on the mountainside kept cycling through his mind. Try as he might, he couldn't make them stop.

In Deathlands, violent acts always had a familiar form and shape, like something copied over and over: deeds of murder and mayhem committed out of greed, hunger, lust, revenge and sheer stupidity. Though the details, the circumstances and victims differed from one instance to another, they were similar in scale and scope.

What had happened at the mountain ville was different.

If the place had ever had a name, there was no one left alive to reveal it. What had been done there made the hellscape's standard inbred chillers, coldheart robbers and insane barons seem like dimmies playing in a very small sandbox.

This wasn't like the legendary massacre at Virtue Lake, where it was said even the flies on the dog shit were dead. Despite the campfire tales that painted Trader and his cohorts, Ryan Cawdor included, as senseless, murdering monsters, Virtue Lake had no perpetrators, only victims; it was the result of an unfortunate coalescence of events. A bad hand of cards.

The luck of the draw had nothing to do with what had happened high on the mountain. Beyond excessive, as pointless as a cataclysmic act of nature, it bore the unmistakable signature of its creator. The companions had not only viewed this grandiose handiwork before, they had almost been made part of it more than once. There was just one such artist in all the hellscape—an artist who mimicked a wrathful, mindless god.

Magus.

Ryan coasted the bike down the side of a shallow gully, then powered over the soft sand of the wash, building speed to climb the opposite bank. Krysty's arms tightened around his waist as the bike went momentarily airborne, crow-hopping over the lip.

The suffering of the innocent and the weak in Deathlands was a given, as were the angry forces of nature unleashed by the apocalypse more than a century before. Drought, pestilence, fire, earthquake, eruption, storm, flood, famine were things the companions were powerless in the face of. But the cyclone that was Magus, that cut a path of destruction and horror across the Deathlands, could be halted with bullet and blade, and for the sake of their own continued survival, had to be stopped.

They had fought Steel Eyes before, never losing but never completely winning, either. The monster always seemed to find a way to slip from their grasp at the last second, leaving a stalemate and the threat of doom still hanging over their heads. What they were about to do this night, they were doing for themselves. Avenging the slaughter of the helpless, and the misery left in its wake, was the icing on the cake.

Despite the kerchief covering his lower face, grit crunched between Ryan's back molars. He would have spit it out, but he was already losing too much moisture. Sweat peeled down the sides of his face, down his spine and rib cage. The bike wasn't moving fast enough to cool him down. Riding in slow motion, with the taste of mud in his mouth, time dragged on and the exertion was constant. The convoy's dust cloud was too far away to see; besides, he had to focus on what was directly in front of him. Strain built up in his arms and lower back, even in his fingers, as they gripped the handlebars and feathered throttle and brakes.

Gradually, the eastern hills grew larger until they towered above. The chain of peaks was about four hundred feet high, with saddles between the rounded summits. They were glowing an even warmer shade of red as the sun began to set. When Ryan glanced down at the fuel gauge, the needle was bouncing on empty. If he was running on fumes, they were all running on fumes.

A dirt bike appeared out of the heat waves in the near distance, coming toward them at a leisurely pace, Ryan signaled for the others to stop and shut down their bikes at once. By the time the albino rode up, they had dismounted and were stretching out sore muscles.

"Well?" Ryan said as Jak dumped his bike onto the sand.

"Stopped base of hill, mile ahead. Circled wags, make camp."

"We'll hide the bikes here and go the rest of the way on foot," Ryan said. "We've got to take control of the high ground above them. Me and Ricky will circle around behind the hill and come down over the crest. When we attack, we attack from all sides at once. Everyone has to be in position before we lose the light. We have to be able to see these bastards. We can't have them coming at us out of the dark. If there's no wind, belly crawl in, close enough to pitch the grens into the middle of the camp. If there's any breeze, come at them from downwind so the enforcers don't sniff us out."

"If we're that spread out, how will we know when to attack?" Mildred asked.

"You'll be in position long before we will," Ryan said. "Watch the hillside above the camp. I'll blink my flash once. Wait a count of twenty so Ricky and I can close in from above, then let it nukin' rip."

Krysty stepped up to him, slipped her arms around his neck and pulled him down for a long, lingering kiss. "That's not a goodbye," she said as she drew back a little. "That's a see-you-later, lover."

He looked into her emerald eyes and saw concern in

their depths. It was mirrored by her mutie hair, which had contracted into a mass of tight curls. For sure, it was the last night on earth for *somebody*—at this point it was a coin toss who or *what* that somebody was going to be, them or Magus.

"It's never goodbye," he told her, gently brushing her cheek with the tips of his fingers.

Waving for Ricky to follow, Ryan turned for the hills and didn't look back. They set off at a brisk pace, beelining across the plain to the foot of the nearest saddle. With Ryan in the lead, they climbed the crumbling slope using scrub and boulders for handholds. As evening fell, the sweet scent of the sage seemed to grow stronger and stronger. The scattered saguaros cast long, skinny shadows across the slope, and the air temperature began to drop.

At the base of a giant cactus, a mutie jackrabbit with a hairless face as pink as a newborn baby stared at them, its body frozen like a statue. Its foot-and-a-half-long ears stood erect.

"Muy sabroso," Ricky hissed through clenched teeth, drawing a slim throwing knife from his sleeve. Arm cocked back, eyes locked on his target, he held the blade by the tip.

The teenaged boy seemed to be growing bigger by the day, and he was always hungry, always thinking about his next meal. "Not now," Ryan said in a low tone. "Jackrabbits scream. Focus. Tune out distractions."

Once they had crossed over the saddle and began to traverse the shadowed far side of the mountains, he stopped worrying about noise giving away their approach. The view east under a cloudless sky was of another, even wider stretch of desert plain, which ended at the horizon in staggered rows of desolate, ruddy hills.

That they had ended up here—bodies sun-blasted, throats parched, with sand in their boots, on the verge of closing the book on Magus—was the result of a singular chain of coincidence. It had started in the relatively fertile valley on the other side of the eight-thousand-foot mountain. Steel Eyes's handful of human sec men had slipped away from their camp for some recreation and joy juice in the nearby ville's tiny gaudy house. They had gotten so drunk while waiting in line to be serviced by a lone slut, who was puffing away like the little engine that could, that they'd blathered on about their employer, the convoy and the direction they were all headed next. A day later, when the companions showed up at the gaudy house en route to points north, the sec men were long gone and the slut so sky-high on jolt she was talking nonstop and tap-dancing in a puddle of her own piss.

After verifying her Magus story—the gaudy master had overheard it, too—the companions traded an assortment of extra gear, including one fully functional, single-shot 12 gauge with a broken buttstock, for six skinny swaybacked horses. They picked up the convoy's trail just outside the ville and followed it up a steep, winding, predark mountain road. The going was slow because they had to stop often to let the horses rest. They spent one sleepless night beside the disintegrating tarmac.

By Ryan's reckoning, they were two full days behind Magus when they reached the edge of a broad meadow bordered by tall pines and a small stream. According to the gaudy master, Magus's likely next landing spot was just the other side of it. Continuing on the ruined road would have led them directly to the ville but cost them the element of surprise. Ryan guided them a ways into the meadow, then stopped the single file of riders with a raised hand. He listened hard, but there was not so much as a bird tweet or a bug chirp.

From her perch behind him on the horse, Krysty pointed at the thick, waist-high grass to their right. She said softly in his ear, "Something there. It's moving…"

Jak was already standing tall in his stirrups, eyes fixed in the same direction.

Ryan signaled for the albino to dismount and circle around behind, drew his panga from its sheath and quietly swung down from the horse. He had walked no more than twenty feet when he saw something bright red among the green. He thought he glimpsed a stout black body beneath. Whatever it was, it turned to the left and disappeared. He followed, wading through the lake of tall grass.

Jak was moving toward him, the sun reflecting off white hair and skin. He had his arms outstretched, and he was smiling.

When Ryan took his next step, it was met by a burst of noise from in front of him. A blur of angry birds with flaming red heads, thick black-feathered bodies and flapping, four-foot wings, shot from cover. As the buzzards rushed past him, scuttling away like gigantic swarthy chickens, he instinctively swung the panga, smacking one of them on the pate with the flat of the blade. Stunned, the bird sat down hard, beak gaping, wings spread and twitching. It stank like a slaughterhouse; there was fresh blood smeared on its chest feathers. Its stomach was grossly distended, the contents so densely packed and heavy that, like its brethren, it couldn't fly.

That didn't bode well.

He waved for the others to dismount. They left the horses to graze in the meadow and, spreading out, weapons at the ready, advanced to the edge of the clearing. Nestled among the trees, the nameless ville had once looked like something out of a predark storybook: tiny central square with bandstand, on either side of which stood a school, city hall, church with tall steeple, movie house, stores. Because of its remote location, it had survived Armageddon pretty much intact. And had apparently provided sufficient protection to a support a limited population.

Past tense.

The central square and surrounding street was littered with bodies. It looked as if it had rained dead people and dead dogs. Many of the corpses were torn into pieces: arms, legs and heads ripped off and flung. The buzzards had been hard at the best bits—the eyes and tongues—leaving three gory craters in every upturned face.

Some of the humans had been more carefully disassembled.

In the school gymnasium they found a makeshift surgical theater. The hardwood floor was smeared with swooshes of blackened, congealed blood. The air was thick with the stench of death and swarmed with flies. Dissected organs lay piled on the bleacher seats: hearts here, lungs there, eyeballs in a plastic bucket. The horror hadn't ended very long ago. The blood in the tiled showers was still red; it stood in pools where the butchers had hosed themselves down afterward.

At the far end of the predark basketball court, a man in a lab coat was hanging from the rim of the hoop, by the neck, by his own belt; his belly had been slashed from sternum to crotch. Greasy gray intestines looped around his ankles. He had a large irregular purple birthmark on his right cheek—it looked like a silhouette of Texas.

"By the Three Kennedys," Doc had gasped through the kerchief over his nose and mouth, "that poor soul's wearing his guts for garters!"

The entire ville had been chilled; everything alive had been ground up and spit out. What Magus had been looking for, if anything, was a mystery. Replacement parts for a deteriorating body? Recreation for a deteriorating mind?

In the end the reasons didn't matter. What was done was done.

Only this time there would be payback.

After Ryan and Ricky had skirted the back side of the desert hills for a goodly distance, he sent the young Latino up to a summit to recce their position relative to the enemy camp.

"Wags at the bottom of the hill after next," Ricky said when he returned. "No campfire that I see."

Minutes later they belly-crawled over that summit, then descended to just below the ridgeline. Over tops of sagebrush and boulder, Ryan could see the five wags parked in a ring, bathed in rosy light as the sun slipped behind the peak of the mountain. Ricky was right; there was no campfire in the center. He peered through the Scout's scope. There were no milling figures. No one seated, either. No sign of Magus. No lights on inside the Winnie.

Ryan didn't give the attack signal as planned. There was no one to attack.

He and Ricky moved carefully down the slope. He slipped between two sets of bumpers, his longblaster held waist high. The Steyr's 7.62 mm round packed enough wallop to drop all of the hellscape's large predators; it figured to be more effective versus enforcers than 9 mm handblasters, but that was a proposition yet to be tested. As the last light began to fade, the other companions emerged from the shadows between the wags, with weapons raised.

A quick search of the parked vehicles turned up nothing.

"Where did the rapscallions go?" Doc asked when they reconvened in the center of the camp.

With head lowered, Jak was already circling the perimeter. He stopped abruptly and pointed at a patch of churned-up dirt that led past the pickup with the cab-mounted machine blaster. "This way," he said.

The trail was wide and easy to follow, even as night fell. It ended a short distance away, farther along the base of the hill, where the bedrock had been cut away, carved into an unnatural arch. Before they stepped under it, Ryan and the others knew what they'd find: a redoubt's vanadium-steel door.

The massive portal stood ajar, and weak light spilled out from inside.

With weapons up, they slipped single file through the gap, into a tunnel with a polished-concrete floor. Ryan stared down at the mass of rusty, overlaid footprints in front of them. There were way more than thirty-five sets of feet. The toes were headed in both directions—in and out. The redoubt had been breached many times in recent memory.

"By the Three Kennedys," Doc said, "that is somewhat dire…"

He wasn't looking at the overlaid footprints and drips of enforcer sweat, which turned the tracked-in dirt dark brown in spots. His attention was focused on the painted metal warning sign hanging on the wall. In eight-inch-tall letters it read:

SECURITY LEVEL RED ALPHA
UNAUTHORIZED ENTRY WILL BE MET BY
LETHAL FORCE
TURN BACK NOW

Cartoon silhouettes below the lettering showed helmeted soldiers with automatic longblasters shooting down a running man, woman and child.

"Think it still applies?" Mildred asked.

"Only if skeletons can fire M-16s," J.B. said.

"After more than a century, such threats do tend to lose their teeth, my dear Mildred," Doc said, displaying his own remarkably fine set.

"We don't know what defenses this place has," Krysty stated. "But we sure as hell know what's gone in ahead of us. Fighting enforcers in close quarters means big noise. Our element of surprise is going to disappear quick."

"We could wait for the stinking *pendejos* to come out," Ricky said. "Booby-trap their wags. Blow them all to hell and back when they try to drive off."

"What if they're planning to use the mat-trans to jump out of here?" Ryan queried. "What if they have no intention of ever coming back? We could wait outside this redoubt until we're skeletons, too."

The companions said nothing. He could see from their expressions his point had sunk in.

"We've got to find out what Magus is doing here," Ryan went on. "We've dealt with enforcers in a redoubt before. The tight spaces belowground will make the incendies even more effective. Think about it—chain-reaction fireballs!"

"I do like the sound of that," J.B. admitted.

One by one, the others nodded. None of them wanted to abandon their quarry after so long a hunt and with the finish almost in sight.

Her eyes gleaming, Krysty said, "Let's go fry us some big, fat lizard butt."

"Before we do that," Ryan said, "we've got another little job on our plates."

At a trot he led them back to the circled wags. "Only way anyone is leaving this camp is on foot," he said as he unsheathed his panga. With that he slashed the blade across the sidewall of the Winnie's left front tire, dropping the wheel to its rim with a sudden whoosh.

The companions needed no further instructions. They spread out in the near darkness and quickly cut all the tires on the wags.

As they returned to the redoubt entrance, Ricky said to no one in particular, "There's lots of gas in the wag tanks for our bikes. And water in the Winnie."

"Ah, the unbridled optimism of youth," Doc said with a laugh.

J.B. chuckled, too. "Yeah, the kid thinks we're actually going to live through this."

"J.B., what do you mean?" Ricky asked.

"Wait until you come toe-to-toe with an enforcer, my boy," Doc told him, "then the veil will be lifted."

The far end of the tunnel was blocked by a blast-proof sec gate, steel bars backed by armaglass, which stood open. Along a bowed-out section of wall near the entry, the snouts of three M-60 machine blasters protruded from a single, horizontal firing slot. Against the wall opposite was a six-foot-high backstop on skids, designed to absorb blasterfire and minimize ricochets. The backstop was decorated with lines of 7.62 mm bullet holes at waist height. They looked as though they'd been drawn with a yardstick. Above and below the holes were irregular patches of brown—ancient crusted blood spatter.

With the others standing well clear, Ryan swept his hand over the electronic eye set in the wall above the blaster muzzles. Nothing happened. The motion detector was out of commission.

After passing through the sec gate, Ryan peered around the corner at the inside of the blaster turret. The trio of M-60s was controlled by a mechanized cam apparatus that had linked triggers and arc of fire. Someone had stripped out the guts of its electronics; wires were cut and hanging loose, circuit boards smashed. The threat on the entrance sign wasn't hollow. And Krysty was right—this place had its own built-in set of challenges.

"Listen up," Ryan said, "some of the redoubt's automatic defense systems might still be operational. There's no telling what other kinds of traps are still armed. If we follow the footprints, the path should be safe. If we find chills on the floor, we'll know to take another route."

"I don't think we're going to find chills," J.B. said as he stared down at the mishmash of rusty footprints. "I get the funny feeling Magus has been here before. Most of the tracks are from barefoot drippers."

It was something that Ryan had already noticed. The enforcers never wore boots and had very wide, very distinctive, four-toed feet.

"If Steel Eyes already knew about the existence of this redoubt," J.B. said, "if it's been a regular stop, then whatever's inside must be rich pickin's, and there's probably a shitload of it."

"Forget about scav," Ryan said as he began passing out the incendies. "First and foremost, we're here to put Magus on the last train west. From here on, we're triple red. This doesn't look like a typical redoubt. Keep your eyes open and the chatter to a minimum."

Ignoring the elevators, they took the stairwell down. In case things went off the rails, it gave them the possibility of a fighting retreat. Dusty footprints decorated the first landing. Magus and the enforcers had followed the same route.

As the companions descended, the whine of a power cycle drifted up from below. It grew louder and higher in pitch until it was a piercing, sustained scream.

"Know what?" Krysty said. "I think Magus is about to make that jump you talked about."

It didn't sound like the power-up of a mat-trans unit to Ryan. From the noise level, the energy involved had to be immense. "We need to move faster," he told the others. "Before they do whatever they're going to do..."

At the next floor down he took the lead through the stairwell access. A few redoubts had their own unique layout, based on the main function of the installation.

The companions knew this place was different, and they didn't have time to search the place blindly; they needed a map to recce from. And, though the redoubts all sported wall-mounted maps on every level, the diagrams were not necessarily located in the same place.

The concrete corridor opened onto an expansive room lined with comp stations in cramped little cubicles. Ryan had seen such setups before, and they always reminded him of chicken coops—without the stink. The low ceiling had collapsed in places, raining squares of acoustic tile on desktops and floor. There were no bodies, no skeletons, just row after row of gray office furniture coated with a century-thick layer of dust.

The floor-plan map of the redoubt was screwed to the wall, behind a sheet of Plexiglas, beside another bank of elevators.

Mildred swept the plastic clean with her palm. "There," she said, tapping the cover with a fingernail. "The mat-trans is four levels down and on the far side of the redoubt."

At a dead run, they retraced their route, and once they reached the staircase, they took the steps two at a time.

The footprints were petering out, but drips of enforcer sweat glistened on the metal front edges of the treads. They looked like sprinkled raindrops—but, to the companions, smelled like scalie piss mixed with wag fuel.

Through the door four levels down, Jak took point with his .357 Magnum Colt Python, following the sweat trail like a bird dog. It led them through a long, straight corridor to another sec check, this one more daunting than the first. A short section of the corridor was bracketed at either end by steel-barred and arma-glass gates, which stood half open. Between the gates was a designated kill zone. Machine-blaster posts were staggered on either side of the hall: get past the first, get nailed by the second. Cameras looked down from all four corners of the ceiling. On the wall to the left was a lone, armored window with a small microphone speaker and a metal sliding bin beneath. The sign beside it read:

NO UNAUTHORIZED PERSONNEL
BEYOND THIS POINT
NO WEAPONS
PLACE SECURITY CARD IN TRAY
OBEY ALL COMMANDS
ENTRANTS SUBJECT TO CAVITY SEARCH

As he read the sign, Ryan could feel the vibration of the generators through the soles of his boots. His skin crawled with static electricity. To send that kind of charge through hundreds of thousands of tons of concrete required an unimaginable amount of power.

An unpleasant thought occurred to him. If Magus knew they were in pursuit, this could be a trap. If a nuclear bomb was involved, if its countdown mechanism had already been activated, there was no escaping back the way they'd come. If Magus intended to jump away at the last second before detonation, their only hope was to do the same.

With Jak ahead of him and Krysty close behind, Ryan moved past a pair of elevator doors in the wall on the left. As Ricky, Mildred and Doc followed, a cheerful chime rang out: *ding-ding*. The sound stopped all the companions in their tracks. The elevator doors rolled back smoothly.

Backlit by the car's ceiling bulb was a lone enforcer. It was so wide it seemed to fill the entire doorway. The surface of its skin was covered with an array of ridges and knobs, like a crocodile's. Sweat beaded and then oozed down its wide belly and dripped steadily off the underside of its pot roast–size scrotum, pooling on the floor between massive, bandy legs.

Throwing back its head, it let loose an earsplitting roar of outrage.

The cry was answered a fraction of a second later by tens of thousands of foot-pounds of concentrated blasterfire. Five different calibers of bullets and shotgun rounds knocked the creature onto its heels and slammed it into the back of the car. Wild ricochets pocked the floor and sidewalls with holes and slashes, as the din of firing continued. Chunks of the enforcer's thick hide were blown away, revealing shiny blue bone beneath. The point-blank volley seemingly had no other effect. The slugs weren't through and through; there was no blood—red, blue, green or yellow.

One by one, their blasters came up empty; the shooting dwindled. Before they could all reload and resume fire, the enforcer had recovered. As the elevator doors began to slide closed, it lunged through the haze of trapped blaster smoke. The four-inch-long amber talons on its thumbs held the doors' leading edges apart, and it stuck its lumpy head through the gap. Yellow eyes slitted, wide, toothy maw grinning in anticipation, it took in seven defenseless victims, all within easy reach.

Mildred yanked the pin from a red canister, paused, then gently rolled the cylinder underhand onto the elevator floor. Fountaining white sparks, like a roman candle, the thermite gren sputtered between the enforcer's thighs, directly under its prominent gonads.

A very different kind of howl erupted from its throat when a second later the gren fully ignited and took the puddled chemical sweat with it. The resulting blast of four-thousand-degree heat sent Ryan and the others staggering away, shielding their faces with their forearms. Even though the enforcer was engulfed in fire, head to foot, it crumpled the edges of the elevator doors trying to pull itself free.

There was no escape.

In seconds the car's thin steels walls began to melt around it. The enforcer reeled back from the doorway, arms thrashing. Flames roared upward, burning through the roof of the car, as though it was made of candle wax, and sucking the air in the corridor into the elevator shaft, as if it were a giant chimney. As the enforcer collapsed, the car broke free of its cables and plummeted downward.

Ricky's dark eyes widened in disbelief. During the brief, one-sided firefight, his De Lisle carbine had been stuck firmly at port arms. "Were you shooting it in the head?"

"Shit, yeah," Jak said, dumping six smoking hulls from his Python.

J.B. clapped a hand on the youth's shoulder and said, "Those knobby, sweaty bastards die triple hard. Don't worry, kid. You'll get used to it—mebbe you'll even get a shot off next time."

Ricky shrugged. "Next time I'll know where to aim."

The muffled crash of the elevator car rolled up the shaft. It was a long fall to the bottom.

Ryan heard more bellows of fury—seemingly coming from all directions at once. It sounded like three hours past feeding time in a mutie zoo.

Retreat was definitely no longer an option.

"We've got to reach the mat-trans," he said. "Don't waste ammo. Use the grens to clear a path. Let's go!"

With that, he and Jak led the full-out charge down the corridor. One hundred feet ahead was an intersection with another corridor. As they neared it, Ryan waved for Jak to slow down. They stopped and peered around the corners as the others stormed past. In the dim overhead light, way down the corridor on the right, he could see lumpy heads bobbing toward them. It was the same story when he looked in the opposite direction.

He and Jak rolled incendies both ways, then without waiting to see the effect, chased after the others. Ryan knew the thermite grens would keep the enforcers back, but only the first wave, and only temporarily.

In front of them, Krysty, Mildred, J.B., Doc and Ricky disappeared into a doorway on the left. Then the floor jolted violently under Ryan's boots, sending him slamming shoulder first into the wall. Concrete dust rained down from the ceiling. Dozens of levels below, the generator's whine died away, like a falling artillery shell, and the corridor lights winked out.

For an instant it was so dark Ryan couldn't see the end of his nose. Pitch-black, but not quiet. Over the pounding of his heart, he heard what sounded like dozens of bare feet slapping the floor. The generator re-covered after only a second or two, starting the climb to peak power, and then the lights came back on.

When Ryan looked behind them, he saw a corridor filled wall to wall with wide bodies, and they were bearing down fast. "Run, Jak! Run!" he shouted.

The entrance to the mat-trans unit's control room stood open. Ryan was the last across the threshold. He spun around, located the keypad and, desperately hoping that the usual codes worked in this redoubt, punched in the one that would close the door. It worked. Breathing a sigh of relief, he quickly entered another to lock out access.

"We're too late," Krysty said as he turned. "We just missed them."

He'd already guessed that. In a single go, something had drained the tremendous power load to zero.

Ryan rushed past panels of blinking, multicolored lights and the madly chattering, predark machinery, into the anteroom. The door to this mat-trans had a porthole, and he could see the tendrils of jump fog slowly lifting. Though his view was obscured, there were no feet below the mist and no slumped bodies on the floorplates near the door—just shiny smears of sweat.

There was no way to tell where or how many of their quarry had gone. Or even if Magus had jumped with them.

A resounding boom from a foot or fist against the outside of the control room's door put an end to that train of thought. More banging followed, and under the rain of blows, the barrier began to bulge inward. Amber thumb hooks poked between the edge of the door and its frame, bending back the double-walled steel as if it was pot metal.

It wasn't going to hold.

Krysty pulled out a red canister.

"No!" he said, catching her hand by the wrist. "If we use incendies in here, we'll end up cooking ourselves and the mat-trans."

Behind them, a knobby arm reached through the gap, a hand flailing clumsily toward its prey

"Into the chamber!" Ryan ordered as the anteroom entry was pried open.

The companions piled through ahead of him. Once inside, he shut the door, which didn't have the usual lever for a handle. He dogged it with the locking wheel—just in time. On the far side of the porthole, inches from his face, enforcers tore madly at the hatch. The locking cams of vanadium steel were too strong for them, but the tips of their amber talons scored the glass, crosshatching it.

Ryan knew he had only seconds before the automatic cycle started. He lunged for the unit's Last Destination button.

At almost the same instant, Doc shouted from the rear of the chamber, "Wait, Ryan! Do not press—!"

But the button had already clicked under his thumb.

"By the Three Kennedys, look here. Look at this!"

The floorplates beneath his boots throbbing with pulses of light, Ryan pushed past the others and glimpsed what he hadn't been able to see before: a second porthole door, the mirror image of the one they had entered through. He pressed his face to the arma-glass and saw nothing. What was on the other side

was not only devoid of light, it swallowed light, like a
bottomless hole.

Gray fog materialized near the chamber's ceiling.
As Ryan breathed in the stinging mist, his head began
to spin, then his knees gave way. He crumpled to his
back on the floorplates. Beside him, Krysty and the
others were already down, writhing and screaming.
Jumping had never hurt before—the fog had always
produced a merciful blackout. Mat-trans units never
had two doors. Mind racing, he tried to make sense
of it.

Then something incredibly powerful seized his
wrists and ankles and stretched them in opposite directions. He roared in pain, certain that every tendon
and joint would break under the accelerating pressure,
but they didn't—instead, the opposing forces pulled his
body thinner and thinner, as if it were made of rubber.

He couldn't make it stop; he couldn't even slow
it down.

Chapter One

Once again Veronica Currant found her attention wandering across the luxuriously appointed dining room, past the dark leather booths, crystal chandeliers and liveried waitstaff. It came to rest on the TV above the Manhattan restaurant's bar. Because the presidential inauguration was less than a day away, media was replaying the whole "lost ballot" business in excruciating detail: the characters in the Florida GOP implicated in the computer tampering conspiracy, and the Supreme Court decision that had ultimately determined the outcome of the election. The country was sick of hearing about it, and so was she. She just wanted it over with. After all, there were checks and balances built into the system, no matter who was elected. The Republicans had had three successive terms in the White House since 1980. How bad could a Democratic President be?

The tall, gaunt man on the other side of the table tapped his water goblet with a silver spoon to get her attention. "We were discussing terms on a multibook deal," Noah Prentiss reminded her.

It took an effort of will on her part not to stare at the swollen red knob of his nose and the constellations of tiny starbursts on his cheeks.

Prentiss was an alcoholic, low-rung literary agent. His low-rung client—a small pudgy man who bit his nails—sat to his left. They had turned their half of the white linen tablecloth into a veritable Jackson Pollack of red-wine spills, meat juice and grease spots, bits of discarded gristle, drips of Caesar dressing, shreds of romaine and escaped bread crumbs.

"Kyle and I have discussed the matter at length," Prentiss went on, "and feel a raise in advance is appropriate on the next Clanker contract."

Clanker was one of the eight-book series Veronica edited for a New York City paperback house. The central character of the same name was a steampunk cyborg—coal and wood fired.

"No one writes Clanky as good as me," Kyle Arthur Levinson boasted, somewhat thickly after four martinis and a half bottle of cabernet.

Veronica looked from one man to the other but did not reply. Silence in answer to a question was a negotiating technique she had learned from the five-foot-two pulp-fiction publisher, cigar-smoking entrepreneur and renowned tightwad who was her boss. It was a strategy that put the opposition at an immediate disadvantage.

If she had chosen to, she could have listed many reasons why Mr. Levinson didn't deserve more book contracts, let alone a raise in pay. He never turned in his assignments on time. Despite the advance outlines to the contrary, he wrote the same story over and over. Clanker aways ran short on energy at a crucial moment in the plot and broke up some chairs or bookshelves to burn in his brass firebox, thus saving the day. Levinson cannibalized action and sex scenes word for word from his own books. He never researched or fact-checked his work. He never read books by the other ghosts in the series, which created conflicts with canon. None of

these issues set him apart from the rest of the stable—
to one degree or another, all the writers were guilty of
the same offenses. So why should he get more money?

Prentiss had an answer for that.

"Remember," the agent said, "Kyle's been on this
series from the start. He helped build its current global
audience."

"I'm the one who invented ol' Clanky's catch phrase,
'Stoke me!'"

That was hardly something Veronica could forget.
Levinson used that tag line at least fifty times in every
book, and she had to go through the manuscript and
personally remove forty-five of them. Truth be told,
"his" catch phrase for Clanker was stolen from "Stalk
me!"—the catch phrase from another of the company's
series, Slaughter Realms. Which in turn had been lifted
from "Stake me!"—the catch phrase of the house's
vampire line, Blood City.

Sometimes in the middle of an excruciating edit of
one of his Clankers, she caught herself wishing he'd
write "Choke me!" so she could strangle him with a
clear conscience.

"We have come up with some numbers we'd like to
run by you," Prentiss said, holding out a slip of paper.

Veronica took it and put it in her purse without looking at it. "A decision like this has to come from the
top," she said. "I'm sure you understand…"

"Of course," Prentiss said. "I understand completely.
Now, how about a little something sweet?"

Levinson was already scanning the dessert menu
with keen interest.

Half an hour later Veronica was starting to feel hungry. She'd had only sparkling water to drink, a seafood

risotto and an undressed green salad. Not wanting to prolong the ordeal by ordering more food, she paid the tab with a company credit card and left agent and client happily nursing their third brandies. She knew her boss wouldn't grouse about the bill. A $300 lunch was peanuts compared to actually giving Levinson a raise. Effective stalling cost money but paid off big time down the road when the writer became desperate. And sooner or later, writers always became desperate.

Outside the restaurant, the January temperature was in the high thirties; it felt colder because it was so damp. She thought about walking the five blocks back to the office but changed her mind. She had a big pile of manuscripts to edit at home, and she wanted to get out of her high heels and into a pair of comfy slippers. After hailing a passing taxi and getting in, she gave the driver the address of her apartment in the East Village.

Her thoughts returned to the Levinson problem.

That there were always worse writers out there had been pounded into her by painful experience. "Better the bad writer you know" was the company's long-standing philosophy. To overcome the failings of the stable, failings all too apparent to readers of the various series, and to keep her job, she'd had to master the relevant facts and skills herself. She had learned about weapons, tactics, martial arts, survival, engineering, astrophysics; the list went on and on. Despite the fact that she was only twenty-six, she was a mother figure to the writers she herded—a dispenser of sustenance, corrector of embarrassing mistakes, protector and defender. They were babies, all of them. Some white-haired or hairless, some toothless with age, but still helpless, whining babies.

The cab pulled up in front of her brownstone on a street lined wall-to-wall with similar narrow, multi-story houses, all of the same, roughly 1850, vintage. Sickly, leafless trees grew out of spike-ringed holes in the sidewalk.

After paying the cabbie, she climbed the steep front stairs, unlocked the door and stepped into the small foyer. As she started up to her second-floor apartment, she considered blowing off work, putting her feet up and reading a good book for a change. A rumble from the floor above startled her. It sounded like a stampede of elephants. Looking up, she saw huge, dark figures lumbering down from the landing. They were as wide bodied as NFL players. The marble staircase shook under their combined weight. She flattened her back against the wall to keep from being trampled.

As they poured past, she saw there were eight or nine of them, all dressed in a kind of uniform: royal-purple satin hoodies and black satin jogging pants. She couldn't get a clear look at their faces because of the hoods and because they were moving so fast. She did see and recognize the skeletonized buttstocks of AKS-74U "Krinkovs," some of them slung under the hoodies, the abbreviated autorifles looking like children's toys. In the middle of the pack, apparently being guarded by the others, was a spindly, frail individual.

Was that Bob Dylan? she thought, turning to look as they crossed the foyer below and trooped out the front door. A rumor had started going around the block that morning that the famous balladeer had bought the brownstone next to this one, but no one had actually seen him yet. What was Bob Dylan doing in *her* building? The odd smell left in their wake made her wrinkle her nose.

When she peered over the second-floor landing, her heart sank. Her apartment door was standing wide open. Without thinking, she crossed the hall and rushed inside. The place had been trashed—furniture overturned, lamps broken, pictures knocked off the walls as if a whirlwind had struck. The television, stereo and computer were untouched. It smelled like a meth lab.

"Talu, Petey!" she called. "Lucy!"

The cats didn't come.

She found all three hiding, wide-eyed, in a corner under the bed. Much to her relief, they were unhurt.

Nothing seemed to be missing from the bedroom; everything was just as she had left it. The autographed black-and-white photo of a bearded, smiling Robertson Davies sat atop her dresser.

Oh crap, the Eagle! She jumped up and tore open her closet door. Behind cartons of neatly packed summer clothes on the top shelf, the lock box was still there. She opened it with the keypad and looked down with relief at the Bengal tiger–striped .44 Magnum Desert Eagle snug in its fitted foam case. It had been a strange gift from an even stranger man—restraining-order strange.

Robert Marx, in addition to being bipolar and a con man, had authored a few books for the company's Western soft-core-porn line, Ramrod—that series' catch phrase was both obvious and literal. Veronica had never dated Marx, never saw him once outside the company offices, but he had become so enamored of her that out of the blue, he'd given her this $2,500, illegal-in-NYC pistol—the world's most powerful handgun, in fact. Something Marx thought incredibly funny.

Primarily to defend herself against him—and people like him—Veronica had learned at a range in Connecticut to shoot the monstrous thing. She'd initially had serious problems with muzzle control because of the weapon's weight—four-and-a-half pounds, fully loaded—and its tremendous recoil. To master it, she'd had to strengthen her wrists and forearms with dumbbell finger curls.

A loud, sudden noise from the living room made her stiffen. It sounded like something heavy had fallen. Maybe one of her floor-to-ceiling bookshelves had crashed to the floor.

They're back! was her only thought.

Veronica kicked off her heels. With the ease of much practice—and without chipping a nail—she slapped home the pistol's loaded magazine and chambered the first fat wadcutter round in the stack. Snatching the custom-molded earplugs from the case, she thumbed them into place as she moved to the bedroom door. When she burst into the living room with the auto-pistol in a two-handed grip, ready to fire, there was no one there. Above the toppled chairs and scattered manuscript pages, a weird gray mist swirled in the air.

Something terrible was about to happen. She could feel it in the pit of her stomach.

Firmly planting her feet, she aimed the Eagle at the churning, expanding cloud. As she stared over the iron sights, it occurred to her that she had finally and completely lost her mind.

Chapter Two

The pain didn't stop when Ryan went blind in his one good eye.

Or when he stopped breathing. Or when his heart stopped beating.

Consciousness and sensation stubbornly remained while his body stretched and stretched, like a strand of spit, until it was a slithering ribbon a molecule high and a molecule wide. Until it was light years long. The cries of his companions were an unbroken wail, which he vibrated to, like a plucked guitar string.

It was nothing like the jump nightmares he had experienced before. The random, twisted horror stories peopled by ex-lovers, bloodthirsty muties and archenemies of his past were at least a comprehensible agony, with beginnings, middles and ends. There were no time signposts in this version of hell, nothing to separate one excruciating instant from the next. He was being stretched and stretched, but to where? To what? Had they been tricked into an endless loop of matter transfer, never arriving, forever in transit?

And the worst part of all: he had hit the button. Magus's victory, their defeat, was by his own hand. His own bastard hand.

Suddenly the pressure seemed to ease a bit; before he could come to grips with the change, it reversed entirely. Instead of stretching, there was compression. Violent, dramatic compression at both ends, like g-forces trying to crush him flat, to drive the back of his head into the base of his spine, his ankles into his hipbones. Caught between the downward and upward forces, his insides were squashed. He just managed to roll onto his side as he projectile-vomited.

Choking and gasping for air, Ryan could feel the smooth floor beneath his cheek and temple.

He opened his eye and could see a dim light in the heart of the swirling fog.

They had arrived. Somewhere.

As he crawled toward the brightness, he felt as if he had been run over by a convoy of wags. His skin crackled strangely, as if tissue paper had been stuffed under it. The others were moving on all fours, also apparently unable to stand. He counted the dark shapes on either side of him—all were accounted for.

"Triple red," he said, or tried to say. His voice came out as a hoarse and almost inaudible croak.

None of them, himself included, had the strength to do more than drag their blasters along.

The edges of the porthole doorway were obscured by the dense, low-hanging fog. As he advanced hand over hand toward the center of the light, the hard glass turned into something softer under his palms and then his knees.

The gray mist began to lift from the floor. The door stood open.

He saw a pair of bare feet in front of him—small, pale, female feet, with red-painted toenails. As the fog dissipated, the woman came into full view. She was young and dressed as no Deathlander he'd ever seen—

not even a baron's wife. Her clothes looked new and were of a strange style: a jacket tailored at the waist and a knee-length skirt snugged around the hips, both cut from the same shiny gray cloth. In her ears, there were sparkling jewel studs, what Ryan thought to be diamonds from pics he had seen. Her shoulder-length hair was brown with red highlights, her small nose freckled.

But what commanded his attention was the enormous gold handblaster she held pointed at them, hammer cocked back to fire. The hole in the business end looked as big as a sewer pipe. The slide and frame were black striped, like the pelt of a tiger. From her stance he could tell she knew what she was doing, and the yawning muzzle stayed rock steady. Her fingernail color matched that of her toes.

"This isn't happening," she said, a look of horror in her eyes. Then it passed and she said, "Don't move, any of you!"

Ryan tried to speak and couldn't make his throat muscles obey. A faint, wheezing noise escaped his lips.

To his right, Ricky was still retching, but nothing was coming out of his mouth. He had already vomited all down the front of his T-shirt. It was on his cheeks, his neck and in his hair, too. The youth's tan face looked deadly pale as he struggled to control the spasms.

The others seemed to have better weathered the storm—at least they weren't still puking. Some of the decorative beads in Mildred's plaits had broken, and the braids were undone. Jak had a shallow, bleeding, horizontal cut on his chin. Doc looked dazed, but no more than unusual.

The room where they had materialized was small and cramped. Ryan had never seen so much predark stuff concentrated in one place, but it lay in scattered, broken heaps on the Oriental carpet. A steady grinding noise was coming from the other side of the tall windows—it sounded like hundreds of wag engines all revving at once, interspersed with occasional horn blasts. When he glanced behind them, the open entrance to the chamber they had exited peeked in and out of gray mist.

"Where are we?" Krysty asked, glowering up at their captor. "What ville is this?"

"'Ville'?" the woman said. "It's Greenwich Village. Who the hell are you? And where in hell did you come from?"

"Look at this place, Ryan," Mildred said. "They must have just passed through here. They have to be close."

He stared down at a broken, framed photo on the floor. A woman in fatigues and a boonie hat was standing behind the corpse of an immense wild boar—at least five hundred pounds, he guessed. She had a bloody spear in one hand and a bloody combat knife in the other and was smiling through her camo face paint.

It was the same woman who was holding them at blasterpoint.

"Who is 'they'?" the woman demanded. "Do you mean the bastards who wrecked my apartment?"

"The bastards we're chasing," Ryan said, his power of speech recovered. "Which way did they go?"

Before she could answer, a whooping, rhythmic siren erupted from outside.

Figuring that if the woman was really going to open

fire on them, she would have already done so, Ryan rushed to the bank of windows, and the others followed.

As Mildred looked down on the street she said, "Well, that makes a nice change."

The enforcers' elephantine wedding tackle was no longer on display; they had put on pants. Even so, the width and heft of their bodies was unmistakable as were the blocky shapes of their heads inside tight purple hoods. And they were still barefoot.

The lone siren quickly became a deafening chorus. The enforcers rampaged along the sidewalk below, breaking into the small wags jammed end to end— strangely enough, the row of wags looked almost new. The muties rammed their fists through driver windows, ripped the doors from their hinges and tossed them over their shoulders. The wags sagged heavily to one side when enforcers jumped in and began tearing wires from under dashboards, presumably trying to start the engines without keys.

Magus was nowhere in sight.

The woman with the big blaster joined them at the window. "I am definitely losing it," she said, her weapon now pointed at the floor. "Those things aren't human."

A doorway across the street burst open, and a tall man in a robe ran down the stairs. He crossed the street, carrying a yard of polished wooden club, fat at one end, a knurled knob at the other. With the club cocked over his shoulder, he yelled over the din of alarms for an enforcer to get away from his shiny personal wag. Snapping the driver's door free of the hinge, the creature spun at the waist, flinging it sideways like a gigantic buzz saw. It struck bathrobe man amidships and nearly cut him in two. The impact left him sprawled facedown on the pavement, in the middle of a spreading puddle of gore.

Try as they might, the enforcers couldn't seem to get the commandeered wags running. In frustration, holes were punched through the roofs, steering wheels snapped off and windshields kicked out onto hoods.

"Is it just me," Doc said, "or does this all seem a bit chaotic for old Steel Eyes? It hardly reflects the usual high level of advanced planning…" The old man was confused by what he saw outside.

"The clockwork man likes things to go like clockwork," Ryan agreed.

"Mebbe his brain's stripped a gear?" J.B. said, without tearing his eyes from the escalating destruction below, wondering how all of the wags had survived looting and scavenging, where the gas had come from.

"Ryan, if we don't get Magus now…" Krysty said.

"You're right," he agreed. "Keep the incendies ready. We're going to have to get in close to maximize the effect."

As they moved for the door, the woman once more raised her blaster. "Who are you?"

"No time for introductions," Ryan told her. "Shoot us in the back if you want, but we're going after them."

Jak led them out the apartment door and down the marble stairs.

"Toss the grens inside the wags if you can," Ryan said as they crouched in the foyer. "Locate Magus."

They burst through the building's front door two abreast, but had descended only the first few steps when autofire rattled from the far side of the street.

A rain of bullets spanged the concrete treads and wrought-iron railings and crashed through the glass in the entry behind them.

With hard cover more than thirty feet out of reach, Ryan had no choice. He turned and pushed the others back through the doorway. Otherwise they were going to be cut to pieces.

Inside the foyer, Mildred said, "Enforcers were doing the shooting, I saw them."

"That's a new wrinkle," J.B. said. "They never touched blasters on the island."

"They were firing AKS-74Us one-handed," Mildred continued, "waving them around like garden hoses."

More high-velocity slugs zipped through the door's broken glass, cutting tracks down the wall plaster and knocking chips out of the staircase.

"Why are they using blasters now?" Ricky said. "We can't chill them with bullets. Why do they need blasters?"

"To make us keep our distance and hold our fire," Ryan said. "Magus is part human and can be hurt with bullets. Did anyone see the bastard?"

Heads shook no.

Another sustained burst of autofire raked the building's entrance, forcing them to press their backs against the wall. The opposition's ammo supply seemed endless.

"They're going to get away, Ryan," Krysty said after the shooting stopped. "Gaia, they're all going to get away."

AFTER THE SCRUFFY strangers trooped out, Veronica stood amid the ruins of her living room, unable to take her eyes off the gray cloud and the dark, ovoid shape lurking behind it.

If it was real, she reasoned, then everything that had just happened was real.

With the Eagle raised to fire, she looked inside the chamber, saw that it was empty. She gingerly touched the edge of the doorway with a fingertip and got a powerful static shock that made her jerk back her hand. There was actually a little flash and an audible crackle.

It was not a dream.

The creatures outside were real. Mr. Crawford's body in the street was real. Eye-patch man and the others weren't lifted from some low-budget '80s John Carpenter film—they were real, too.

Automatic gunfire clattered in the street. What with that and all the car alarms going off at once, it sounded like video clips of Beirut. Then bullets smashed through her street-facing windows, angling up and digging ugly holes in the plaster overhead. The original 1850s ceiling medallion took the worst of it.

As if she wasn't pissed enough.

"Hosers!" she shouted.

Avoiding the broken glass underfoot, she ran back into her bedroom. From the closet, she pulled out a pair of running shoes and slipped them on. Then she took the cross-draw, leather chest holster from its hook on the wall behind her clothes, inserted the Desert Eagle and strapped it across her suit jacket. Its twin pouches held 8-round magazines of .44 Magnum bullets.

The weight of the fully loaded harness felt good.

A DIY curriculum of advanced combat and weapons training had not only helped her keep her job, it had taught her that, unlike the authors she wet-nursed and contrary to her own expectations—and the expectations of those who thought they knew her—she was absolutely fearless. It turned out danger flipped her secret switch. Where others feared to tread, Veronica Currant jumped in with both feet.

Born to raise hell and take scalps.

And now, out of the blue, she had been given the chance to fight monsters. Not monsters in lamentable purple prose. Not in a mindless video game. But in the flesh. It felt as if her whole life had been leading up to this moment.

The cats were still hiding wide-eyed under the bed and wouldn't come when she called and made kissing sounds. They weren't going anywhere anytime soon.

She yanked the Eagle from its sheath. Kicking the debris from her path, she exited the apartment. As she looked over the hallway rail, more bullets crashed through the front door, a story below.

The strangers were out of the line of fire, squatting along the walls of the foyer, clearly pinned down. Eyepatch, the albino, the black woman, the guy with glasses and fedora, the brown kid, the statuesque redhead, the senior citizen with walking stick—they were variations, permutations of the series' characters she lived with on a daily basis. Prototypical crusty, hard-bitten badasses, a melange of signature guns and knives in abundance, dressed like homeless people.

And of course, they had suddenly and remarkably come to life.

"This way!" she shouted as she rounded the foot of the staircase. She led them down the hallway to the back of the building and out a rear entry. She turned to the left and descended another short set of steps to the backdoor landing of the building's below-ground apartment. The door looked solid, but for someone who had mastered violent-entry techniques, it wasn't. Expelling a grunt, she executed a front kick, planting her foot in precisely the right spot. With a crunch, the door splintered away from the deadbolt and lock plate and swung slowly inward.

"There's nobody here. Don't worry," she said as she stepped through the entrance. "Owner's still at work. Go on through to the front. We can come up from below street level, get cover from the parked cars."

The leggy redhead raised an eyebrow at the word *we*, her expression undisguisedly suspicious and hostile, but the Latino kid with vomit on his shirt and the old man beamed at her. They all seemed taken aback at the apartment's furnishings.

The fedora-and-glasses guy pointed at the calendar on the kitchen wall. "Wow, that's an old one," he said.

Veronica thought the remark was odd since it was the current *Sports Illustrated* Swimsuit Edition, and the model in question—blonde, tanned, microbikini, zero body fat, draped over the stern of a vintage speedboat—was all of twenty.

"Don't put your eyes out staring," the black woman said, giving him a hard shove from behind.

Taking them through to the living room, Veronica opened the front door, which led up to the street.

Eyepatch put a hand on her shoulder and stopped her from taking point. "This is as far as you go, lady," he said. "Trust me, you have no idea what you're getting yourself into."

He held up a red canister. She recognized it at once from her extensive research. Thermite. Four- to five-second delay fuse. Undo safety clip, pull pin, release safety lever. Throwing range, twenty-five meters.

"Let's clear a path, Jak," Eyepatch said to the albino. "Right through the windows, into their laps."

The albino pulled out his own thermite grenade. Veronica thought that the canister's color was a disturbingly close match to his eyes.

They pushed past her and climbed to the top of the short flight of steps. The others hung back, just below the level of the street. Safety levers plinked off. The two men chucked hissing grenades.

Eyepatch and the albino didn't appear ready for what happened next—because they didn't duck.

Massive overlapping explosions rocked the ground, sending them flying backward, arms and legs flailing. As they crashed down on top of their equally astonished friends, the concussion blast emptied window frames up and down the street. A wave of blistering heat washed over the stairwell, then car alarms a block away started wailing.

"Dark night," the man in the fedora said as he regained his feet. "What was in those wags?"

"Let's do this before they recover," Eyepatch said, unslinging his Steyr Scout. Then he scrambled back up the steps, with the others close behind.

Despite the warning for her to stay put, Veronica brought up the rear, Eagle at the ready. The pall of greasy black smoke that hung over the sidewalk made it hard to breathe. Inside the towering, twin fireballs at the curb, there was nothing left but twisted car frames and axles. The spindly sidewalk trees were burning furiously, as if they'd been doused with gasoline, and the cars fore and aft of the thermite strikes were on fire,

too. Monsters in purple hoodies had given up trying
to jumpstart a ride. They lumbered across the street
and disappeared behind the parked cars. She followed
the strangers as they took cover away from the heat
and smoke, next to a pair of cars farther up the block.
As she ducked beside the rear passenger door, autofire
rattled at them from the opposite sidewalk. The driver
side of the sedan absorbed a torrent of bullets. The left-
hand tires both blew out, glass shattered and the car
quivered on its suspension. Just above her head, slugs
zipped through the front compartment and sparked on
the concrete steps behind them.

She had gone through live-fire drills in a Georgia
backwoods training camp. This was no drill; these
shooters weren't trying to miss. No way could she get
off a shot from her position without putting her head
in the ten-ring.

Then Eyepatch, the Latino kid, the black woman
and the redhead jumped up from the ends of vehicles
and returned fire.

The albino was already in motion, scampering like
a white spider between car bumpers. With an under-
handed, bowling-ball pitch, he skipped a sputtering
red can across the street and under the car the shooters
were firing from behind. Then he dived back over the
front hood amid a flurry of bullets. He landed with a
shoulder roll and came up crouched on the balls of his
feet, grinning madly.

An instant later a tremendous boom shook the street.
The jolt dropped Veronica hard onto both knees. As she
caught herself, she thought she saw a shadowy blur of
car door and hood sailing high overhead, then a wave
of withering heat made her whimper.

Grenades of that type didn't explode, she knew. The car's gas tank hadn't exploded, either. Not enough time had elapsed for the heat to reach combustion point. The monsters themselves had exploded, like they had five pounds of short-fused C-4 stuffed up their butts.

She peered over the windowsill and saw the surviving monsters break cover and take off down the sidewalk in the direction of Washington Square Park. Their blocky heads and wide shoulders bobbed over the tops of the cars. The monster in front held the one she'd thought was Bob Dylan, carrying the form as if it were a small child—or a ventriloquist's dummy— legs bouncing up and down at the knees.

When the strangers popped up from behind cover, so did she. Taking stable holds against the vehicles and trees, they all opened fire at once. Eyepatch worked the Steyr's bolt like a machine, punching out shot after scope-aimed shot. She could see his bullets striking the backs and heads of the retreating monsters, plucking at the fabric, the impacts staggering them as they ran.

Veronica knew her ballistics. For some reason, what should have been certain kill shots with 7.62 mm NATO rounds wasn't.

She tracked the moving targets over the sights of the Eagle but held fire—without a clear shot, no way was she going to send .44 Magnum slugs sailing down her own street.

The opposition seemed to have a destination in mind.

As they disappeared around the corner, Veronica's new friends leaped from between the cars to give pursuit. Eyepatch waved for her to stay put.

"No, lover," said the redhead, a strange glint in her eyes, "let her come along if she wants to."

Again bringing up the rear, Veronica holstered the Eagle, as it was awkward and heavy to carry in hand while running.

The monsters crossed West Fourth Street against the light, bringing the afternoon traffic to a screeching, horn-honking halt. They took off along the wide sidewalk that bordered the south side of Washington Square Park, scattering pedestrians and sending them fleeing into the trees. The panicked screams brought a pair of horse-mounted cops onto the sidewalk. As they drew sidearms on the approaching purple-hooded crew, their steeds suddenly spooked, reared and, with minds of their own, shot off back into the park.

Farther ahead at the corner, a helmeted motorcycle cop jumped the curb and, with the bike's siren wailing, cut off the monsters' path. He drew and rapid-fired his service automatic pistol, but it didn't slow the charge. The monsters swept over him. Then, like a CG movie stunt, something that shouldn't have been possible in real life, both Harley and rider were tossed forty feet in the air and came crashing down on the stopped traffic.

The motorcycle's siren abruptly cut off on impact, but more were coming from all directions and getting louder by the second. The police response would be the Emergency Service Unit—ESU—NYC's version of SWAT. That was not a good thing. Veronica wanted to yell a warning to the others that armed civilians would be shot first and asked questions afterward, but couldn't because she was struggling to breathe and keep up the headlong pace. Though Eyepatch and the rest were running hard, they kept looking around. They seemed disturbed, even apprehensive about the surroundings, the people, the traffic, the city skyline.

A half block ahead of them, the monsters poured down the steps to the West Fourth Street subway entrance. As they closed in on it, the rattle of rapid gunfire rolled up from belowground. It sounded like pistols, not AKs.

They paused at the edge of the stairs to catch their breaths.

"Why are they running from us?" the Latino kid said. "They're stronger, even without blasters. Why they not stand and fight?"

No one answered him.

Hat-and-glasses guy was staring up at the tall, wall-to-wall buildings, as if he'd never seen the like before.

"Dark night! This isn't Deathlands," he gasped. "Where in nukin' hell are we?" To Veronica it looked as if he was on the verge of hyperventilating.

The black woman put a hand on his back and tried to calm him. "We're in New York, J.B."

Eyepatch didn't seem to notice his friend's distress. "We've been here before," he said. His attention was focused on the traffic on the street beside them; he seemed to be looking from one license plate to another.

"What year is this?" he asked Veronica.

In the context of what had already happened, the question didn't seem all that strange. "It's 2001," she said.

"By the Three Kennedys," the old man groaned, "we have jumped back in time."

Veronica blinked at him in disbelief. "You're from the future, then?" she asked dubiously. As she uttered those ridiculous words, an uncharitable thought popped into her mind: Wow, it must really suck.

Eyepatch didn't confirm or deny their origins. Instead he asked another question. "What month and day is it?"

"It's January 19." A thoroughly assimilated New Yorker, she added sarcastically, "Why? Do you people have somewhere more important to be?"

"Anyplace but here and now would be just fine," Eyepatch said. "The world ends at noon tomorrow."

Chapter Three

When the bundle of meat and metal in its arms shrilled a command, the enforcer cut hard right and started down the stairs that led below street level. Its brethren followed in lockstep. They had been to this strange-tasting, chaotic, crowded place many times in the service of their shambling master. The fact that they had never before missed the designated landing spot, never met opposition on arrival or taken a casualty did not make it uneasy. They were trivial concerns compared to the inconceivable power the master had shown them over and over.

The power to loot the past and change the future.

As it descended, a rush of warm air rolled up the concrete steps, propelled by the pressure of a subway train moving in a tunnel beneath them. The enforcer sampled the gritty wind with its tongue. Mixed in with inanimate molecules of soot, of petrochemical solvents, of greasy, spoiled food and lavatory-cookie perfume was the flavor of living bodies, hearts pumping hot, red blood and skins oozing a watery sweat. The aroma of humanity did not perk its appetite.

It wasn't a predator.

It didn't kill to eat, or kill because it hated; it killed because it could.

At the bottom of the stairway, subway riders starting

up for the street took one look at the mass of hooded, menacing figures coming toward them, spun 180 degrees and fled in the opposite direction, scattering across the concrete concourse.

The wide entrance floor was bisected by a barrier of stainless-steel turnstiles and a security kiosk. On previous visits they had paid to ride, according to local custom; this time, however, the master was in a rush and waved for them to hurry ahead. The brethren started hopping the turnstiles, which brought a pair of uniformed NYPD Transit Police charging out of the kiosk to intercept them. Obviously intimidated by the size and number of the fare cheaters, they drew their 9 mm sidearms.

"Stop!" one of them shouted over the sights of his handgun.

The black communication device on his hip chirped and crackled. A disembodied voice announced, "Ten-double-zero, officer down," then gave a description of multiple, identically dressed suspects fleeing the scene on foot and their last known direction of travel.

With the master cradled in its arms, the enforcer easily jumped the turnstile's spokes.

"Stop or we'll fire!" the policeman repeated, eyes wide as he and his partner, pistols held in two-handed grips, closed distance.

From ten feet away the two cops started shooting. Instinctively, the enforcer shielded the master from the flurry of bullets with its own body. The hits to its torso and back barely registered as such—its sheer mass absorbed the shock of the impacts; its armored endoskeleton deflected the projectiles from vital organs. It did feel the hits to the side of its head, though; as its skull was violently jarred again and again, bright white lights flashed behind its eyes.

Bullets ricocheted off it in a wide arc, spraying across the concourse, with nothing to stop their flight but human flesh and bone. A male in an olive parka and watch cap was hit from behind; his knees buckled. An elderly female took a slug in the chest, sagged and toppled, spilling the contents of her shopping bags onto the concrete. Other bystanders dropped at random, as if their strings had been cut. People began screaming. The few who realized what was happening pressed their faces to the floor.

One of the cops circled to the front—from his aim-point, trying to line up a head shot on the master. Before he could fire, the enforcer shifted the precious dead-weight to its left arm and hopped forward with both feet. Toe to toe with the policeman, it struck with its free hand—a precise blow, perfectly timed, with more than three hundred pounds of mass behind it. The amber thumb hook drove into the corner of the man's left eye socket, through and under the bridge of his nose and out the opposite socket. For an instant they were frozen, the impaler and the impaled, then the handgun slipped from the cop's fingers and clattered on the concrete. With a brisk snap of its wrist, the enforcer wrenched off the face, from forehead to upper jaw, like a cheap plastic lid, leaving behind a yawning red crater and ex-posed tongue. A gargling noise burst from the officer's throat as he collapsed, then blood began to fountain.

The other cop staggered in retreat, the slide on his empty pistol locked back. Behind him, one of the breth-ren ripped a turnstile from its mounting and with a downward, single-handed blow, drove one of the fat, stainless spokes through the crown of his head. The massive surge of pressure inside the skull made both eyes pop out of their sockets, but the policeman never felt it. He was already dead.

As master and disciples advanced toward the platform entrances, the screams and shouts behind them grew louder and louder. Humanity was waking up. Commuters in winter coats and hats rushing up from the trains parted like a school of panicked baitfish. While some darted for safety, others flattened themselves against the walls or fell helplessly to their knees. Those who froze in their tracks midconcourse were either bowled over and trampled or grabbed, broken and flung out of the way.

The half man/half machine in the enforcer's arms shuddered and made a clanking, grinding noise—like a wag throwing a tie-rod.

The master was laughing.

Then the grating, steel-scraping-on-steel voice said, "Faster! Hurry!"

They trooped down more flights of stairs, smashing and hurling human obstacles out of their path. When they stepped onto the middle of the subway platform, the nearest waiting commuters hurried for the other exits. On the opposite platform, a crowd stared at them uneasily.

From down the tunnel to the right came a rush of warm wind, signaling the approach of a train—one going in the opposite direction.

"Cross the tracks!" the half man/half machine shouted at them. "Now! Run!"

The enforcer carrying the master didn't expect an explanation. That it understood the reasons for an action wasn't required. Its brain was no match for the master's, even without its comp enhancement. The only thing required was that it did as it was told. With the other brethren, it jumped down from the platform onto the soot and grease-blackened rail bed.

"Watch out for the electrified rail," the master reminded it.

As the enforcer stepped over the high-voltage track, between the ceiling supports, the wind gusted harder. It tasted ozone and rat shit in the steady breeze, and when it looked down the dark tunnel it saw the headlight of the train bearing down on them.

The humans on the platform were yelling and waving for them to go back. When they saw the hooded, assault-rifle-armed heavyweights were going to make it safely across, they turned and raced for the exits.

The brethren jumped up onto another deserted platform.

Seconds later the long, low train squeaked to a stop beside them. The doors to all the cars slid open and commuters flowed onto the platform, moving quickly past the enforcers, looks of astonishment on their faces. When the brethren entered the middle door of a car, they forced a mad exodus of riders out either end. Commuters pushed and shoved to escape.

"Put me down," the master said.

The enforcer obeyed at once, carefully lowering the half man/half machine to the floor of the car. As it did so, there was a rumbling sound and a vibration beneath them, then more shrill squeaking as a train going the other way came to a stop at the opposite platform.

Through the speakers overhead, an automated voice warned travelers that their car doors were about to close.

"Don't look in the other train!" the master screeched as all the doors whooshed shut.

Another command without explanation.

But too late this time. It had already turned its head. The train opposite was only a few feet away; plates of grease-smeared window glass faced each other across the narrow gap. It blinked its eyes and immediately turned back.

With a stomach-wrenching lurch, they accelerated away from the station.

The two trains had been side by side for only a second or two, but the afterimage of what it had seen through the hazy windows, in the strangely flickering, interior lights was burned into its mind.

Standing in the aisle of the opposing train, it had seen itself, the master and the others.

Even the two brethren who had fallen.

Chapter Four

A handful of people dashed up the stairs from the subway as if hell was on their heels. They ran past Ryan and down the sidewalk. Wailing sirens closed in all around. The wags on the street were stopped bumper to bumper, engines idling, horns honking, drivers shouting. So much noise, so many wags. So many people packed into such a small space—faces looking down from thousands of windows onto a gray canyon, which snaked between towering buildings. The concrete was cold against his palm. He smelled wag exhaust, saw the overcast sky above—though he felt like a speck of dust sucked down into the spinning gears of a vast and angry machine, it was all real.

All happening.

"Magus is heading for one of the underground trains," Mildred said. "If we don't catch up quick, we're going to lose the trail."

Unslinging his Steyr, Ryan waved for the others to follow. As he descended the stairs, the honking, wailing din turned into a screaming din. Wide and low-ceilinged, the concourse echoed with cries of pain and anguish. As the companions jumped the turnstiles, dazed people struggled up from the floor ahead of them. Seeing the group's weapons, some pointed and screamed at them. Some pleaded for help as they pulled on limp arms, trying to raise loved ones who were obviously past raising. Some just sat weeping, with their faces buried in their hands.

"Ryan, wait," Krysty said, catching him by the arm. "How are we going to stop the enforcers? We can't use thermite in here. Look around. There are too many innocent people."

"They're all going to be ashes in less than twenty-four hours anyway," J.B. said.

"But not by our doing," Mildred argued.

"We'll figure that out when we find Magus," Ryan told her.

The trail the enforcers left behind was easy to follow, even in a full-out sprint. It consisted of broken bodies—some still crawling, most not. It led them through a doorway and down a long flight of stairs.

As Ryan stepped onto the empty platform, a shrill horn sounded. In front of him, the low silver train was already in motion to the right. He got a quick but unmistakable glimpse of purple-hooded behemoths clogging the middle of one of the cars before the train disappeared into the tunnel.

Across the tracks, beyond the row of ceiling supports, the opposite platform was empty—no passengers, no train.

"What do we do now?" Ricky asked.

Ryan turned to the woman with the unholstered, tiger-striped blaster. She didn't look rattled by what she'd just seen, which surprised him. She looked really, really pissed off. "Which way is that train headed?"

"North to Herald Square," she said.

"How many stops in that direction?" Mildred asked.

"It isn't the number of stops," the woman said. "They could get off anywhere, change trains, reverse direction. If you don't know where they're going..."

"We don't know where they're going or why," Ryan said.

"Nukin' hell!" J.B. exclaimed, screwing down his fedora with one hand. "We did this for nothing? We're going to die for nothing?"

"Attention," a voice bellowed through the speakers above the platform. "Attention, all subway passengers. This station is being cleared for security reasons. Repeat, this station is being cleared for security reasons. Until the procedure is complete, no more trains will be stopping here. For your own safety and the safety of those around you, please remain calm and follow the signs to the nearest street exit. If you need help, NYPD officers will be available to assist you."

"What's going on?" Krysty asked.

"The ESU is about to clean house," the woman with the tiger-striped blaster said as the announcement began to repeat.

"Combat-trained, militarized police," Mildred explained. "Automatic weapons. Grenades. Snipers. Explosives."

"This place is about to be assaulted by men in black uniforms, battle helmets and armored vests," the woman added. "They will see us as armed suspects at the scene of a mass murder or terrorist attack. They will shoot on sight. We have two choices. Abandon our weapons now, blend in with the other passengers as best we can before they sweep in and hope to hell they don't review the station's closed circuit video before we manage to get out—"

"We're not going to throw away our blasters," J.B. interrupted.

"That's a nonstarter," Mildred agreed.

"The other choice is to follow the purple hoodies down the tunnel," the woman said.

"But they are on a train, my dear, and we are on foot," Doc said.

"I don't mean follow them down the tunnel to catch them," the woman stated. "I mean go down the tunnel to get out of here. ESU will clear the station first and then move on to the tunnels. If you want to keep your guns and stay alive, we have to escape while they're busy elsewhere."

"Do you know the way?" Ryan asked.

"Yeah, as a matter of fact, I do," the woman said as she holstered the big gold blaster. "Follow me. My name's Veronica, by the way. Veronica Currant. But you can call me Vee."

They quickly exchanged names; there was no time for handshakes.

Overhead the loudspeaker voice boomed, "Attention subway passengers. Attention subway passengers. If you are injured and unable to move or find yourself trapped, please remain calm. Do not resist the approaching armed police officers. Obey all their commands. They will take you to safety and medical help as quickly as possible."

Vee led them down to the end of the platform, then jumped down onto the rail bed. "Stay away from that," she said, pointing to the left, at the third rail.

Ryan had already noticed the red warning sign that read Danger High Voltage. The lights in the tunnel were dim and widely spaced; the air rank and humid.

A thick coating of black grime covered its walls and coated the clustered pipes and cables that ran along them.

They had trotted maybe fifty yards when Vee stopped at a barely visible hatch-style door on the right. It was unmarked. With a grunt, she leaned on the locking lever, and the door cracked open. "This is a tunnel-maintenance access and emergency exit," she said. "From here we can get to the street."

She leaned through the doorway, then a weak light came on inside.

"How do you know so much about this place?" Mildred asked as they filed into the cramped space. "Do you work here or something?"

"No, I just pick up odd, interesting tidbits in my job," she said.

A very steep stairway led up, so steep there were support rails along both walls. When they shut and dogged the hatch door, it muffled the racket from the station. They ascended in silence, except for the sounds of their breathing.

Ryan could feel the strain in his thighs as he put one boot in front of another. They had done a lot of full-out running and fighting in a very short time span. Not to mention the aftereffects of the chron jump. J.B.'s comment about their sacrifice being all for nothing tried to go around and around in his head, but he shut it off.

The game wasn't over yet, not by a long shot.

Not while they still drew breath.

At the top of the stairs, they found a long, darkened hallway with broad puddles of standing water on the floor. Steam pipes and conduit hung low above them; what looked like banks of generators and transformers, and their controlling circuit panels, stood behind locked cages of heavy wire. When Vee opened the exit door to an alley, the grinding din was back—wag horns, the steady growl of engines, sirens, now mixed with unintelligible bullhorn commands. They moved quickly between high, windowless brick walls, around a hard right corner to the mouth. The street leading to the subway entrance was now blocked off with police and emergency vehicles and flashing lights. Helicopters zigzagged across the sky overhead. No one had time to marvel at what was going on outside.

"Our position appears untenable," Doc observed.

"Then we go back to her place," Ricky said, nodding in Vee's direction. "We get in the machine and go back home to Deathlands."

"That isn't possible," Vee told him. "What you see happening on this street is what's happening on my block. That's the response when people get killed and cars get blown up. The whole area will have been cordoned off by armed police with helicopter overflights. No way in or out."

"We shouldn't have chased Magus onto the street," J.B. opined. "We should have just followed at a distance until we had a chance to chill him, with no witnesses. Now we're as dead as everyone else in this city. That apartment is our only way out."

"Even if we could get back into her building, J.B.," Ryan said, "even if we figured out the mat-trans's controls and somehow made it to Deathlands, I think we'd arrive at the same redoubt with enforcers clawing at the door."

"So," Krysty said, "if the city sec men don't kill us, the enforcers at the other end of the chron jump will.

And if we survive here until the twentieth, the nuke strikes will take us out anyway."

"That doesn't leave many options," Mildred stated.

"Except to have one hell of a send-off," Krysty said.

"The mistake was all mine," Ryan told them. "I brought this down on us. We should have waited outside the redoubt for Magus to come back. From the moment we set foot inside that place, we were fucked."

"Stuck between a rock and another rock," Doc said soberly.

They had been caught in countless tight spots in the past—or more correctly in the future—but they had always been able to figure a way out. This time perhaps not. A question occurred to Ryan: Could a person really die a hundred years before he was born? He kept it to himself.

"We still have some time left," Vee said. "Can't we change the future somehow? Avert this nuclear attack? What do you know about it?"

She sounded remarkably calm for someone who'd recently learned the world was going to blow up in a matter of hours, Doc thought.

"Precious little that would help that cause, my dear," Doc said. "An all-out missile exchange between the United States and the Russians on January 20, 2001, created a global, nuclear holocaust that ended much of civilization. That conflagration and its aftermath necessarily complicates the unraveling of the whos, the wheres and the whens. Which one, if either, started it is unknown. It could have been initiated by a third party or a computer glitch—or misinterpreted data. Miscommunication, even. Because we don't know the precise chain of circumstances that triggered Armageddon, altering the course of those events becomes difficult if not impossible."

"If you're thinking of warning someone about nuke-day," Krysty said, "who would listen?"

"You're right," Vee agreed. "No one is going to listen."

"You believe us?" Ricky asked.

"After what I've seen with my own eyes today, I'd believe anything you told me."

"What's happened to us is triple bad luck, and there's no way around it," Ryan told the others. "But it doesn't change why we're here. Or what we can do in the time we have left. One way or another we can still make sure Magus never leaves this place."

"Chill half-metal bastard," Jak spit.

"We need to get off the street and figure out how," Ryan said.

"We can go to my office," Vee told. "It will be closed for the night by the time we get there. I have the keys. No one will bother us. We can cut through the alleys and stay out of sight."

As they trooped single file down the sidewalk, away from the subway station and the police barricades, a man in a peacoat stepped from a doorway and, smiling broadly, accosted Ryan. "Snake Plissken!" he exclaimed. "I thought you were dead!" Then he laughed like a mutie hyena.

Ryan kept walking. It wasn't the first time he had heard that line.

To his back the man shouted, "Hey, Snake, *Escape from L.A.* blew chunks!"

Chapter Five

Angelo McCreedy lowered his copy of the *Daily Racing Form* as people poured up the steps from the Thirty-Fourth Street–Herald Square Metro station. In his classic black chauffeur cap, black three-piece suit and tie and black leather gloves, he leaned against the stretch limo's front fender. If his pickup didn't show soon, he was going to have to move the limo from the taxi stand and start circling the block—the cabbies lined up behind him were starting to get restless. Exiting subway travelers seemed in an extra big hurry this afternoon, maybe because of all the sirens going off. A major accident was the cherry on top. It could louse up traffic for the rest of the day.

As he folded his *Form* and tucked it under his arm, a mass of shiny purple appeared at the top of the subway stairs.

Man, those are some big dudes, he thought.

They looked almost identical, like octuplets. They were in matching outfits and had the same height and build. The tight hoodies kept their faces in shadow. They all sported what from a distance looked like very expensive alligator boots. All except the littlest one, who was being carried like a child.

Some kind of cripple, he thought. Poor thing had metal feet.

McCreedy's heart did a skip-tee-doo when the purple bunch turned and came right at him. His face flushed with fight-or-flight hormones. He wanted to retreat around the front of the vehicle but couldn't make his legs move quickly enough. He didn't notice the assault rifles they carried until the two-horned, front sight of one was jammed up under his chin.

The eyes shadowed by the hoodie top were yellow. Not yellow brown or yellow green. Yellow yellow, as in a daisy. And the pupils were elliptical slits that ran vertically, like a reptile's. The double-wide holding the gun had on a rubber, alligator Halloween mask; it and the daisy eyes had to be some kind of prank. Then the mouth opened, and he saw the rows of small, pointed teeth and the flicking tongue.

As he sagged back against the fender, the creature holding the cripple leaned the little one's head close to his ear. McCreedy opened his mouth to cry for help, but no sound came from his throat.

It had only half a human face, the rest was metal. The eyes were both metal. As the fan-bladed pupils opened wider, they made a whirring sound like the aperture of a cheap video camera. Guy wires and grommets connected its cheeks and jaw. Where living flesh abutted the stainless steel it looked angry and infected. It shouldn't have been alive, but it was.

In a voice that sounded like wing nuts rattling in a tin can, it said, "You will drive us."

As McCreedy was bum-rushed around the front bumper to the driver door, he kept thinking that this couldn't be happening. In desperation he looked to the slowly passing cars for help, which was absurd—it was Manhattan. No help was forthcoming.

The limo sagged heavily, springs squeaking as the purple crew began piling into the rear compartment, invisible behind the black-tinted windows. Rough hands shoved him behind the wheel and slammed the door. The monster who got in the front passenger seat carried a very short, very deadly-looking assault rifle. It was only then he noticed the wicked amber hooks on both thumbs.

"Keep the privacy screen down," the little one said. "Do exactly as I say, or your brains are going to end up on the hood like three pounds of bird shit."

"Yes, sir," McCreedy managed to croak. "Where do you want to go?"

The grating voice rattled off the address of a university hospital on the East Side. The bigger ones hadn't made a peep. He wondered if they could even speak. Without signaling, he pulled away from the curb and forced his way into the sluggish flow of traffic.

As they crept forward, he considered cracking a joke to break the ominous silence: "Hey, how 'bout those Mets?" But the eye-watering, cat-piss smell wafting from the limo's passenger compartment made him change his mind.

Like a meth ho's thong, he thought.

He glanced warily back in his rearview. They sat as still as statues on the white leather upholstery. If, in addition to being armed, stand-on-two-legs giant reptiles, they were tweakers, no telling how they would take a joke. Screw it, he needed to bail on the limo. Just get the heck out and quickly, before things got even worse.

McCreedy studied the traffic ahead. If he had a sufficient gap in front or on either side, he could floor the gas, open his door and roll out. To shoot at him, they'd have to get out on the opposite side and fire over the roof or around the bumpers. By the time they did that, he would be running against the direction of traffic, keeping his head down, using the cars for cover. He'd seen the same scenario pulled off lots of times on TV and in the movies. And what choice did he have anyway? He was fairly sure if he didn't do *something*, he was going to end up dead.

As he crept his fingers down to unfasten his seat belt, a horn of the assault rifle's front sight hooked under his nose. As if the monster had read his mind.

"Drive!" said the voice from the back.

At one point during the twenty-minute trip, he thought he heard snoring coming from the back. When he turned up the entrance ramp to the hospital complex's parking lot, the limo was riding so low the frame scraped on the concrete. Metal face directed him to the main building, which covered half a city block and was at least thirty stories tall.

McCreedy stopped in a patient-loading-and-unloading zone. He wondered what the heck they were doing at a hospital. If the little one needed an oil change and filter, Jiffy Lube had faster service.

A reptilian hand seized his neck and squeezed. The amber thumb hook rested against his jugular vein.

"You're coming with us. Get out slowly."

All of them piled out, the little one moving on its own in front of him in the middle of the pack. With an odd, herky-jerky gait, it passed through the automatic double doors.

The entourage drew immediate attention from staff and patients. Like a circus act. Or a rap ensemble.

"Wait just a minute, please." A pair of uniformed,

armed security guards stepped up to block their path. "Are you here for medical services or to visit someone?" one of them asked.

"Out of the way," the little one rattled.

The guards exchanged quick, concerned looks but did not budge. Their hands dropped to the butts of their holstered sidearms.

McCreedy started to shout a warning about the assault rifles, but before he could get a word out, the scaly hand tightened on his neck, shutting off his air and the flow of blood to his brain.

The reptilians didn't need guns to handle the situation.

One of them simply reached out and grabbed the big, burly men by their faces, gripping eye sockets and chins in either hand, pulled them over double and hauled them squealing through an open doorway. The door to the side room slammed shut. From the other side came violent, crashing sounds. It was over in seconds.

When the monster reappeared, McCreedy saw, inside the hood, below the slitted yellow eyes, a toothy smile.

Seeing them coming four abreast, hospital workers and civilians cleared a path, flattening against walls or slipping out of the way into rooms and alcoves, in some cases abandoning patients on gurneys and in wheelchairs to their fates.

They turned into the first elevator in a bank of four. The car groaned under their combined weight. One of them—maybe Metal face, he couldn't see who—pushed a button on the control panel. The doors closed; the car jerked, then began to smoothly drop. It was a tight fit; it smelled really bad and something was leaking from somewhere—puddles were spreading underfoot.

McCreedy looked up from his shoe tops and kept his eyes focused on the back-lit indicator above the door. They passed *P* for parking, then *B*—for basement, one through four, before stopping at *B5.*

The doors opened onto a windowless, drop-ceiling hallway lit by overhead fluorescents. The reek of form-aldehyde made a nice change from the aroma in the elevator. A rainbow of color-coded stripes on the facing concrete-block wall indicated the routes to various departments on this level: Pathology, Medical Records, Maintenance, Central Disinfection, as well as others.

They trudged down the corridor, made a hard right and filed through a doorway placard-labeled Bioengineering and Nanotechnology.

On the other side of a floor-to-ceiling glass wall, people in white face masks, hair covers and sterile suits were bent over rows of workstations. Everything was white on white.

One of the workers looked up from a binocular microscope. When he saw the mob standing on the other side of the glass, he rose and stepped to a sliding door. He cracked it back a scant couple of inches, pulled his face mask down under his grizzle-goateed chin and said, "Yes, how can I help you gentlemen?"

"Where is Dr. James Nudelman?" Metal face said.

"Jim went home sick today," he said, his eyes darting from one purple hoodie to the next. "He left before noon. He probably won't be back until Monday. Can I take a message?"

"And where is home?"

The goateed man opened the door wide enough to

step through and slid it shut behind him. "Who are you, exactly?" he asked.

One of the reptilians reached out, caught the man's right forearm in its hands and, with sickening ease, snapped it in two. Goatee let out a piercing scream and dropped to his knees, chin lowered to his chest. Masked faces on the far side of the glass turned to stare.

"Where is home?" the little one repeated with impatience.

Through clenched teeth, the man gave up the address. McCreedy recognized it as a building near Central Park.

"Good thing you work in a hospital, eh?" Metal face said.

"You mean because you broke my fucking arm?"

"No, because there's a morgue handy."

A purple-hooded monster loomed over the kneeling man.

McCreedy shut his eyes. He had a pretty good idea what was coming next.

Chapter Six

A person of unidentifiable sex and age, swaddled in many layers of cast-off, filth-blackened clothing, smelling pungently of his or her own bodily waste, pushed a shopping cart packed with assorted reclaimed rubbish—discarded toilet seat, lengths of rusty pipe, stacks of cardboard, rags, bottles, unmated shoes—into Doc's headlong path down the alley.

Whether the lunge was meant to simply attract his attention or to cause him some kind of injury, he reacted without breaking stride, long legs nimbly sidestepping the front of the cart. As he did so, his silver-handled sword stick hissed through the air and cracked the cart pusher a modest blow across the right cheek.

As if he was flicking a fly out of midair.

"Bas-tid! You bas-tid!" the him or her shouted in outrage.

Doc kept running. The complaint barely registered over the cooing, achingly familiar, female voice in his head.

"Theo, Theo…"

As he sprinted alongside the companions, fragments of his past were coming at him like a hail of rifle bullets, zinging into the front of his head and out the back. A razor-sharp jumble of agonizing been-there, done-that's, memories that spanned the two-hundred-plus years of his unique existence: walking the grounds of Christ Church College with his Oxford dons in the late 1880s; picnicking with his family in Omaha on the Fourth of July, 1896; being trawled against his will to an underground prison in the late-twentieth century, then being cast forward in time beyond the coming Armageddon to Deathlands, and there, further degraded, forced to service hogs for the amusement of Baron Teague's head sec man, Cort Strasser.

He had a bit of a memory of later, chilling stickies by the dozens, as they hung in mating chains on the side of a ruined, predark highway overpass, until all he could smell was burned cordite and aerosolized blood.

And then there was the present existence.

His experiences in late-nineteenth-century London, England, and various cities of the United States hadn't prepared him for Manhattan in 2001. He had usually been kept sequestered in ultrasecret redoubts after being trawled to the 1990s. Though he had access to printed and digital media during that confinement, he never had been directly exposed to the realities of civilization in the twenty-first century. The surrounding noise, the wags, the smells, the tall buildings, the sea of pavement, all the people, added up to a full-sensory scour that grated his every nerve end raw.

"Theo, Theo…"

His dear wife Emily's voice vibrated softly inside his head. It was the voice of a ghost. She had died two centuries before, as had his beloved children, Rachel and Joylon. He knew it wasn't real, but he couldn't make it stop. He had traveled through time on three occasions now. A human body could endure only so much of it, he thought. He knew that the shock of transit did fundamental damage to the workings of the human mind. He had succumbed to insanity's embrace many times in the past, but of late, he had remained fairly lucid. Perhaps this occasion was the straw that finally broke the camel's back.

For an instant, the black pit of insanity seemed to yawn before him, obliterating his awareness of present and past. As if they belonged to someone else, his legs kept driving.

No, not now, he told himself. Not here.

Not with the entire twenty-first-century New York police force and the full weight of calamitous history lined up against them.

For the sake of your companions, gather your wits, man! Doc urged.

To the steady beat of boot soles on pavement, he started singing a tune under his breath. It had been popular in Omaha, the year he was stolen from the embrace of his family.

"When you hear a dem bells…"

He couldn't help but crack a smile when he got to the chorus of the old minstrel song, "There'll be a hot time in the old town tonight." It was ironic, if a bit premature. The "hot time" in question—at one hundred million degrees, ten thousand times hotter than the sun—was still roughly a day away. And it was not going to be a party anyone returned home from.

In a single, blinding instant, everyone and everything around him was going to be deconstructed, erased from existence. He had no loved ones of his own left alive to contact, to warn, to say goodbye to. None of the companions did, except for Mildred. This was, after all, the time period in which she had been born and lived. He wondered if she would try to touch base with relatives. No, they thought she was in suspended animation in a cryo tank.

Maybe she still was?

That possibility gave Doc pause. Was a version of Mildred on ice, even as the Mildred he knew kept pace beside him, beaded plaits of hair bouncing in rhythm to her footfalls?

Time travel was a riddle wrapped in raw bacon. After you had turned it over and over in your mind, examined it from all sides, just when you thought you had it figured out, it slipped from your grasp.

They ran and ran, stopping only when they had to come out of an alley to cross a wide street. The scale of the city as seen from ground level was daunting—seemingly endless blocks of towering buildings jammed side by side.

Head lowered, panting hard, Doc waited with the others at an alley mouth while a daisy chain of police cruisers roared by, roof lights flashing. After letting the wags pass, they hurried to the opposite side of the street, then continued down the alley.

After another 150 feet, Vee signaled for a stop. "This is my work building," she said.

The bottom floor had no walls, as such. Behind heavy wire, steel bars and an electronic gate, many shiny wags sat parked in painted, numbered spaces on an immense pad of polished concrete.

Vee stepped up to the keypad beside the gate and punched in a code. Something clanked and then the gate smoothly rolled back.

"There are motion-detector video cameras in the

parking lot and elevator," she said. "They're connected to the building-security desk in the lobby. Keep your heads down and guns well out of sight. There's an audio mike in the elevator, too, so it'd be best to keep quiet."

Doc buttoned up his frock coat so the LeMat buckled on his hip wouldn't show.

There was a second keypad next to the elevator. Again, Vee entered the correct code. The doors slid open and everyone piled in. Then she hit the button for the twenty-second floor.

When the car stopped, they stepped out onto a plush, dark red-carpeted hall, on the far side of which was a wall of glass that looked out onto the street. It was almost dark, the opposing sides of the man-made canyon dotted with tiny rectangles of light. So many cubby holes stacked one on top of the other and edge to edge. Moving closer to the glass, Doc got a bit of a bird's-eye view of traffic on the wide avenue below. Because of the effective soundproof construction, he couldn't hear the noise it made.

The name of the publishing company was emblazoned across the wall behind him in foot-high, stainless-steel letters.

The others lined up in front of a water tank, taking turns at the tap. The paper cups it provided were ridiculously small. He was so thirsty.

Hungry, too. Light-headed.

Doc cleared his throat to get Vee's attention, then nodded at the food and drink behind the heavy glass of massive machines farther along the wall. "We could use some sustenance, as well," he said.

"I don't have any money," she confessed. "I didn't

think to bring a purse to a gunfight." After a second's pause she said, "The world is really going to end? You're sure about that?"

"Touch my hair," Krysty said.

"Why?"

"Just touch it."

Vee raised her hand and reached out with her fingertips. Before she could make contact, the hair on that side of Krysty's head retracted, winding up in tight coils. She jerked back. "It's alive! My God, it's alive!"

"That's the legacy of what is about to happen here," Krysty said. "I was born a century after the nukecaust."

Without another word, Vee took a red fire ax from its glass case on the wall and, bracing her legs, applied it liberally to the fronts of the machines. Plastic bags and bottles and aluminum cans cascaded to the floor among a shower of bright fragments.

"Help yourselves," she said. Then she turned to Ricky and said, "But why don't you go wash up first? The restroom is through that door."

"Rest room?" Ricky queried.

"A place where you can find water and paper towels," Vee explained.

"Yeah, kid," J.B. said, "you're going to put us off our feed. Go rinse the dried puke off your face."

Ricky was blushing as he pushed through the door.

When Mildred shot J.B. a disgusted look, he said, "What? He needed to clean up, didn't he?"

"He isn't the only one, pal," Mildred stated.

They each gathered up handfuls of bags and drinks, then Vee led them to a large room with a long table surrounded by well-padded chairs on wheels. One wall was plate glass, floor to ceiling; the other three were covered with framed, poster-size blowups of book covers and smaller portraits, presumably photos of the books' authors.

Doc spread out the bounty on the table in front of him. He had only a rough idea of what was inside each package. Salty or sweet, or both, he didn't really care. He started ripping open the plastic and stuffing the contents in his mouth.

Krysty pointed at a photo on the wall and said, "Ryan, isn't that…?"

Doc turned to look. The book in question was from the Slaughter Realms series, entitled *Iroquois Armageddon*. Beside it was a photo of a man smiling smarmily; it was someone he recognized.

Daniel Desipio.

The very same Fire Talker who'd nearly got them chilled by the Matachìn pirates. Not a time traveler, per se, he had been put in cryostasis to protect the world's population from the genetically modified, viral poison that lurked in his blood. A century later, the Lords of Death had thawed him out to serve as their weapon of war. Going from ville to ville, telling campfire stories to earn his keep, Desipio—with the help of local mosquitos—spread the deadly plague.

"How could you possibly know *him*?" Vee said. "The slimy little weasel disappeared a couple of years ago, took his multiple-book advances and vanished off the face of the earth. The publisher keeps his photo up there to remind us that writers can't be trusted."

"We don't know him," Ryan said flatly.

"But we did happen across some of his novels in the future," Doc continued, even though Ryan's expression said "Shut the fuck up." In Doc's opinion there was no

harm in a diversion from the current, dire situation—
a brief respite would afford them the opportunity to
regroup mentally. Besides, he wanted a better picture
of how Vee's mind worked.

"A century after nuclear war, the books still exist?"
she asked.

"It turns out their construction and materials are
very resilient," Doc said. "The books resist burning.
Starting a campfire with torn-out pages is an exercise
in futility. The paper smolders and blackens and gives
off a good deal of dark smoke but that's about it. I found
the main characters in the stories very imaginative. Iroquois Ninja Princess. Ragnar the Viking. Nav Licim,
the goggle-eyed leader of the Celery people. How did
the author come up with all that extraordinary detail?"

"He didn't," Vee said. "It was handed to him by our
in-house team. We call it work for hire. The company
owns the intellectual rights."

Doc looked from one garish book cover to the next.
Some of the genres hadn't existed in his day. What on
earth was a *Clanker*?

"I'm curious," Vee said. "How did you all manage
to get here if the world in your time is destroyed?"

"Technological remnants of this time that were protected from nukeday's EM blast are still functional,"
Mildred told her. "Some are so top secret very few
people in your day knew of their existence. In the future, no one knows how to repair these systems. Replacement parts are nonexistent, and their operation
is pure guesswork."

"We were chasing Magus and his enforcers," Ryan
said. "We didn't realize we were stepping into what
turned out to be a time hole."

"It was an accident," Doc added.

"Which one is Magus?" Vee asked.

"The little spindly one," Krysty said.

"Why were you chasing him?"

"Actually," Doc said, "Magus is more of an *it* than a *him*, my dear. At some point in the past, when it was still a *he*, perhaps certain bodily injuries were sustained. Or it is possible they are an accumulation of smaller insults over the span of a lifetime. Or perhaps parts wore out and had to be replaced. The end result is a creature half metal, half flesh and bone, perhaps with a computer-assisted brain. Whatever human sensibilities it had before this unholy transmogrification, it is entirely devoid of them now."

"It sounds like the series' character Clanker, only he's entirely steam powered," Vee said.

"Steel Eyes is real," Mildred said, "like Hitler or Pol Pot. Only with less of a conscience and all of the continental United States to make nasty in. Not for a political cause. Or a social agenda. Or for economic gain. For fun. Because it amuses."

"No one stands up to this Magus?"

"That's easier said than done," Mildred said. "Deathlands has no centralized government. No standing army or police force. Pockets of civilization are organized like a feudal system, where the most ruthless rise to the top and defend their turf with bands of armed sec men. There are no heavy industries, trade is limited. Boundaries between what's known as baronies are loose and always in dispute. The human population is small, widely spaced, and the only communication is by word of mouth. The general chaos makes survivors vulnerable to organized, mobile, systematic mayhem."

"What is Magus doing here?" Vee asked.

"There have been rumors going around for decades," Ryan said, "that Magus routinely time travels to before the nukecaust to gather weapons and supplies required for operations in Deathlands. Raw materials that are no longer available. Things that aren't made anymore."

"The past is like Magus's Costco," Mildred said.

"At the Deathlands' end of the time hole," Ryan went on, "we found evidence that it had been well used by Magus and enforcers."

"Why would Magus come to this time, so close to the nuclear holocaust?" Vee asked.

"That's a good question," Mildred said. "Of all the times to pop into, why this one?"

"Mebbe Magus has no choice," Ryan said. "Mebbe the hole can't be adjusted to come out in an earlier time."

"You mean it's a permanent route?" Krysty queried. "Like a mountain tunnel or a train track?"

"Sure, why not?" Ryan said. "Or originally the exits in the past and future could have been moved, but some of the controls got damaged. Who knows?"

"The last train west, literally and figuratively," Doc said.

"Or Magus can't figure out how to run them," J.B. added.

"Or Magus thinks moving the time hole is too big a risk," Mildred said.

After a pause Vee asked, "Who or what are enforcers?"

"We do not know who they are," Doc said. "What they are is incredibly dangerous and difficult to dispatch. We came across them once before, in prior skirmish with Magus. It is possible that, like Krysty's remarkable hair, they are genetic anomalies."

"Wait, I have an idea," Vee said. "I think we may be able to track Magus. Let's go to my office."

Doc found the way her face had suddenly brightened most appealing. She was a take-charge, and very attractive, young lady. He realized how much he was looking forward to watching her handle that gargantuan pistol in a firefight.

As they packed into Vee's relatively small office, Doc noticed the way Ricky was gaping at her with puppy-dog eyes. The boy had scrubbed his face and neck raw in an attempt to please their hostess. It was sophomoric, to be sure. Comical. Doc was taken aback at the level of irritation it aroused in him.

Vee stepped behind her cluttered desk and removed a small black box from her desk drawer. "This is a police-radio scanner," she said as she plugged the unit into a power bar at her feet. "We can monitor all the emergency calls coming in. If Magus is as sick and evil as you make out, there's going to be a trail of destruction left behind. If we know what's been done and where, we might be able to figure out the direction Magus headed and get there first."

When she turned on the scanner, it let out an incomprehensible howl of noise. It took a second or two for Doc to disentangle and interpret the overlapping, frantic voices. He couldn't understand the code numbers being shouted out, but the locations of the associated events were all different, and the crimes in question apparently simultaneous and ongoing.

"How many Maguses are there?" Vee asked.

Chapter Seven

Wearing a six-power magnifier loupe and a headlight, Dr. William Ransom labored over the naked brain of one Nile Carstairs, a sixty-three-year-old man with a massive, invasive but benign brain tumor. In the twelve hours that had elapsed since the first incision was made, the OR's boom box had run through much of the discography of the psychedelic '60s in San Francisco. He had laser cut and cauterized to the best of Jefferson Airplane, the Dead, Big Brother, Steve Miller Band, Creedence, and Country Joe and the Fish, before moving south to L.A. and the Doors. It would be another two hours before they could staple back the lid of Mr. Carstairs's skull.

Though the operation was grueling and incredibly draining, it had taken his mind off the Democrat about to be crowned King of America.

From the boom-box speakers Jim Morrison was belting out "This is the end..." when the neurosurgeon heard the sharp bark of gunshots. He raised blood-smeared, gloved fingertips from the man's parietal lobe.

Around the operating table, the surgical team froze, as well; above their face masks, their eyes were full of confusion and alarm. They weren't in an inner-city ER, where wounded gangbangers were sometimes finished off by their competition. Their hospital was an Upper West Side edifice that provided cutting-edge medicine. And they were on the fifteenth floor, with layers of security between themselves and the street.

Gunshots clattered in long bursts. Machine guns, he was sure. And they were rapidly coming closer.

"Wha…? Wha…?" Mr. Carstairs moaned, his speech a bit thick-tongued because of the mild sedative he had thumb control over. He would stay wide awake during the operation, but immobilized, his head held in fixed position with a Mayfield clamp. This was necessary to ensure he retained full neural function as the huge tumor was slowly and painstakingly excised.

The double doors to the operating room burst open, and two huge figures in matching purple hoodies rushed in, smoke curling from the barrels of their machine guns. More purple hoodies poured in behind them.

It was Dr. Ransom's worst, wake-up-sweating nightmare. The top of his patient's skull lay on a gauze pad in a stainless-steel tray, and the skull's delicate contents were exposed to the air.

He stepped away from the operating table, shielding the helpless patient with his body. "You can't come in here!" he shouted. Ignoring the guns, he waved frantically for them to retreat. "Get out! Get out quick! You've broken the sterile field. This is a brain operation!"

A much smaller purple-hooded intruder shuffled out from between the mass of brawny bodies, moving with a decided limp. Dr. Ransom recoiled when he saw the face. The eyes looked like steel hen's eggs. It was smiling at him, only most of the mouth was gone, replaced by stainless plates.

"No," it said in a grating, inhuman voice, "it *was* a brain operation."

One of the big bruisers effortlessly backhand-brushed Ransom aside and without hesitation reached for Mr. Carstairs's cranium.

"Good grief, no!" Dr. Ransom cried.

The strange-looking hand took a firm hold on the brain and then made a fist, crushing it. Gray goo shot out from between the fingers, spattering the chests of the green-gowned surgical team. From the neck down, the patient's body went rigid, then relaxed; the heart and brain monitors flatlined.

One of the assisting doctors fainted, toppling over backward as his knees buckled. His head hit the tile floor with a dull thud. The rest of the team retreated from the table, their hands raised in defense or surrender.

A pair of purple hoodies seized Dr. Ransom by both biceps, lifted his bootied feet from the floor and carried him out of the OR and down the hallway, as if he weighed nothing at all.

"What do you want?" he cried. "What do you want?"

"That's a surprise," the metallic voice replied from behind him.

The small one was being carried, as well, only cradled in two arms like a sack of potatoes.

"I can pay you anything you want. Anything…"

"I know, you're a god in mortal form. You shit gold ingots. But it's not your money or your shit that's required. It's your expertise."

"You mean it's about your physical issues? Take me back to the OR. Take me back and I'll help you! Whatever you need, I can put the entire hospital's resources at your disposal!"

"That's a problem, Doctor."

"Why?"

"Because then I'd spend the rest of my life in a maximum-security prison. What needs to be done, needs to be done elsewhere. Or perhaps a more accurate term would be else*when*."

"What on earth are you talking about?"

"I want you to do some tinkering on me, all right, but not now. You're going to do it a hundred years in the future."

"You're insane!"

"Doctor, I'm far worse than that, as you will soon discover."

The pressure being put on Ransom's arms was making him lose all feeling in his hands. He could see the sides of his captors' faces as they bore him along. They had crocodile skin. Dark, ridged, horny. And their eyes were yellow.

Surely this can't be real, he thought. But it couldn't be a dream, either. He remembered getting up at 4:00 a.m., showering, shaving, eating eggs Benedict for breakfast while he checked the value of his stock portfolio online, driving to work, reviewing the latest laboratory results on Nile Carstairs, then suiting up and washing for the scheduled six o'clock start of the surgery. If it was real, where was the hospital's armed security!

He had his answer when they reached the elevators. Three uniformed officers lay sprawled facedown on the floor. The pool of their mingled blood was peppered with bright brass shell casings.

Stepping over the corpses, the crocodilians carried Dr. Ransom into the elevator. They held him suspended as the rest of the horde packed in behind them. When the doors closed, the acetone-ether stench in the car made his head spin and his eyes water.

As they marched three abreast down the ground-floor hallway to the street exit, he assured himself there was still the chance of police intervention. But no police were waiting outside. Sirens shrilled in the distance. A black stretch limo sat idling at the curb, its rear doors standing open. The front passenger window was down; there was no one behind the steering wheel.

Over the limo's roof, across the wide street, Dr. Ransom saw a mob of people hurriedly exiting the door of a posh restaurant. They all wore red, white and blue hats, carried banners and balloons and were roughly the same age, but they weren't of the same political stripe. Some were supporters of the about-to-be-crowned Democratic President; others were Young Republicans, rightfully still disgruntled over the November election results. On the eve of the presidential inauguration, they were taking their differences to the sidewalk.

Ransom's shrill cries for help were lost amid the shouting, screaming and shoving match that ensued.

Under different conditions, he would have cheered on the forces of the GOP. But stuffed headfirst into the limo, he had bigger fish to fry than proposed capital-gain hikes and the threat of universal health care.

Chapter Eight

Lieutenant Zach Nathaniel stood calm and detached amid the chaos of the precinct's war room. All departments were represented, even Traffic Enforcement. Uniforms and support staff were running around like headless chickens. Every phone on every desk was lit up and ringing. No one was answering them. He glanced at one of the video monitors mounted on the near wall; it was tuned to a local TV station. Public panic was understandable, given the press coverage. The news crews had gone Orson Welles–*The War of the Worlds* hysterical.

In this storm-tossed sea, he was commander.

The mayor and the chief of police had a press conference scheduled in a few minutes. They would be requesting calm and asking people to stay where they were—whether it was offices, stores, whatever—as long as it was safe and behind locked doors. The point was to keep the public from venturing onto the streets to return home, something that would put lives at risk and complicate the situation for law enforcement. Three hours after the first incident, there was no way to deny that the city of New York was under attack—the only questions were by whom and why. In a rare moment of bipartisanship, the still-sitting Republican President and the Democratic President-elect had broadcast statements of sympathy for the victims and their families and promised all available federal support in resolving the crisis.

Nathaniel raised his coffee cup to his lips, found the liquid cold and bitter, promptly spit it back and set down the mug. Across the low-ceilinged room, plain-clothes detectives were still sticking pins in the huge, street-by-street incident map of the city. All the crimes had occurred within an hour of each other, a coordinated blitz attack, which seemed to have stopped temporarily. Maybe the latest crimes hadn't been discovered yet? Or maybe the perps had stopped their murder spree to grab a snack? There was a small army of them at work, all dressed in purple satin hoodies, black tracksuit pants and alligator boots—an army sans fashion sense. As the evening wore on, fatality numbers had continued to climb: commuters, shoppers, security guards, hospital personnel and patients, bystanders—virtually anyone unlucky enough to wander into their path.

And hostages had been taken. The list read like a hospital-staff register: immunologist, neurosurgeon, cybernetician, protheticist, roboticist, electrical engineer, cardiovascular surgeon, thoracic surgeon, ophthalmologist, orthopedic surgeon, organ transplant/anti-rejection specialist. All had been kidnapped from different Manhattan institutions in separate lethal attacks. Only one incident broke this pattern. A doctor had been killed, but there had been no kidnapping, nor even attempted kidnapping.

It was tragic and confounding.

Nathaniel could see a lone crazy with a grudge against a particular doctor or hospital going berserk with a gun. That had certainly happened before. But this was different. This was organized, efficient and synchronized. The perps weren't using just *any* guns; early reports indicated they were armed with full-auto AKs. The kidnappings of these particular individuals wouldn't jeopardize the running of the hospitals; they were all specialists, the best of the best in their respective fields. To this point there had been no ransom demands sent to the hospitals or the doctors' families. No terrorist proclamations or bag-over-the-head video feeds, either.

It was as if someone was trying to start their own goddamn hospital with conscripted labor. But where? And why? Only one thing was clear—this was no joke. Not with NYPD officers and civilians down and an unknown number of armed suspects still on the loose.

Nathaniel turned to look as surveillance video from the West-Fourth-Street-station attack started to roll on one of the other big-screen TV monitors.

"Shut up! Everyone shut up!" someone behind him shouted.

Then, when the din continued, "Shut the fuck up!"

The show began with the perps jumping the turnstiles, their features hidden by the purple hoods. They were all massively muscled, like 'roided out bodybuilders.

"Can you freeze the video, please," Nathaniel called out to the officer running the playback. "And zoom in on the hands."

After a second, the motion of the scene stopped, and a horny, dark-colored hand filled the screen.

"What the heck is that yellow hook?" a detective

one desk over exclaimed. "An extra-long fingernail? Some kind of gang thing?"

"That's no fingernail, Ramirez," someone else said. "It looks more like a claw."

"Doesn't look like skin on the fingers, either," another detective volunteered. "Hand could be in some kind of glove with the claw attached."

When the video resumed, there were even more questions.

"Why is the little guy being carried?" someone asked. "Could he be wounded?"

The playback showed a transit cop rounding on the perp who was lugging the smaller person. Gunshots cracked and the slide of his weapon cycled back and forth as he rapid fired at close range.

It looked as if he was nailing the big guy square in the head again and again. Nathaniel could see it jolting back in time with the impacts. Was the perp wearing body armor on his *skull*?

In the background of the shot, civilians started dropping as though their strings were being cut.

"The bastards are killing people indiscriminately," Detective Ramirez said.

"No, look closer," Nathaniel told him. "Their automatic weapons are still slung. The bystanders are getting hit by ricochets off that wide fucker's head— friendly fire."

As the pair of transit cops were shown going down hard, the room rang with shouted obscenities. Curses were still pouring forth when the surveillance camera caught a second group of suspects vaulting over the turnstiles. There were eight of them, normal sized but athletic.

"Jesus, who the heck are they?" someone asked.

"Freeze and zoom in," Nathaniel ordered.

"What the fuck?" Ramirez said. "That guy in the lead looks like Snake Plissken!"

Yeah, Nathaniel thought, as if this wasn't weird enough. One of the women was dressed like a proper Manhattan business woman, except for the big hand-gun strapped to her chest. The other two females looked scruffy, as if they hadn't washed their clothes or showered in days.

Were they the rearguard of the purple people? The mop-up crew?

As they ran down the concourse, they weren't shooting anyone, even though their weapons were drawn and there were plenty of unmoving targets of opportunity. Of course it was always possible they had already run out of ammo.

The video jump cut to a subway platform. It showed the purple crew crossing the tracks, then taking a train in the opposite direction.

"Why did they do that?" Ramirez asked. "Are they morons? Don't they know we can see where they're going?"

He was right; that didn't make sense, either.

Add one more to the growing list.

By the time the Plissken gang reached the same platform, the trains in north- and southbound directions had come and gone and it was deserted on both sides. After a brief discussion that the video-camera microphones couldn't pick up, they jumped down into the northbound rail bed and disappeared into the tunnel. That could have meant they had become accidentally separated from the purples.

Or that they had a different mission to complete.

"Get stills of their faces and descriptions sent to all units, and hand them out to the media," Nathaniel said. "Let's find these bastards."

A uniformed cop approached him and said, "Sir, witnesses from the explosions in the Village are waiting for you in the interview rooms."

"I want to show them a feed of the metro attack. Arrange it at once."

"Yes, sir."

Detective Murphy was waiting for him in front of interview room one.

"Who have we got in there?"

"Mrs. Adela Blair, age eighty-one, widow, claims to have seen everything from her top-floor apartment."

Nathaniel entered the interview room, with Murphy following. He took a seat and introduced himself as commander of the detective squad. The white-haired woman on the other side of the table was tiny, maybe four foot five, her face made up like a doll, heavily powdered, big rouge spots on her cheeks and bright red lipstick bleeding into the creases above her upper lip. She was wearing one pair of dark-rimmed glasses and had a second pair in pearlescent pink suspended on a lanyard around her neck. Mrs. Blair seemed remarkably clear-eyed and sharp for someone who had just escaped a war zone—the indomitable Manhattan spirit in full force.

The door opened behind them, and the uniform wheeled in a monitor and DVD player. After quickly plugging them in, he handed Nathaniel the remote and left.

Before starting the video, he told the woman, "If you see anyone you recognize, just say so."

"There!" she said, pointing almost immediately. "Those look like the same monsters who blew up our block and fired machine guns."

"Are you sure?" He glanced down at the glasses around her neck.

"Of course I'm sure," Mrs. Blair snapped back. She held up the glasses in question. "These are for up close. My corrected distance vision is perfect. I was wearing my distance glasses the whole time."

Nathaniel fast-forwarded through the slaughter to the second group of suspects, then zoomed in on their faces, one by one. When he got to the woman in the business suit, Mrs. Blair's eyes suddenly widened.

"That's Veronica!" she said in astonishment. "Veronica Currant! She lives in the brownstone three doors down from me. Such a lovely young woman, always so well dressed. Keeps cats, like me. She's a book editor. She works for a publisher in Midtown. What's she doing with *them*?"

Now, Nathaniel thought, we're getting somewhere.

Chapter Nine

Dr. James Nudelman tossed another double handful of chopped cabbage into the huge pot and watched the mush of overcooked green contents quickly return to a rolling boil. He wasn't home sick as he'd told his colleagues; he was home experimenting. On the other side of the spacious, spot-lit, marble-counter-topped kitchen and across the sunken living room, floor-to-ceiling windows revealed a panorama of twinkling lights above the tops of Central Park's dark trees. The greatest city in the world absolutely throbbed with power.

Polluting, expensive, nonrenewable power.

All that was about to change.

The world was about to change, thanks to him.

Over the course of two years, the physicist PhD had turned the pricey, five-room, eighteenth-floor apartment he'd inherited from Granny Nudelman into his own private laboratory, stripped off the wall-to-wall Berber carpeting, cleared all but one of the rooms of furniture and redecorated it after the style of a chemical plant. Chest-high rows of twelve-by-eight-by-eight black plastic boxes divided more than half the interior space. The battery terminals on the ends of the cases were linked by heavy electric cable; inside each was thousands of neat stacks of a specially laminated paper that had been presoaked in copper chloride. Suspended by heavy chain from the ceiling, at intervals above the rows were twenty-gallon translucent plastic tanks filled with a lemon-orange-tinted fluid. Spiderwebs of clear tubing containing this liquid ran from the bottoms of the tanks to the tops of the rows of boxes.

The whole system was drip fed. Tubing at the bottoms of the stacks was clustered and duct-taped in bundles to the floor, leading off to the bathroom. Gravity pressure forced the waste products of the chemical process straight into his spare-room's toilet. With this prototype design and a DC-to-AC inverter, he had successfully powered a toaster, blender, fan and clock radio. And now, the thousand-watt benchmark: a burner on his electric stove.

If Granny Nudelman's apartment smelled like a public urinal, there was good reason.

The impossible dream of a reusable, pee-powered battery had become a reality.

Standing in the rising, cabbage-reeking steam, staring out at the twinkling lights, he saw a brave new world. Urine would never again be flushed away. It would become a precious commodity, something to be saved, gathered, trucked to pollution-free power plants. He envisioned Manhattan's 8.3 million sets of kidneys, 8.3 million bladders working in unison around the clock, seven days a week to produce enough clean energy to light the largest city in the United States.

Thomas Alva Edison might have given the world light, but James MacArthur Nudelman would supply it with endless, renewable power.

Yellow is the new green, he thought .

Of course there were still a number of critical questions left to answer. Was the technology really scalable?

What were the limits of the current system design? How far could the life span of laminated paper cells be extended? He had to wait until his contract with the university expired before taking his ground-breaking discovery to the next level, otherwise he would have to share the patents and royalties with the institution— something he had no intention of doing. Ensuing steps were going to require serious venture capital, but he was confident he would find it with very little difficulty.

Although secrecy was vital, he had been forced to involve select members of the hospital cleaning staff in his experiments. He had had no choice. By himself he couldn't supply sufficient quantities of urine to fuel the electrochemical process. For many months he had been paying cash under the table for topped-off catheter bags. These were hush-hush transactions conducted in the facility's parking garage. He lugged the bags home in an ice chest in the trunk of his car.

Behind his back he knew his black-market suppliers referred to him as "the pee-o-holic."

Let them scoff, he told himself. In the future, every time someone stands or sits to relieve himself they will think of me and be eternally grateful. Instead of "taking a piss," they will call it "taking a Nudelman."

With the cabbage hard on the boil and banks of scented candles burning on every horizontal surface, he removed a can of spring-bouquet air freshener from an open case at his feet and sprayed liberally between living room and the entry foyer. The other people on his floor had been complaining bitterly that the hallway outside his apartment smelled like a zoo. The boiling cabbage, the vanilla candles and the aerosol helped to mask the odor of his clandestine operation.

Waving the container back and forth, like a beauty queen on a parade float, he retraced his steps. Halfway to the kitchen, from behind, there came a terrible crash. As he instinctively hunched at the sound, the solid wood front door of his apartment splintered from the hinges and triple dead-bolt locks, cartwheeled past him and landed on the steps of the sunken living room.

He jerked his head around, thumb frozen, still pressing the can's spray button.

Huge figures in purple and black poured through the ruin of his entryway. The faces under the hoods looked dark and warty, eyes as yellow as the fluid in the suspended tanks.

The container in his hand hissed, sputtered, then ran out of propellant.

One of the intruders stepped from between the others. Across its arms, it carried a smaller individual who was dressed in the same style.

Nudelman backpedaled from this advancing apparition until his spine hit the edge of the marble countertop. In the U-shaped kitchen there was nowhere to run. The intruder held the small person cradled not three feet away. The face was mostly hidden by the hood's overhang and the intense backlight of the ceiling spots. He stared dumbfounded at the bare foot that dangled before him.

The pale toes, arch and instep were flesh and blood and distinctly human, but the rest of the appendage was steel. A set of overlapping plates appeared to supply articulation at the ankle joint, with some kind of connected, through-and-through axle. Everywhere it abutted metal, the flesh looked angry and inflamed, and there was green pus.

In short, it was a prosthesis from hell.

"Dr. Nudelman," a rasping voice said, "gather up whatever material you will need to continue your work. You are coming with me now."

How many times in the dead of night had he replayed a variation on this dark fantasy? That the Chinese or Russians would break in and steal him and his discovery, that he'd be locked away in a concrete prison of a top-secret research center and never seen or heard from again. But they didn't look Chinese or Russian. Nor a goon squad hired by one of the big oil and power octopi. Their strange, dark and bumpy skin, the cruel amber talons on their thumbs, the width of their bodies and the blocky shape of their heads—they all looked alike, and they didn't look human.

The pack of huge bodies shifted slightly, and he saw they had already taken a human captive—a slender man dressed in a black limo-driver's uniform, complete with shiny cap. One of the creatures at the rear had him by the back of neck and lifted up on tiptoe.

"Who are you?" Nudelman asked, trying desperately to stall for enough time to think through his options.

"I am your master," the little person told him, "from now until you draw your last breath." Then it reached up with a steel claw and tossed back the purple hood.

As Nudelman recoiled, he felt his bladder sphincter release, but there was no flood of hot wetness down the front of his pants.

The littlest monster had scared him pissless.

Chapter Ten

Mildred glanced up at the big analog clock on the wall of Vee's office and couldn't help but do the math, adding the hours left in this day to the countdown to noon of the next. In the hellscape, time wasn't measured in seconds, minutes and hours. Few people had a watch that worked. No one asked what time it was. The sun rose and fell. Night, with its attendant terrors, dragged on and on until dawn. In Deathlands the experience of time passing was unique to each individual, norm or mutie, not some kind of by-mutual-agreement shared reality.

In this remote past that she so well remembered, seconds were seen as hard currency. Spectator sports counted down to zero before they were won and lost. Fortunes made or disappeared to the ticking of global clocks. Lives lived, ordered by an artificial heartbeat, a punctuation mark that divided present from past. What was unreal in the Deathlands was real here, as real as the constantly moving second hand.

Time was slipping away, and the punctuation mark to end all—the ungodly fires of hell—loomed certain.

"There's only one Magus as far as we know," Mildred told the editor.

"Why aren't the police saying what was taken in these attacks?" Krysty asked.

"Actually they are saying," Vee said. "And it isn't 'what,' it's 'who.' Police radio code for a kidnapping is 207. That code has been repeated over and over from different locations. It means there have been multiple, almost simultaneous kidnappings at various Manhattan hospitals."

"What's 187?" Jak asked.

"Homicide," Vee said.

The albino gave her a pained look.

"Chilling," Mildred translated for him. Scattered among the 207s there had been a lot of 187s. The enforcers were doing plenty of what they did best.

"Although the police aren't saying who was kidnapped," Vee went on. "From what you've told me about this cyborg creature, I think we can assume the targets are medical specialists who can help repair its physical and mechanical systems."

"I think you're right," Mildred said. "Hospital departments and staffing in major cities are pretty much the same across the board, from institution to institution. If just any neurosurgeon, ortho doc or transplant doc were needed, it would be one-stop shopping. Magus must be kidnapping *particular* specialists, otherwise there'd be no reason to strike so many locations."

"Do you think the repairs will be made here, in this time?" Vee asked.

"Not with Armageddon less than a day away," Ryan said. "Magus has to be taking them back through the time hole to Deathlands."

"Are there medical facilities there?" Vee asked.

"Only the crudest imaginable," Mildred said. "Think of the Wild West in the 1880s. But Magus has made many trips here for looting. The hellscape is vast. Who knows what's been hidden away. And where." She was thinking of the vast redoubt system.

"My dear Vee," Doc said, "the only thing certain is that Magus is a tactician of the first order. He always seems to be a few steps ahead of pursuit and always has an escape route or two. The ultimate purpose of unfolding events remains a mystery to everyone but our steel-eyed foe."

"Even if, as you say, there's only one Magus," Vee said, "there has to be a lot of those enforcers here. So far there have been more than a dozen attacks by eight or ten of them."

"Maybe they're already here," Ricky suggested.

"Entirely possible," Ryan said. "We don't know how many enforcers went through the time hole ahead of Magus, or when. They could have already been stationed close to their targets, waiting for the signal to attack."

"This is all very interesting," J.B. said with a frown, "but how are we going to find the bucket of bolts?"

"There's only one way out of here that we know of," Ryan said. "And right now it's surrounded and blocked off by armed sec men. Magus has to be stashing his victims someplace fairly close to the time hole, waiting for a chance to jump back to Deathlands."

"The victims could be stashed, but maybe the looting campaign isn't over," Mildred stated. "Magus has more than a day before the hellstorm to collect whatever else is on the to-steal list."

"Every bad guy leaves a trail of bread crumbs," Vee assured them.

"Speaking of which, we need more food," Krysty said. "And we need it now."

"We might not have the chance to eat again soon," Ryan agreed.

"I can phone in a to-go order and have it delivered to the security desk downstairs," Vee said. "What would you like?"

"I don't care, as long as it's not that plastic-wrapped shit," Krysty said.

Vee seemed at a loss. "Pizza? Burgers? Thai? Mexican? Sushi?"

"Just get whatever will be delivered the quickest," Mildred said.

Vee got up from her chair and left the room.

When the editor returned she said, "The food will be here in ten minutes. I need someone to go down to the ground floor with me and help carry it back."

Doc and Ricky rose from their chairs at the same instant.

"I'll go," Ricky said, beaming.

"Perhaps the lovely lady should do the choosing," Doc countered.

Glaring at each other across the table, they looked as if they wanted to start throwing punches. Mildred realized at once what was going on, and it was hard to keep from laughing. The world was about to end, and the geezer and the kid were squabbling over a woman neither of them had a chance in hell with.

Vee had it figured out, too. Smiling sweetly she said, "Mildred can help me with the food. She knows how to fit in here if we get questioned. And her appearance will draw less attention from security. If they ask, I can always say she's one of our writers."

Mildred wasn't sure that was a compliment.

"The conference room will be a more comfortable place to eat," Vee said. "We need to keep monitoring the police calls. And keep a record of any new attack locations as they come up. Write down the time, as well, so we can figure out a direction of travel." She shut off and unplugged the scanner, and she carried it with her as they headed back to the long table.

After the unit was back online and crackling with frantic chatter, Vee unstrapped her Desert Eagle and set it down beside the scanner and a legal pad and pen she had picked up along the way. "If we take firearms into the lobby, Mildred, it will bring a visit from the police," she said.

Though it made her uneasy, Mildred left her Czech-made ZKR .38 revolver and holster on the conference table.

On their way down the hall, Vee stopped at the vending machines. She picked up the fire ax and gave both machines several whacks, breaking loose their pot-metal cash boxes.

"Just like an ATM," she said as she gathered up handfuls of one-dollar bills and stacked them into two fat bundles.

After the elevator doors closed and the car began to descend, Vee looked at her and said, "Do you have living relatives in this time?"

"Yes, I do."

"Do you want to contact them? You can use the office phone when we get back."

"You mean, do I want to say goodbye?"

"Well, yes…"

"They think I'm frozen in a tank in some cryofacility, Vee," Mildred said. "They said goodbye a long time ago.

"If I can't protect the people I love from what's coming tomorrow, scaring them in their final hours seems just pointless and cruel."

When they reached the ground floor, the delivery man was waiting at the security desk, which was manned by a pair of seated, uniformed guards. Six big white paper bags sat on the counter in front of them.

"I don't know those security men," Vee said softly. "Let me do the talking."

As they neared the counter, the aroma of hamburger and fries made Mildred's mouth water. How long had it been? A hundred years? It seemed longer.

Vee counted out sufficient singles to cover the cost of the food, then handed the rest to the delivery man.

His eyes widened as he accepted the wad of cash. "Ma'am," he said, "there must be fifty bucks here."

"Do me one favor," she said.

"Sure, what?"

"Spend it all tonight."

"Deal!" he said, turning quickly for the exit.

As they gathered up the six bags, Mildred noticed that both guards were armed with 9 mm Glocks and wore body armor under their uniform shirts. That stuck in her mind because she didn't remember building security ever carrying guns or wearing armor, except in banks or big city hospitals of course.

One of the guards said, "Whoa, that's a lot of food, ladies. Got a party going up there on twenty-two?"

"No, we're stocking up for an all-nighter," Vee said. "Final tweaking of a book. Got to get it ready for the printer."

"Good luck with that."

Mildred smiled and nodded and followed Vee back to the elevator.

When the car doors closed behind them, the aroma of charcoal-cooked meat and deep-fried potatoes became overwhelming. Her stomach began to growl ominously as she held the hot bags to her chest.

"Do you miss the food?" Vee asked as the elevator climbed.

"Not until now. I'd forgotten."

"What do you eat in the future?"

"Trust me, you don't want to know. It will put you off eating for a week."

They trooped into the conference room, set the bags on the table and started passing out paper-wrapped, double bacon cheeseburgers and grease-stained bags of French fries.

Mildred watched Jak sniff carefully at the sandwich he held in both hands. Then he took a huge bite of what had to be his first bacon cheeseburger. He groaned as he chewed, then gulped it down.

"Don't eat the paper," Vee told him as his mouth gaped to take bite number two.

"Or your fingers," Mildred added.

The others were already hard at it, cheeks stuffed like chipmunks, jaws grinding away vigorously.

As Mildred raised her own sandwich to wet lips and parted teeth, then crunched through the toasted, seeded bun, the copious mayo, ketchup, lettuce, pickle, red onion, sliced tomato, crisp bacon, melted cheddar and two juicy, charbroiled meat patties, she saw a pair of tiny red dots, like dancing insects, on the other side of the plate-glass window.

They weren't insects.

And they weren't dancing.

She spewed her mouthful of burger across the table and into the lap of an astonished J.B.

Chapter Eleven

Lieutenant Nathaniel watched from the shadows at the mouth of the alley across the street from the target building. There was a damp chill to the winter night but no precipitation, air temp just above freezing. He wore body armor and a black knit hat. The right side of his black nylon NYPD windbreaker was pulled up and tucked behind the holster of his Glock 19, clearing the path for a quick draw. Like a string of paper cut-out silhouettes, men in black combat fatigues and balaclavas, full-body armor, carrying bulletproof riot shields and M-16s ran soundlessly, in formation, down the other side of the street, toward the building's front entrance.

Nathaniel keyed his secure, tactical com link and spoke into the headset microphone. "Team Bravo, this is Operational Command. Request an update. Over."

After a brief pause, the bud in his ear crackled, and the gruff voice of the Emergency Services Unit leader replied, "Ten-four, Command. All rear exits secured and sealed off. Team Alpha is in position on roof opposite. Team Bravo entering front of target site now. Suspect contact is in estimated less than ten, repeat contact in less than ten."

After looking at the building's location, which was surrounded by other high-rise structures, they had decided not to helo drop a fourth team onto the roof in advance of the main assault. They didn't want to risk alerting the suspects with rotor noise and echoes off the other buildings. The plan was to disable all but one of the lobby's elevators, then ascend to the twenty-second floor, using that car and the two emergency staircases. Once the suspects were engaged by the three-pronged assault force, the helicopter would land and the fourth team would close the trap from above. With all escape routes blocked, the suspects had nowhere to go.

It was surrender or die.

"Confirm when you are in position to engage," Nathaniel said. "Acknowledge."

"Ten-four that. Out."

Not often, but sometimes, things just fell into place.

The positive identification of one of the suspects in the metro attack had led Nathaniel in short order to the company that employed her, which had led in even shorter order to its location. A quick phone call to night security at the building revealed that eight individuals had been caught on video at about 5:30 p.m. entering the premises through the parking lot. Security had recognized one of them as Veronica Currant, and she had input the necessary entry key codes. The suspects had taken the elevator directly to the twenty-second floor and had not left the building.

Nathaniel immediately ordered a full-force response—mobilization and deployment of the precinct's police, tactical and EMT units. Without lights or sirens, and out of sight of the target floor, squad cars had sealed off the connecting streets, blocking access to the building. Minutes later he and the ESU vans had arrived on scene. A pair of armed ESU personnel had borrowed the uniforms of the private security guards and then taken their places at the front desk. They had orders not to fire unless directly threatened; their primary function was to observe activity on the video monitors and report suspect movement inside the building.

Kidnapping seemed to be the major part of the gang's MO. In all but one incident, a citizen had been taken away. Even though video showed the suspects hadn't brought hostages in with them, that didn't mean they hadn't taken prisoners after entering, from the floor they were on or others above or below. If the perps were in fact holding anyone captive, the element of surprise combined with overwhelming force could save innocent lives.

Tactical units had still been assembling outside when Currant had informed the security desk she had phoned out for food to be delivered. Nathaniel had been tempted to take out whoever came down to pick it up and thereby reduce the odds, but the assault teams had been nowhere ready to close the net. He'd reasoned if the gofers didn't return promptly with dinner, the other suspects would know something had gone wrong and would have the chance to prepare for attack. Nathaniel had told the disguised officers to sit tight, let the suspects collect their food and go back up.

When the time came, ESU would be going in first. Given the situation and attendant department protocol, it was the only option. There would be casualties, he had no doubt, but with any luck they would be one-sided—the *other* side. The sniper teams on the roof directly above him had a clear line of sight into the twenty-second floor offices. From initial reports, they had all eight suspects in view. All were in the same room. No hostages in sight, just viable targets.

The shooters were waiting for the green light, which was ultimately his call. He had no qualms about giving the command, but he had made it clear to the ESU leader how important it was to keep some of the perps alive if possible—they could provide valuable intel on the locations of the other suspects, the ones in purple. He was confident that ESU personnel would show more restraint under the circumstances than his precinct's beat cops or even his detectives. They were better trained. Better armed. Better shots. And because they worked as a cohesive unit, they were less likely to go rogue and take individual revenge for the killings of their fellow NYPD officers.

The identified suspect, Veronica Currant, turned out to be a Canadian citizen living in the U.S. on a work visa. Age twenty-six. Single. No roommate. Educated at the University of Toronto's Massey College. When contacted by Canadian authorities, her family had had little information to offer. They didn't know the last names of her friends at work or the names of anyone she was dating.

Currant had no traffic citations. No wants or warrants in the United States or Canada. No prior arrests in either country. No New York state weapon permit, but a computer records check had turned up several occasions when she had legally purchased ammunition at a gun range in Connecticut—the total purchase amounted to nine boxes of .44 Magnum wadcutter rounds. When contacted by Manhattan police, the range owner remembered her and the weapon she'd had in her possession, because it had been a fancy

semiauto Desert Eagle—and because it was a whole
lot of gun for someone five foot five and 115 pounds.
The range owner had been certain Currant had bought
more ammo than she'd used on his targets.

Preliminary checks with the FBI and its Canadian
counterpart, the Royal Canadian Mounted Police—
RCMP—had revealed she had no connections to any
known terrorist organizations. The Canadian Security
Intelligence Service had nothing on her, either. She had
worked for the same company for three years, paid her
taxes and rent on time.

Hardly a usual suspect in a case like this.

Not that this case was in any way usual.

It got worse. Way worse.

Fingerprinting the metro turnstiles would have been
a total waste of time had it not been for the Closed Circuit Television—CCTV—footage. When they zoomed
in the video, they could approximate with some degree
of certainty where the suspects' fingers had touched
the stainless-steel entry barriers. Of course, considering the number of hands that had also touched the
turnstiles, pinpointing single sets of prints was still an
incredible longshot.

But once again, things had fallen into place—sort
of.

They had drawn blanks on six of the unknown suspects, but got a hit on the seventh, the black woman
with the plaited hair. Three of the fingerprints on the
turnstile belonged to a Dr. Mildred Wyeth, who had
applied for and received a concealed-handgun permit.
According to the permit application, she had competed
on the U.S. national team and silver-medaled as a
pistol shot.

Just when it looked as if they had their second suspect nailed down, the bottom dropped out. A further records check showed that Wyeth had nearly died on the operating table in December. An MD involved in cryogenic research, she was put into cryostasis and was flown to the Shelley Cryonic Institute in Minnesota. The woman in the metro video only vaguely resembled the driver's license photo taken in 1998. She was black, yes, but her face was thinner and instead of an unruly Afro, she had beaded braids. On the CCTV she moved like a trained athlete or a battle-seasoned, elite soldier, not a deskbound academic.

But as everyone knew, fingerprints didn't lie—no two sets were alike. The video showed the woman's bare hand touching the steel in the exact spot where the fingerprints were lifted.

How was this possible? It just didn't make sense. The timing was all wrong.

At every turn the case seemed to get more bizarre, and made to order for the tabloids. And the bestseller list. And the big screen. If he closed this one, he knew his story would be worth a fortune. He could even retire early, if he wanted to. But that was way down the road; many perplexing questions had to be answered first. Right now, his only concern was taking the next necessary step—successfully capturing at least one suspect alive.

His earbud crackled.

"This is Team Bravo," the gravelly voice said. "We are in position for dynamic entry. Ready on your green."

The time for reflection was over.

Nathaniel opened the channel on his com link.

"Team Alpha, this is Command," he said. "You have green light. Repeat, this is Command. Alpha you have green light. Take the shot."

ESU SNIPER MATT CARTER knelt behind the raised lip at the edge of the rooftop. His balaclava pulled down over his face, he peered through the Remington M24's Leupold Mk 4 LR/T M3 10×40 mm fixed-power scope. Thanks to the front bipod, the weight on his right shoulder was minimal. Downrange, behind the mil-dot wire reticle, the kill zone was a brightly lit, elongated rectangle in a facade of otherwise mostly darkened windows. Eight people were seated around a long table, eating from what looked like big bags of fast food. He could see them laughing as they stuffed their faces with both hands. They had no clue, didn't realize they'd already been found. Clearly, they didn't expect to be located so soon.

For some, if not all, it would be their last meal.

Finger resting outside the trigger guard, Carter put the crosshair wires on Snake Plissken's chest. Bullet-drop compensation for the 150-yard distance to target had already been clicked into the Leupold. The zero was dead on. Because the rooftop gun was higher than the target, he used the vertical mil-dots to adjust his low hold. With the shot lined up, he focused on his breathing, slowing it until he could feel each beat of his heart.

Plissken would die first, as he appeared to be the gang leader. Cut off the head and all that.

Even for Manhattan, they were a strange-looking group. Survivalist-terrorist hippies or something. The long-haired albino was by far the freakiest of the bunch.

He reminded Carter of a young Johnny Winter, the blues guitarist. The redheaded chick, on the other hand, was totally hot. He realized his concentration was slipping away and shut off the thought.

Ten feet down the roofline to his right, the shooting-team spotter, Joe Gaspers, had binocs on the kill zone. Fifteen feet to Carter's left, Peter Balwan knelt behind a scoped Barrett M82. The semiauto .50 caliber weapon rested on its built-in bipod.

Usually when Team Alpha was called out, it was to bring down one, maybe two targets. In this case there were four times that many, and there was no way to drop them all. The initial problem was the heavily tempered and laminated glass that served as the building's outside wall. Given distance to target, it was thick enough to stop and/or deflect the Remington's 7.62 mm round, and cause a disastrous, first-shot miss.

The plan was for Balwan to break the glass between the 7.62 mm and the first target with the Barrett's 660-grain slug, and then Carter would follow up a split second later with the kill shot slipped through the .50 caliber hole. The sniper team had practiced this sequence of precise shooting hundreds of times, until it was automatic and the separation timing between two dead-on shots less than half a second.

A further complicating factor was the fogging and spiderwebbing of the glass after a .50 caliber hit. It created a milky-white halo and fractures around the impact point, which would spread a good three feet in diameter and partially obscure the view into the room through that window panel.

After taking out the primary, they would move on to

a predesignated sequence of targets, one through six. His bolt-action M24 held five rounds of M118 Match and one in the pipe. The semiauto Barrett's box mag held ten. Once firing started, there would be no time for him to reload.

With exits at either end of the room, the targets could scatter both ways. Carter guessed he might hit three, if he was lucky and if they were slow getting up from the table. The short guy in the beat-up hat, the albino and the old guy had their backs to him and figured to be slowest to react. After the primary target was down, they would track aimed fire across the room from left to right, Balwan breaking glass for him with the .50 before he laid down each shot.

First the leader, Carter thought. He tapped outside the trigger guard with his fingertip. Bang! Riding the imaginary jolt of recoil, he smoothly swung the rifle's sights, cycling the action in his mind, keeping his low hold, placing the mil-dot between shoulder blades of the guy in the hat, tapping the guard. Bang!

Back or front of target, it didn't matter to him.

Dead was dead.

Carter had seen the highlights of the metro video as part of a very rushed mission briefing. Like everyone else in the room, they'd made him furious, but he wasn't angry now. He never surrendered to any emotion when he was behind the gun. Hitting a moving target at distance was about control. Breathing. Heartbeat. Muscles. It required relaxation, then a precise application of finger pressure at a precise instant. Control was the only way to find and take advantage of that perfect moment of calm.

When the command to commence fire came through his earpiece, despite his training and his experience, Carter felt a surge of adrenaline. There was no way to turn off that reaction to showtime.

"Confirm green light?" their spotter asked them both. This to make sure they had all heard and understood the order to apply lethal force.

"Confirm," Balwan said.

"Confirm," Carter repeated. He again slowed his breathing and slipped into a routine, a ritual that had become second nature. He snuggled into the buttstock, then dropped the rifle's safety.

"Laser targeting on," Gaspers said.

Carter flipped the switch at the same instant as Balwan. Laser beams shot across the yawning divide between the buildings, above the deserted Manhattan street. Red dots jostled over the same one-inch space on the outside of the heavy glass.

"On three…" Gaspers said, his binocs locked on the distant window.

As their spotter began the countdown, Carter added the backbeat, which was his timing cue. One-and, two-and…

On three the Barrett roared. Carter didn't flinch; he hit the back beat with smooth finger pressure, and the Remington bucked into his shoulder.

The sound they created together was *boom-bam!* So tightly spaced it could almost have been a single shot and quick echo.

Downrange, the big pane of glass blasted inward. Four feet of its surface turned opaque in a crude circle. A puff of glass dust twinkled as it fell down the front of the building.

Working from the same rhythmic count, unspoken, from the same playbook, memorized, Carter and his partner rained down hell.

Boom-bam!

Boom-bam!

Chapter Twelve

Holding the fat sandwich, watching it drip juice in a puddle on the table, Ryan couldn't help but remember the beefy cheesies from Shadow World's Gloomtown—a sad, sick, toxic and eventually fatal joke on a starving-mad, expendable populace. Although similar in general shape, what he held in his hand was not powdered rock disguised as animal protein and perfumed with synthetic chemical aromatics. It was the real nukin' deal.

The fabled double bacon cheese.

Something loudly and endlessly discussed over countless hellscape campfires while skinned Norway rats sizzled with sharp sticks jammed up their butts and skanky root veg roasted on open coals until their skins turned black. The predinner conversations always hit the same central themes, speculation more or less elaborate depending on the amount of joy juice the campers had swallowed.

"I heer'd they was four inches high and eight across't."

"I heer'd they weighed two pounds each."

"I heer'd you could build 'em anyway you wanted, pickles, no pickles, extry grilled onions, fried egg on top."

"I heer'd they came wrapped in special boxes like old-time birthday presents."

The double bacon cheese was something Ryan Cawdor never thought he'd live to taste.

The first bite was so astonishing, he had to fight to keep from just wolfing down the whole thing. He chewed that bite slowly, eyes closed, savoring the blend of flavors and textures.

This was what the fuss was all about.

He swallowed, then picked up a strip of golden fried potato and bit it in two. It was hot, crispy on the outside, soft in the middle. A man could cry, it was so good.

On the other side of Vee, Mildred spit out a big mouthful of hamburger.

"Down!" she shouted. Then she rolled off her chair to the right.

There was no mistaking the nature of the situation. The six companions—Ryan, Krysty, Mildred, Doc, J.B. and Jak—had fought together so long, had survived so many surprise attacks that their responses were instinctive and instantaneous.

As Ryan twisted to his left, butt sliding off the chair, the ten-foot-tall, six-foot-wide pane of glass directly across the room from him shattered with a loud, crunching pop. Seemingly in the same instant, a heavy slug slapped the wall above him, and an inch from his right shoulder, the chair back took a center hit and rolled backward on its casters.

At the end of the table, the newest and least seasoned member of the team didn't instantly react to Mildred's warning. Jak lunged up from the floor, smashing Ricky with a shoulder, knocking him off his chair and onto the floor.

Ryan glimpsed the window, which was crazed, top

to bottom. A single fist-size hole was in the middle of a wide, milk-white circle. One hole, two shots.

Longblaster fire. It was coming from the rooftop across the street, and they were sitting ducks.

To his left as he snatched his Steyr Scout by its sling, a second pane imploded, sending a whoosh of glittering glass shards across the floor. But he and the companions were already moving low and fast for the exit.

A third window collapsed, also to his left. The table shuddered as a bullet carved an ugly furrow across its width, spraying his head with splinters. Realizing the direction the shooters were team-tracking, he turned 180 degrees and grabbed Vee by the collar. As he dragged her the other way, she reached for the tabletop and grabbed her Desert Eagle and holster.

The shots that came after were wild, a big blaster and a smaller one, no longer coordinating fire. Tempered glass deflected the bullets. Working alone, neither shooter could put lead in the bull's-eye. Mildred ran in front of them for the exit. She slapped the light switch on the way out, plunging the room into darkness.

Pushing Vee ahead of him, Ryan cleared the doorway and put the hallway wall between them and the longblasters.

Down the brightly lit corridor, the other companions leaned against the same wall. None of them appeared to have been hit. Head-size holes had been blown out of the wallboard by the big longblaster. White powder and bits of plaster decorated the magenta carpet.

"Who is shooting at us?" Vee asked. "Is it Magus?"

"Snipering at us is not really Steel Eyes's style, my dear," Doc said.

"Certainly not with enforcers playing on the team," Mildred said. "It's more likely the NYPD. They probably have been on to us for a while. The security guards downstairs were wearing sidearms. Rent-a-cops don't usually come strapped like that. I should have put two and two together, but I didn't think it was possible for them to locate us that fast. Got to figure by now they have the building completely surrounded and an all-out assault on this floor is imminent."

After a quick breath she said, "Are we really going to kill police?" She seemed disturbed at the prospect.

"They don't have a chance of getting past this weekend alive," J.B. said. "But we do, if we can get back to Vee's apartment in time to jump back to Deathlands."

"If we let them take us now, we're as doomed as they are," Ryan told her. "We'll be turned to dust along with everyone else, and Magus will win." As always he was thinking like a natural-born Deathlander: sec men were sec men, no matter the uniform or the flag they fought under. Raise a blaster, pay the price. It was the survivalist code. The companions had every right to live, even if it meant someone else had to die.

The shooting had stopped for more than a minute. It was the lull before the storming.

The attackers didn't want friendly-fire casualties.

They were coming; Ryan could feel it.

ESU LEADER Lieutenant Thomas Holmes stood with head lowered, eyes closed and his Glock 19 in his black-gloved fist as he got the report from Team Alpha's spotter through his earbud. It was not what he wanted to hear. He listened with disbelief, then a flood of anger. "How could you have missed them all?" he said. "Goddammit, I should have taken the shot my-self!"

He let his fingertip slide off the com link.

And the cherry on top: Team Bravo had waited on the emergency stairway landing for a couple of min-utes to confirm the snipers had stood down.

He keyed his com link again and said, "Go, go! All units go!"

He was first through the fire door onto the floor, pistol supported in both hands. At the opposite end of the hall, the other fire door was just banging back. The elevator doors slid open, and the car disgorged more ESU officers.

Kneeling behind and bracing their riot shields on the floor, they created bulletproof cover for their com-rades to leapfrog. Holmes stationed men at the three entry points to keep the perps from doubling back and using them to escape. From either end of the floor, ESU moved from door to door, room to room, closing in on the central point of the conference room. As they conducted their headlong search, there was no clatter of automatic gunfire, only shouts of "Clear! Clear!"

Minutes later the entire force met beside the hall-way entrances to the conference room. It was wall-to-wall men in black. Holmes looked at the faces of those closest to him. Their eyes were wide with shock and anger—the trapped perps had seemingly gone up in smoke.

"Check this floor again. Start over," he said. "Check the heating vents, the ceiling. Every goddamned inch. They've got to be here."

Sweeping off his balaclava, he turned on the light in the conference room.

A cold breeze was flowing through the breached glass panels. There were numerous bullet holes in the wall, overturned chairs; the fast food left behind on the long table was still warm.

No blood.

No sign of them.

"Where the fuck did they go?" he said aloud.

Chapter Thirteen

Vee pushed from the wall and waved for the others to follow. "This way," she said in a voice that she hoped left no doubt she knew exactly what to do. She took them across the corridor, through a doorway and into a small, well-appointed anteroom with a posh desk and chair, phone, computer, file cabinets—the domain of the publisher's executive secretary. She quietly closed access to the hallway, then led them past the desk and through double floor-to-ceiling walnut doors that opened onto her boss's luxurious office suite.

From the corridor outside came the cheery ding of the elevator. Heavy boots tramped down the corridor. It sounded as if they were being invaded by an army.

Vee reached across the wide desk and snatched up a key from the base of the green-shaded lamp. Crossing to the rear of the room, she motioned to the private washroom and ushered the others inside. It had a white marble floor, countertops and backsplash. The walls were dark walnut paneling. There were no windows. There was no other exit. She pulled the door shut.

"What in nukin' hell are we doing in here?" J.B. asked as he took in the surroundings.

"A reprise of Custer's Last Stand, perhaps?" Doc suggested.

Vee ran a fingertip along the edge of the wall until

she found the latch. When she pressed it, the entire panel popped open on concealed hinges, revealing what looked like a very narrow gray metal elevator. The front spanned just six feet. She slipped the key in the doorframe's lock. When she turned it, a motor whirred and the metal doors opened from the middle, revealing a car longer than it was wide, but just barely. The enclosure was lit by a bulb in an opaque circular housing in the ceiling.

"Get in, hurry," she urged.

Seven bodies brushed past her and packed into the small space, toe-to-toe. She pulled the external panel closed as she backed in, then pushed a button on the brass console. The doors slid shut. Then the car began to drop.

They were all pressed tightly against one another. There was hardly any air to breathe, and what there was smelled like unwashed bodies, gun oil and burned cordite. Doc stood behind her, young Ricky in front—the teenager was almost nose to nose with her. He had a serious but rapturous look in his brown eyes, as if he was trying to drink her in. Doc was trying to make conversation in her left ear. He wanted to know how she had learned about the secret elevator and where "by the Three Kennedys" it was going to take them.

Meanwhile, something hard was poking her low in the back.

She hoped to hell it was the silver lion head of his cane.

"It's a long story," she said over her shoulder, trying to shift away from the prodding, verbal and otherwise.

In fact it was more than a long story; it was the *same* story.

It had come from the publisher's Strike Force Thirteen covert-military-action series and a novel penned by none other than Kyle Arthur Levinson, the same author she'd had lunch with earlier—it was difficult for her to comprehend how radically her life had changed in just a few short hours. The writer had thought it would be hysterical if Strike Force Thirteen blew up his publisher's offices, killing everyone and everything—down to the mail clerk and the potted plants. The company seemed to attract authors with adolescent senses of humor, so that in itself wasn't a problem. The problem was Levinson had the Strike Force heroes base jumping twenty-two stories while the whole building exploded above them—this in full view of the NYPD, who had the building cordoned off with squad cars, ESU and sharpshooters. In Levinson's novel the heroes managed to land without a scratch and then escape three hundred cops on foot, while trailing their chutes behind. There was no explanation for this remarkable feat. Not even an attempt at explanation.

Chomping on the butt of his cigar, the publisher had glanced up from her synopsis of the absurd climactic scene and said, "Fire this fucking idiot, then fix it."

Easy for him to say.

Levinson had numerous book contracts outstanding; he was one of the most prolific writers in the stable, so practically speaking, he couldn't be fired, at least not in the short term.

And Vee was the one who had to figure out and then write a new ending to the novel. Levinson couldn't be trusted to do the revisions himself; that had been tried before, with disastrous results. The setting of the final action scene had to stand as written; the whole plot had been leading up to the building's destruction. She had to find another way for the heroes to escape.

And it had fallen into her lap.

Enter Ivana, a stunning, leggy, blonde Russian woman in her early thirties, who the publisher said was an up and coming literary agent. In Vee's experience, New York literary agents could almost always speak English and usually wore clothes under their knee-length sable coats. When the publisher introduced Ivana to her, the Russian had uncrossed, then recrossed her long legs while lounging in one of the executive suite's leather armchairs—it was an indelible, Sharon Stone–*Basic Instinct* interrogation moment. Only there was no way to tell if Ivana was a natural—down there she was shaved as smooth as a baby's bum.

A week later, in the middle of a major publishing crisis, Vee had barged past the executive secretary before getting clear permission to breach the inner sanctum. As she'd entered, the door to the private washroom had been swinging shut. The publisher's face a furious purple, he'd jumped to his size-seven feet from the leather couch. Before the shouting had begun and she'd been driven from the room, Vee was certain she'd seen a smear of red lipstick on the fly of his gray pinstripes.

In her four-inch heels, the publisher's presumed mistress had to be a foot and a half taller than him—hard to miss. Ivana had never entered the floor from the main elevators, but Vee could always tell from the lingering scent of her expensive perfume whenever Ivana paid a secret visit to the boss in his office.

So she'd figured there had to be another way in and out.

It had given her a quick fix for Levinson's unbelievable ending—just add a hidden elevator and put Strike Force Thirteen in it—but by then, her curiosity had been piqued. She'd called the elevator company that serviced the building. And had gotten nowhere. They'd denied the existence of a fourth elevator. But after she'd circulated the question to friends on other floors, a woman who worked at an ad agency upstairs had pulled her aside and told her about the *real* private elevator. The ad execs used it to sneak call girls in and out, during and after business hours.

The publisher never used it as an entrance or exit himself. He came and went via the main elevators along with everyone else. It was for special access only.

Once Vee had started her after-hours search, it had taken her all of ten minutes to find the secret catch along a seam of the washroom's wall. The spring-loaded panel had swung out, revealing the elevator doors and a conventional key lock. She'd already known where the key was. Her boss was, if anything, predictable. He kept the key in plain sight on the tooled brass base of his antique, bankers' desk lamp. Since no one else knew about the elevator, there was no reason to go to the trouble of hiding it.

Doc was still whispering in her ear when the car lurched to a stop. The panels opened silently—there was no telltale ding. Vee stepped out of the sardine can into a short, windowless corridor that ended in a heavy metal door and took a deep breath of fresh air.

"Where does this lead?" Ryan asked as he moved past her to the barrier.

"Not to the parking lot," she said.

She'd figured that out on her first trip down, long before she'd ever reached the bottom. If the entrance/

exit door had opened onto the parking lot, call girls would be videoed driving in and out, and they'd need the key code to open the gate. No way would big-time execs give hookers that access. They would need to be in complete control, ride down in the car, take their entertainment back up with them, return them the same way—all without being seen.

Vee moved to the metal door, inserted the same key and unlocked it. The door opened outward; the hinges were on the inside. It didn't open far, a little more than a foot, then it hit something solid and stopped.

Peering around the door's edge, she saw the side of a white-and-red EMT truck, blocking the exit. It was parked very close to the wall, no doubt to allow other traffic to move past. Its idling engine made a steady low rumble.

Without a word, she squeezed through the opening.

Down the alley, a hundred feet to the right, was a squad car. Its light bar was flashing, but there was no one inside or standing nearby outside. She pushed the door back a little, creating a crack between it and the vehicle so she could look in the other direction.

The main police presence seemed to be concentrated inside the building's parking lot. Through the bars and wire of the security fence, she could see at least a half-dozen squad cars and that a black ESU van had pulled in past the gate. The EMT truck's tall, boxy body and the open door completely blocked them from line of sight. It was a narrow window of opportunity. Their rear was totally exposed.

"Come quickly," she said to Ryan and the others. "The police can't see us. Get into the back of the truck.

There's probably a driver sitting inside in the front. He or she needs to be prevented from raising an alarm."

Jak easily slipped through the gap between door and frame. Moving by her, he opened one of the rear doors and disappeared inside. Vee expected some evidence of a struggle, the truck rocking on its suspension, maybe a cry for help or a thud or two, but there was nothing. When she climbed into the back of the vehicle with Ryan and J.B., Jak was holding a short-bladed black throwing knife to a terrified young EMT's jugular. The blue-uniformed man had his hands raised in surrender.

"Don't kill me. Don't kill me," he pleaded over and over.

As the others jumped in and shut the back doors, Ryan and J.B. pulled the unresisting paramedic into the rear compartment and pushed him onto a seat on one of the two gurneys. Mildred found rolls of surgical tape in a medical kit, and they bound his hands, feet and mouth before strapping him down.

"Don't give yourself a heart attack," Mildred told the EMT as she leaned over him. "Try to relax. As soon as we're clear of the police, we'll cut you loose unharmed, I promise."

"Who's going to drive this wag?" J.B. said.

The answer was obvious: Vee was the only one who knew the city. She shouldered him aside and got in behind the wheel. The statuesque redhead followed her into the front compartment, climbing onto the passenger seat.

"Brace yourselves," Vee said as she buckled her safety harness, then reached for a pair of switches on the dash. The truck's siren screaming and its light bar flashing, she dropped the engine into gear and stomped the gas. As she barreled past the cordoned-off parking lot, the uniform cops standing around turned to look, but they didn't jump in their cars and follow in pursuit. An EMT vehicle leaving a crime scene Code Three was not unexpected.

At the mouth of the alley, Vee braked hard. "Hang on!" she shouted over her shoulder, then cut a right turn onto an empty street. The truck's rear end fishtailed wildly. For a second she thought she was going to lose control and roll the damned thing. She heard her passengers slamming into the walls and floor as she powered out of the skid. Over the engine's howl, her new friends were cursing her. In her headlight beams, at the end of the long block ahead, was a barricade of parked, white squad cars. She was doing fifty, sixty, then seventy, and the barrier was coming up fast. There was no choice—she couldn't stop and chat. She aimed the truck between the front bumpers of facing vehicles in the middle of the row. If the heavy wagon hit with enough force, it was possible she could knock the lighter cars aside and plow through.

Seeing her speed, seeing the flashing lights, hearing the siren, the uniform cops hopped into their vehicles and backed them out of the way, clearing a path for her just in time.

She shot the gap, holding a steady seventy-five, roaring down the wide avenue's center line. In front of her, for as far as she could see, was more empty nighttime Manhattan street, deserted sidewalks. When she checked her side mirrors, there was still no pursuit.

They'd somehow managed a clean getaway, just like the one she'd written for *High-Rise Hell*, except for the exploding building, of course. It made her want to laugh, so she threw back her head and let fly.

Krysty looked over at her as if she was stark, barking mad.

As they approached the next corner, Vee slowed to a sedate thirty and turned left. After going another two blocks at moderate speed, she turned right, then shut off the siren and lights.

They rolled along in silence. Even though they were now well away from the action, traffic was extremely light for the time of evening. A car here, a car there. No taxis, no city buses at all. She guessed people were keeping off the streets because of the terror attacks.

"Hey, Vee," Ricky said from the back. "How did you learn to drive this wag so good?"

"Well," Krysty corrected him automatically.

"Research," she said.

Chapter Fourteen

Looking in the limo's rearview was like touching the tip of his tongue to a rotten tooth; every time Mc-Creedy did so it made him wince, but he couldn't stop doing it. The dully gleaming metal eyes and the bizarre jaw contraption reflecting back at him were like a fatal highway accident.

Magnetically horrifying.

In a screeching, metal-on-metal voice that hurt his ears, the little one cranked out directions—the most monstrous backseat driver imaginable. It made his mother-in-law seem a rank amateur. The breath gusting through the open privacy window was a million times worse, too. It smelled as bad as a bloated, week-old dead dog in August. And unlike his mother-in-law, the little guy seemed to have a detailed street map of Manhattan etched inside its head. It knew exactly where it was going and the precise route it wanted to take to get there.

McCreedy followed the directions as quickly as he could. He wasn't thinking about where he was driving; his primary concern was obeying without question. He kept remembering what had happened at the hospital—it was an abject lesson in don't-frustrate-the-little-one. He was almost certain he was going to die before the day was done. There didn't seem to be any way around it, but he didn't want the means to be having his head ripped off his neck.

Ahead on the left, a spot-lit American flag flew from a stanchion on the front of a seven-story gray stone building. When he drove closer, he realized it was a police precinct station.

The grating voice ordered him to stop in the middle of the street, opposite the arched, ground-floor entrance.

A desperate ray of hope surfaced. Maybe they had decided to give up and turn themselves in, he thought.

The limo's side doors opened, and the creatures in the back started piling out. An exodus that made the vehicle rock on its springs. The little one didn't seem to have much to say to the big creatures. There had been no command to get up and get out. It was as if they could communicate without words.

If they were surrendering, he thought, as a claw hand gripped his shoulder and pulled him out of the driver's seat, why were they taking along machine guns?

The precinct house looked as if it had been built in the 1930s. Squat, square and stodgy. McCreedy was bum-rushed through the arched entrance. Beyond it was a long, windowless, marble-floored foyer lined on both sides with uncomfortable-looking, scarred oak benches—a kind of unofficial waiting room outside police confines and a way station for crime victims, their families, their lawyers and the lawyers and families of the recently arrested. The benches were full.

As the purple entourage marched past, led by the limping, half-metal abomination, the assembled people froze in their seats, their chatting and squabbling ceased and the expressions on their faces shifted from sadness, pain and anger to horror.

You ain't seen nothing yet, McCreedy thought.

The entryway ended in a set of modern, presumably bulletproof, double glass doors. In the brightly lit room on the far side, McCreedy could make out a large, raised wooden desk. It looked like the kind of thing a judge would pound a gavel on in a courtroom. A man in a black uniform sat behind it, preoccupied with shuffling the sheaf of papers in front of him. When the desk sergeant looked up from his work and saw the wall of purple hoodies staring back at him, his lantern jaw dropped. Then his face turned red. Rising to his feet, he slapped something on the side of the desk.

A panic button, as it turned out.

A piercing Klaxon alarm sounded at about the same instant the creatures applied the soles of their bare feet to the doors. The tempered glass crunched, went opaque and buckled, held together by only thin layers of membrane. Not for long. Claw hands ripped open gaping holes, and the big boys poured into the station. McCreedy was dragged through the emptied doorframe, his shoes slipping on the fragments of glass. When he glanced over his shoulder, he saw the people on the benches running the other way as fast as they could, out the main doors.

In front of him, the desk sergeant drew his sidearm and took aim from his elevated position. His mouth opened and he shouted something, but it was impossible to make out what with the Klaxon blaring.

Seeing the gun pointed his way, McCreedy tried to duck, but a taloned hand caught him by the neck and lifted him upright, on tippy toes. It was like being clamped in a vise.

McCreedy wanted the cop to kill them all; he really did.

Until the shooting started and then all he wanted was for it to end.

Bullets coming at close range from one direction were bad enough, roaring past his head like freight trains, but the freight trains didn't stop. They made hard right and hard left turns; they veered up and down.

The creature who held him fast wasn't using him as a human shield; it didn't need one. Nine-millimeter bullets from the Glock slapped into and zinged off its head, in the process cutting slashes in the satin hood.

Stuff was blown off.

Off the head, itself.

Off the skin, hide, whatever.

Bits of it peppered and stung the right side of his face. He wiped his cheek with his fingertips and felt hard fragments, but there was no blood.

Though it seemed like much longer, the desk sergeant expended his fifteen rounds in as many seconds. By the time the slide on his weapon locked back, a double-wide had hold of him from behind. There would be no reloading.

Through the bullet rips in the hood, McCreedy saw shiny blue where the heavily corrugated skin had been blasted away. Was it bone under there? Could it be metal? It looked wet, but there was no sign of bleeding.

Dropped back on his feet, he was shoved past the duty desk. Behind him, he could hear the sergeant's sustained scream between pulses of the Klaxon. Then the screaming stopped. The alarm continued.

As the purple mob lumbered down the adjoining hallway, he struggled to keep up—it was either that or be trod under. The little one had no such worries; it was being carried like a dummy again. The odd pot-shot zinged overhead, but there was no concentrated resistance. Through open doorways, McCreedy saw officers and civilian employees taking cover behind desks and file cabinets.

If the creatures' goal was to kill a bunch of cops in their own house, they were letting a lot of them slip past. If the mission was to free fellow monsters held in the precinct's jail, how and when had the police managed to subdue them? He had seen no evidence that that was even possible. Bullets had no apparent effect. The beasts' physical strength seemed limitless. He doubted that the steel bars of a cell would contain one for more than a New York minute.

He couldn't think of any other reasons for them to be here, for doing what they were doing.

It was like a French horror movie—maniacally gruesome, but even with subtitles, it made no sense.

OFFICER CRAIG WESTER thought the day was going to be totally boring. He was stuck behind a desk after a beat-down incident involving a robbery suspect. One kick to the head too many, and as luck would have it, the action had been caught on a tourist's video camera.

Now he was running for his life.

The first pulse of the Klaxon emergency alarm had made the hair stand up on the back of his neck. At the sound of rapid pistol shots from the precinct's entrance, he had jumped to his feet. When he'd stuck his head around the doorway, he'd seen the duty sergeant struggling feebly in the grasp of a very wide person in a purple hoodie and more purple hoodies barreling down on him, like a herd of rhinos. He'd recognized them at once as the suspects in a series of terror attacks all over the city. Responding to those attacks had left the precinct house woefully undermanned.

Wester had drawn his weapon, but there'd been nothing he could do. There'd been too many hostiles between him and his sergeant. In a moment of panic— or heroism—he'd turned and now ran down the hallway ahead of the intruders, shouting warnings into the side rooms as he went.

There was an emergency plan in place in case of an all-out, armed assault on the station house. Though such a thing seemed highly unlikely, every officer in the precinct was drilled in the procedure until they could follow it in their sleep. Behind the brass's backs, the rank-and-file referred to it as *Plan Nine from Outer Space* and "fighting Martians."

But as a result of that training, Wester knew exactly what to do.

Ahead of him, the hallway bobbed with black-uniformed cops. They hit the entrance to the fire stairs and flowed quickly and smoothly down them, not quite stepping in cadence but close to it. Wester brought up the rear, last man through the door. He didn't look back.

The alarm sounded even louder inside the stairwell. It would have been hard to think if he had been thinking. But he wasn't. He was acting by rote, like a programmed robot, following those ahead of him, following the action plan like a lifeline. They trooped down the stairs, past the story where the holding cells were, then through the door on the next floor's landing. Their destination, the precinct's armory, was a concrete-lined, steel-reinforced bunker. To reach it, somewhere out of sight in front, an officer used a keypad to unlock the heavy hallway door.

As last man through, Wester pulled the door shut until he felt the lock click. He turned but couldn't start down the steep staircase because there was a momentary bottleneck of black uniforms below him.

When he reached the bottom of the steps, the armory's heavy wire door was open and officers were pouring through into the brightly lit, windowless room beyond.

Above and behind him at the top of the stairs, something hit the other side of the door, hard. The shock wave rattled the walls. It sounded like a battering ram.

Wester knew Plan Nine protocol included the immediate recall of all available units and personnel to the station. Basically, it was "drop whatever you're doing and come running." But from the sound of the battering ram, the shit storm was going to hit long before reinforcements arrived.

When he entered the armory, he was handed an armored vest, a black Kevlar helmet, an M-16, three 30-round magazines and a set of ear protectors. The weight of the automatic weapon felt good in his hands; the earplugs dulled the noise of the alarm and the booming from the door upstairs. He cracked in a magazine but did not touch the charging handle. Again it was Plan Nine protocol. No rounds were to be chambered until the targets were in sight and the command to fire was given. The last thing anybody wanted was the accidental discharge of a fully automatic weapon in a crowded, concrete-walled room.

The armory was equipped with a video monitor connected to the station's CCTV cameras. Everyone was looking up at it, at a massively built, hooded individual who was kicking the living shit out of a steel door. It was caving in under the rain of blows. Behind the kicker were more just like him.

There were none of the usual Martian wisecracks.

"Switch the camera," someone behind Wester said. "Let's see the rest of the station."

The picture changed to the ground floor, but what it showed was even more startling. Cops and civilians were down everywhere, and they weren't moving. It looked as if a tornado had ripped through the station house.

Between the blasts of the Klaxon, the booms of the kicks at the door, muffled gunfire erupted from directly above them.

"For Pete's sake, switch the camera back!" an officer said.

The view on the monitor shifted. In the hallway outside the armory door, three brave cops were taking on a half-dozen hoodies. They had their Glocks up and were blazing away at can't-miss range. Wester could see the suspects' heads jerking at the impacts.

The bullets didn't seem to have any effect.

"They aren't going down," someone in the rear said. "Why aren't they going down?"

As they watched, the purple hoodies stepped right up to the muzzles of the discharging weapons, picked up the officers as if they weighed nothing and drove the tops of their heads into the concrete wall. The limp bodies slumped to the floor below starbursts of skull, brains and blood.

"Who are these fuckers?" the cop beside Wester snarled.

"You mean, what are they," someone else corrected.

An officer at the armory counter slammed the phone down so hard the black plastic base shattered. "I was on the horn to One Police Plaza trying to get some backup here," he said. "She put me on hold! The bitch put me on hold!"

Then the door above them banged open. The rhythmic booming stopped.

"They're coming. Jesus Christ, they're coming!"

A woman's voice in the rear shouted over the emergency horn, "Get in position." It was a female lieutenant and she sounded all business.

Just as they'd trained, eight officers kneeled in front, and five stood behind them.

"Safeties off. Ready your weapons."

Charging handles clattered as thirteen first rounds were chambered. Kneeling, Wester looked through the security screen that walled off the anteroom from the armory proper. The distance between the service counter and the bottom of the steps was less than ten feet. The stairs themselves were just wide enough for two people to pass in opposite directions. The hatch above the service counter was pulled down, closed and locked, as was the entry gate.

"Let 'em hit the wire, then we all open fire at once," the lieutenant said. "We've got plenty of ammo here. The screen should hold them back. Clean shooting, now, just like at the range. Stay on target. Stay calm. Stay sharp. Do your job."

Wester settled the M-16's butt into the crook of his shoulder. He knew he was as ready as he was ever going to be.

When he saw the feet of the first purple hoodie come down the steps, his chest constricted. The feet weren't in shoes, and they weren't human. They looked like the final touch on a full-body Halloween costume.

The first hoodie was joined by a second, then a third. Their bulk practically filled the anteroom. The hoods cast their faces in deep shadow

Then as if on some silent signal, each raised a clawed hand and pushed back their cowl.

They looked…*prehistoric*. Wester had no other word for it. As if they had been hatched out of beach-ball-size eggs buried in the sand of some *Jurassic Park* riverbank. He let go of the M-16's pistol grip to wipe the sweat from his palm.

The purple hoodies were clearly not afraid of what was lined up on the other side of the screen. Their eyes were slitted, the corners of their wide mouths turned up, revealing rows of sharp teeth. It looked as if they were smiling.

One of the cops in the back row let out a scream and cut loose with his assault rifle.

The full-auto burst was contagious. Training and discipline out the window; they all opened fire. Even with earplugs, the clatter of so many automatic weapons going off in a concrete box was deafening.

The cop kneeling beside Wester went down, his right eye keyholed by a ricocheting 5.56 mm round that blew off his helmet and the back of head. Then an officer standing behind him dropped and then another. Bullets whined off the walls. Wester kept shooting,

because through the smoke, he could see the purple
hoodies were still standing, leaning into the torrent of
blasts as if it was a hurricane-force wind. If someone
was yelling for them to stop shooting, it couldn't be
heard over the din. He let up on the trigger only when
the M-16's last shot was fired.

Four hundred rounds of ammo expended at near
point-blank range in an enclosed space should have
done the trick, but it hadn't.

The monsters stepped up to the heavy wire screen.
Then they pulled it apart as if it was made of wet paper.

No time to reload, Wester discarded the assault rifle
and drew his handgun.

As he watched helplessly, a kneeling cop was jerked
to his feet by a purple hoodie, then pulled apart, like
a fly in the control of a small, curious boy. While the
officer screamed, his arms and legs were torn off and
then his torso was sent pinwheeling over their heads
to the back of the room.

Wester shot the grotesque reptilian bastard in the
head, punching out shot after shot at a distance of less
than four feet. The impacts of the 9 mm bullets barely
registered on it. Clear snot streaming from its nostrils, it grinned at him and kept coming. Still firing,
he backed up, aiming for an eye.

A fucking yellow eye.

McCreedy cowered on the staircase, fingers stuffed in
his ears. Below it sounded like World War III. Standing between him and the full-auto meat grinder were
three of the big boys. He knew they weren't protecting
him from the bullets. They were protecting the little
one who stood on the step next to him.

When the shooting finally stopped, he took his fingers out of his ears, but for only a second. The screaming—and the sound of the little one laughing—made him stuff them back in. Steel guy wires slid in and out of its cheek grommets, raising and lowering its lower jaw as it chortled.

It took several minutes for the screaming to end. Fearing that it wasn't really over, McCreedy kept his ears plugged as he was shoved down the steps. In the glare of the fluorescent ceiling light, brutally detached body parts lay scattered all over the floor. There were black-uniformed bodies without heads, arms or legs, blood still leaking from the various ragged stumps.

McCreedy removed his fingers from his ears and covered his nose and mouth with both hands in a feeble attempt to block the stench of spilled gore and voided bowels.

The room's purpose was obvious to him at a glance. The rows of assault rifles and combat shotguns lined up in racks along the walls were a dead giveaway.

Kicking a path through the body parts, the wide boys began gathering M-16s, olive-drab cans of ammo and crates of grenades.

They were using the police station as a gun shop, he realized. A *free* gun shop. It wasn't an aha moment. It didn't explain why creatures like them needed guns in the first place.

A purple hoodie stepped up to him and dumped a half-dozen black assault rifles in his arms. He stood there, meekly holding them until the little one decided they had enough loot.

They started back up the stairs with their burdens, tracking bloody footprints on the treads.

No one challenged them as they walked down the ground-floor hallway and out the front doors. There was no massive police presence waiting for them outside, no rows of squad cars, no phalanx of officers with weapons raised. In the distance he could hear a steady wail of sirens and the string-of-firecracker rattles of full-auto gunfire. The limo was where he had left it double-parked.

One of the big boys popped the vehicle's rear trunk lid. Inside, curled in a tight ball, eyes bugging out with terror was their other captive—Dr. James Nudelman. The strips of duct tape over his mouth and around the back of his head covered most of the big ruby-colored birthmark on the side of his face. McCreedy knew his name from the attack on the hospital. He had no idea why the man had been taken. Why would these creatures hold someone for ransom when they could barge into any bank, rip the doors off the vault, take what they wanted and leave without worrying about law enforcement? It didn't make any sense. Cops couldn't stop them, not even with automatic weapons; he'd seen the proof of that.

The purple hoodie rolled an unprotesting Nudelman to one side like a big bag of dog food, and then they began stacking the stolen weapons and ammo in the trunk. There was a lot of it to stack. What wouldn't fit with the lid closed, they took into the limo with them.

The sirens in the distance didn't seem to be coming any closer. Whatever the police were doing elsewhere in the city, they thought it was more important. Either that, or they knew they couldn't help here.

McCreedy was pushed behind the steering wheel as the limo's side door closed. He felt numbed to his core. Shell-shocked. Utterly lost. With a dry mouth, he babbled a prayer.

"Dear Lord, I know I've forsaken you...I know I don't deserve your mercy...but if just this once..."

"Drive!" the little one shrilled at him through the privacy window.

McCreedy drove.

Chapter Fifteen

Standing up, Ryan leaned into the EMT truck's front compartment. "Looks like we're in the clear for the moment," he said. "We can't just keeping driving around. Pull over, Vee. We need to figure out a plan."

Vee steered the truck to the curb and stopped, leaving the engine idling.

In the distance he could hear the distinct crackle of blasterfire between the wail of sirens.

"We need to pick up Magus's trail, and fast," Ryan said.

Vee reached up to the headliner and hit a switch on the console there. Police and emergency calls instantly blasted through the radio's speakers. "How about that for a start?" she said.

Ryan didn't understand the code numbers or locations being rattled off, but their guide to Manhattan did.

"Now your pal from the future is attacking police stations," Vee said. "That's what we're hearing outside. Three precincts in the south of the city have been hit in the last ten minutes. What's in a police station Magus would want?"

"Weapons," Mildred said without hesitation. "Full-auto assault rifles and stores of ammo."

"You don't have guns like that in the future?"

"We have blasters, guns," Ryan said, "but hardly

anyone is making new ones. And the new ones are very crude in comparison to what you have now. The fine points of steel making and machining have been lost. In our time we rely on the blasters that weren't destroyed in yours."

"What is the point of taking guns if Magus has enforcers?"

"Predark weapons and ammunition are pure gold to the residents of Deathlands, my dear," Doc said. "Hard currency, like jack, jolt and joy juice."

"Magus uses them to trade for slaves and supplies, to bribe favors from the barons and field an army of sec men if needed," Krysty told her.

"But police stations?" Vee said. "Attacking one is like asking to get shot full of holes."

"Bullets not stop enforcers," Jak stated.

"All hell is breaking loose here," Mildred said. "The cops aren't going to be sitting in the barn drinking coffee and eating doughnuts. They'll be out responding to the widespread attacks. The stations will be almost undefended."

"What other source of blasters is there?" Ryan asked.

"National Guard armories, I suppose," Vee said. "But I don't know if there are fully operational ones in the city. I mean, which ones, if any, actually hold stocks of automatic weapons. They're historic buildings."

"Magus is under the same time pressure we are," Ryan said. "Can't go far to get the shopping done."

"Hitting an unmanned National Guard armory wouldn't have the same shock effect, either," Mildred said. "Attacking police stations head-on is a dagger in the heart of America's largest city. If anything, Magus

is all about the gruesomely theatrical. And the eve of
the world ending is the biggest stage that will ever be.
Given the opportunity, Magus is putting on the opening act, warming up a global audience for the headliner, the ultimate terror."

"By the Three Kennedys," Doc groaned, "even for
Magus, that seems over the top."

"How does any of this help us?" Krysty said.

"I've been keeping track of the locations," Vee said.
"Out of twenty-two police precincts on Manhattan,
so far the Thirteenth, Tenth and Midtown South have
been hit. The assaults are zigzagging back and forth,
but seem to be moving in a northerly direction up the
island. If that is a pattern and it continues, the next
stop is the Eighteenth Precinct police station, Midtown North."

"It's all we've got," Ryan said. "Let's go for it."

With lights flashing and siren screaming, Vee
roared away from the curb.

"What about the paramedic?" Mildred said to Ryan.
"I told him we'd let him go when we were clear."

Hanging on to the rear compartment's ceiling, Ryan
glanced back at the man strapped to the gurney. He appeared to be asleep, or maybe he'd fainted from terror.
"We don't want him reporting the wag stolen," he said.
"He stays where he is until we're done."

Ryan turned to look out the windshield. They had
made no turns since the last right; the wide road ahead
was straight as a string. He couldn't see the speedom-
eter over Vee's shoulder, but she was really pouring
it on. The desolate urban landscape zipped past in a
blur. No trees. No dirt. No people. Just asphalt, concrete

and glass. In a way it reminded him of the New York of Deathlands.

Odd to think of the pinnacle of civilization as bleak and inhuman, but that's how he saw it. A vast, cold emptiness. But Deathlands was certainly no picnic in the park, either, and this wasn't his era to judge or condemn. All he knew was he didn't want his life to end here.

He turned and looked back at his companions— J.B., Krysty, Doc, Mildred, Jak and Ricky stood or sat, eyes staring at nothing. Each was lost in his or her own thoughts, but he was sure they all felt the same way.

This was no place to die.

The few wags ahead of them didn't stay ahead for long. As Vee bore down on their back bumpers, they immediately slowed and pulled close to the curb, out of her path. He had read about the different-colored lights hanging over the intersections with side streets. Their purpose didn't seem to apply to the wag they were in. Or Vee just ignored it.

They'd been rolling for about a mile when the radio crackled with a different voice sounding a new alert, but the message was familiar: station under attack, officers down, all personnel return at once.

"Good grief!" Vee said. "That's Midtown North! They're already hitting it!"

"How far away?" Ryan asked.

"We're on Eighth Avenue," she said, as if that would mean something to him. "It's a straight shot to Fifty-Fourth Street and the precinct house. Maybe five minutes if I don't have to slow down."

She didn't slow down; in fact she sped up. The wag's engine screamed at redline. It felt as if the tires were barely touching the ground, as if they were floating over the street. Ryan guessed she was doing one hundred miles an hour or damned close to it. At that speed a minor fuckup, a swerve of the steering wheel, a stray dog in the road, a pothole, and they were going to flip and roll, roll and roll, until the wag was a pile of unrecognizable twisted steel wrapped around a thousand pounds of raw human hamburger.

Over the engine noise, the blasterfire outside got louder and louder—strings of single shots and long bursts of overlapping automatic fire. And there were explosions, too. To Ryan they sounded like the flat whack of detonating grens.

Vee started to slow down at Fifty-Third, past the tallest buildings he'd ever seen. They stretched up and up, he couldn't see the tops, and there were too many stories to count—even if he'd been in the mood for counting them. Then she swung a hard left on Fifty-Fourth. Ryan smelled the smoke a second before he saw the blaze. The odor was like burning tires and roasted pork.

A huge bonfire raged in front of a squat four-story, gray-stone-faced structure with a doorway at either corner of the street-facing side. It was hard to tell, but from the wreckage, it looked as if a police wag in the parking area had been rammed broadside by a big white step van. Both vehicles and the three squad cars parked next to them were fully engulfed in fire.

When Vee stopped the EMT truck in the middle of the street, everybody bailed from the wag with blasters drawn. Through the side window of one of the crushed cop wags, Ryan could just make out the head-and-shoulder silhouette of a body behind the steering

wheel. It had already burned to a blackened crisp. The
flames from the fuel tanks had jumped so high that
they had ignited the red, white and blue flag on the
stanchion at the top of the first-floor facade. The heat
was withering. In the leaping firelight, the building
looked dirty; the pale stone was streaked with stripes
of dark moss or grime.

As Ryan moved for the closest doorway, longblaster
in hand, a deafening sustained burst of autofire came
from above. Muzzle-flashes strobe-lit the darkened,
second-story windows.

Chapter Sixteen

The only light in the limo's trunk was what leaked through the backs of the taillight housings—a weak red glow that occasionally flared brighter when the driver hit the brakes. Though the floor of the trunk was fully carpeted, it was hardly comfortable. The overloaded limo was riding very low on its suspension. Every time it hit a bump, Dr. James Nudelman bounced in the air and came down with a jarring thud. So did the pile of automatic weapons jammed in beside him. Disoriented by the numerous turns the driver had made, he had no idea where he was, except he was pretty sure they hadn't left Manhattan.

The vehicle had made just one stop since his kidnapping. The purple gang had left him bound and gagged in the trunk while they'd attended to another matter. He'd cringed at the first sounds of gunfire from outside; he'd known people had to be dying as a result. The shooting had gone on and on, like the soundtrack for an action movie. When it had finally ended, nothing had happened for the longest time, then the trunk lid had popped open again. In the glow of the courtesy light, a creature had loomed over him with a knobby outstretched hand. It had grabbed him and rolled him to one side. Looking warily over his shoulder, he'd watched as armload after armload of M-16s was dumped on the floor. More and more flat black weapons were piled in, until the heap avalanched, toppling over against his back and head. He had no idea where the guns had been stolen from. Turned to face the wheel well, he couldn't see out of the trunk. Then the lid had slammed shut and he'd been in darkness again.

After about ten minutes of driving, the limo turned and suddenly angled up. Then it hit a big bump and there was a sharp scraping sound, as though the undercarriage was dragging on pavement. A moment later the vehicle stopped. The trunk lid reopened and the reptilians began unloading the heap of guns. When they had emptied the compartment, one of them took hold of his ankles and hauled his legs out over the back bumper. Gathered under a massive arm, he found himself being lugged across a ground-floor parking garage. It was hard to focus because his captor held him so loosely—his head kept bouncing up and down, and he couldn't raise it high enough or long enough to take a good look around. Though he was pressed against the creature's side, his skin rubbing against its ridged hide, he felt no body heat. Under the thin layer of purple satin, it was as cold as a stone.

The reptilian carried him to an elevator but didn't take it. Instead it followed the others through a doorway and down a flight of stairs to a concrete hallway. From the steady hum of generators and the start and stop of pumps, Nudelman assumed it was the building's environmental-system-and-maintenance level. The air seemed much warmer, probably a result of the heat given off by the machinery.

Over the drone of equipment, he heard what sounded like people yelling, but the noise was muffled and he couldn't make out what they were saying. If it was in fact people, they didn't sound pleased. As he was hauled down the corridor, the volume of the shouting grew steadily louder.

When the creature who held him stopped and opened a door, a torrent of frantic noise washed over him. They entered a long, windowless, gray concrete room, harshly lit by banks of overhead fluorescents. On either side of the room, the yellers and screamers were housed in individual, widely separated cells with steel bars. There were at least twenty of them. They weren't cells like in a prison; they were on four wheels, as if they'd been designed for circus animals or use in a medical lab or veterinary clinic. The captives couldn't stand upright; the best they could do was crouch on all fours, and that put their backs against the inside of the ceiling bars and their heels against the rear wall.

Almost all of the prisoners wore the white lab coats of physicians, scientists and engineers, which made him think their captors were in the process of collecting a particular breed of *homo sapiens*, as a dog fancier might do with corgis or standard poodles.

Even inside the long room, it was difficult for him to understand what the other prisoners were shouting about. The sound of their voices had an odd quality— like an echo or reverb effect. It distorted the separation between words, turned them into unintelligible mush.

After a few seconds, his brain sorted out the voices and the words crystallized. Some of the prisoners were cursing a blue streak, while others were making angry, empty threats of criminal prosecution and civil action. They weren't directed at the creature who carried him;

the captives were shouting blindly into space—like madmen.

After being dumped on the floor, Nudelman was untrussed and shoved headfirst into an empty cage. Before he could turn, the barred door clanked shut behind him.

The shouting continued unabated after the purple monster left the room. It was relentless, and it set Nudelman's teeth on edge.

As he glared at the prisoners on the other side of the room, he noticed a blurring of his vision. And in the air between him and them, there seemed to be flurries of tiny glowing sparks. When he tried to focus on these little spots of light, they instantly disappeared.

Using his knowledge of human anatomy and physiology, he immediately put it down to blood rushing to his head and strain on his retinas from cutting his eyes sideways, trying to see where he was going, while he was being carried. The intermittent noise that he had at first determined to be the sound of pumps starting and stopping seemed to be nothing of the sort. The grinding wasn't from a motor. It was too loud, too deeply pitched, and it made the floor and walls shiver. The noise seemed connected to the appearance of the strange sparks. In the pulses between grinds, they were absent. He knew that had to be sheer coincidence— the spots and the slight blurring were a function of his brain and his eyes, not the result of some outside phenomenon. The combination of grinding sound, bright spots and blurring made him queasy. Then a darker thought occurred to him: he could have sustained a serious head injury when the pile of assault rifles had fallen on him.

The man in the cell directly opposite began to beat his balled fists on the barred floor of his cage. He wore blood-spattered hospital scrubs, and his face was cherry red, suffused with fury. He looked vaguely familiar.

"What the hell is going on?" Nudelman shouted over the din. "Who are these things? What are they going to do with us?"

The man in the lab coat kept beating on the floor and ignored him.

"Hey! What is going on here?"

His fellow prisoner threw back his head and unleashed a blood-curdling scream at the ceiling.

Nudelman could see the man was losing it. There was no way to tell how long he had been kept hunched over like a pill bug in the little rolling cage. He tried again to communicate, shouting at top volume over the chaos in the room, slowly and distinctly enunciating each word. "Who…are…these…creatures? What…do…they…want?"

The man in the scrubs looked right at him, but there was no response. It was not only as if he hadn't spoken, it was as if he didn't exist.

Shock, Nudelman told himself. It had to be from the shock of being kidnapped and caged in a madhouse.

The bars that made up the floor of his cell hurt his knees. He shifted his weight, but there was no way to get comfortable. The cage was designed for a much smaller prisoner, say a golden retriever or chimpanzee.

He took in the rest of the room. A thick hose was coiled on the wall next to a water tap. In the aisle between the two rows of cages was a metal-grated floor drain. Nudelman found the sight unsettling. He was beginning to feel pressure in his bladder; soon he was going to have to relieve himself. Were they expected to do their business in their cells, like hamsters, have it fall to the floor beneath, and then at some later time, it would be hosed off down the drain?

Everything that had happened to him so far pointed to a bad outcome.

Were they being held so they could be experimented on? To what possible end? Or perhaps their bizarre captors intended to slaughter, then eat them. He discarded both ideas almost at once. Any person off the street would fill the bill for experiment and slaughter; the preponderance of lab coats in the room meant they had been specifically selected. Their knowledge and specialized skills had put them in harm's way. One thing was clear, there was no national government or rational mind behind it.

As he looked at the prisoner opposite, the grinding noise returned and once more he saw a shower of tiny twinkling lights, like fireflies winking on, then off. As before, he felt as if he was going to throw up. The other man had stopped yelling, perhaps because he was exhausted, but the others took up the slack. His face remained blurred, as did everything else on that side of the room. Again Nudelman got the sense that he knew the man from somewhere. Had he seen him in the hospital? At a medical convention? At a biotech symposium?

No, that wasn't it.

It seemed vitally important to place the fellow. If the two were linked by their past, it could be a way to break through to him. A point of contact might also help explain their current predicament.

A name popped into his head. Danson. No, that wasn't it.

Hansom. No.

Ransom!

Oh God, Nudelman thought. It was Dr. William Ransom! Aka "Wild Bill" for his surgical panache and legendary, three-second fuse in the OR. He gripped the bars of his cage and pressed his forehead against them. Ransom was the foremost neuro cutter in Manhattan, ranked number ten in the world. They had met at a three-day wealth seminar in the Bahamas several years ago. Over umbrella drinks at the poolside bar, Ransom had seemed a likely pee-battery-investor prospect. They had exchanged business cards and talked expensive, big-boy toys—private jets and yachts; Ransom had one of each—and politics and economic theory. Nudelman thought they had made a real connection, and with its disfiguring mark, his face was not easily forgotten.

"Dr. Ransom!" he roared through cupped hands. "Dr. Ransom, it's me, James Nudelman!"

Wild Bill stared right at him, but it was as if he was looking at a blank wall. Tears were streaming down his face and his fingers, his precious surgeon's fingers, were battered from pounding them on the bars.

"Doctor, are you all right?"

The world famous surgeon swept the back of a hand over his contorted face, smearing it with blood, tears and snot.

"Doctor, are you all right?"

Slowly Ransom's eyes rolled back in his head until only the whites showed. Then he took a deep breath and started screaming again.

That set Nudelman's blood boiling. They were no more than thirty feet apart! Elite surgeons were notoriously self-centered and dismissive of those outside their specialty—or those in the specialty but below their global rank—but he and Ransom knew each other! They had talked at length about the failure of Ross Perot's presidential campaign in 1996. So what if he wasn't an MD? So what if he wasn't a big-time cutter? So what if he hadn't flown in to the seminar on his own private jet? So what if he didn't have a three-hundred-foot yacht to sail home in? They had history!

Suddenly the most important thing in the world was to get Ransom to acknowledge the fact that he was alive and a prisoner in the same room. Nudelman waited for a lull in the yelling match with the grinding, then bellowed as loud as he could, "Ransom you fucking asshole, answer me!"

The words cut through the layered din like a cannon shot.

Then the din swallowed them up.

Across the aisle, the world-famous surgeon stared at Nudelman as if he didn't exist.

THE WORLD-FAMOUS SURGEON, a man who could restore life and function to the disabled, who could reanimate the seemingly dead, who routinely held the very seat of the soul in the latex-gloved palm of his hand, crouched on all fours and screamed. He screamed until he was on the verge of blacking out from oxygen deprivation. The inarticulate, strangled cry echoed in the long concrete room. The walls were lined on either side with rolling cages just like his.

Waiting empty cages.

Over the span of a half hour of confinement and iso-
lation, he had gone from shouting "Help me!" to just
roaring as loud as he could. His throat hurt from the
sustained effort. At this rate he knew he would soon
lose his voice altogether.

Why didn't someone answer him?

He had guessed from the trek down to the windowless room that he was in the bowels of a Manhattan
high-rise office building or condominium. There were
usually video cameras in such places. If not, there had
to be security guards or maintenance men. Someone
had to pass by the metal door.

At least in theory.

The empty cages stared back at him. There were
dozens of them. Why so many? he thought. Who else
were they—the horrid creatures who had kidnapped
him—going to put in them?

"Someone help me!" he croaked.

Ransom regularly paid a large number of people big
money to do just that. And not just to help—to serve
his every whim. He paid annual salaries with bonuses
and benefits to the flight crew of his Gulfstream jet,
the captain and crew of his Feadship yacht and the
full-time staffs at his medical offices and mansions
around the world.

Where were they all now, when he *really* needed
them?

The memory of Mr. Carstairs's brains splattering
the team around the OR table came back in a ghastly
Technicolor rush. No doubt about it, he had fallen into
the hands of murderers. Whoever, whatever his captors were, he knew if he did not obey he would meet

the same or a worse fate than his poor patient. The littlest monster had promised him as much.

Under different circumstances, Ransom would have liked to examine that strange creature more closely and at length. As a scientist and physician, he found the *Frankenstein*-esque interface between living flesh and nonliving components both fascinating and remarkable. Such a thing had been thought impossible outside B movies and comic books: metal and muscle crudely joined to create functional movement and a reasonable semblance of life. How had the contraption been assembled and where? Had someone actually designed it, or had it just been cobbled together as needed out of spare parts? Was there a real human brain squatted inside that half-metal skull?

Questions of scientific knowledge aside, whatever the shambling abomination asked of him, he was determined to do without question. He had worked too hard and too long to be snuffed out like a candle flame. He didn't understand the degrading, inhuman treatment he was receiving—it was as if the creatures were trying to break his spirit. Or maybe they just didn't give a damn. At that thought, his face flushed with outrage. What manner of certifiable moron would cage like an animal the eighth most sought after neurosurgeon in the world?

Then he recalled the little monster had said something about taking him a hundred years into the future. That was by far the most frightening threat of all.

It made Ransom think he was in the grip of an insane cult targeting the uber-rich and uber-talented. Is that what the other cages were for? Good grief, he thought, were they going to murder him here in this overheated dungeon, in the deranged belief that it would *transport him to the future*? Like the thirty-nine Heaven's Gate suicides thinking that in death they were going to be taken up by a spaceship hiding behind a passing comet?

For a person so thoroughly grounded in the scientific process and the mechanics of neurobiology, in the purely rational, in experimental fact, the ultimate insult and irony would be to die because of a homicidal maniac's delusion.

That did nothing to explain the appearance of his captors, of course. The big ones were miniature Godzillas, with similar temperaments; the little monster was a demented version of Pinocchio. Nothing on earth looked like that. Nothing acted like that.

And for sure, nothing smelled like that.

Suddenly it occurred to him that the delusion in question might actually be his and his alone. A direct consequence of a brain strangled by an invasive and pervasive hostile growth. Perhaps he had acquired a big old tumor of his own? The possibility made him sag against the hard bars.

Why hadn't he thought of that before?

It explained the hallucinations, both visual and olfactory. Was any of what he was experiencing real? Had a single cancerous cell divided and divided until its tendrils infiltrated his brain like tree roots? Could the beast he had fought for so long and so valiantly have taken residence in his own skull?

He tightly shut his eyes and thought it through, step by step.

If that was the case, if an undiagnosed tumor was causing the hallucinations, if there was no cage, then how had he hurt his aching hands? Why did the bars of the imaginary cage hurt his knees? Why couldn't he stand up without hitting his head?

Every turn in the logical analysis of the situation came full circle to the same dead end. If he was seeing things, he couldn't have hurt his hands on the bars. If he wasn't seeing things, then the mini-Godzillas and the Pinocchio from hell were real, which he knew was impossible.

For a man accustomed to seizing Fate by the balls and squeezing, the situation was now reversed: the balls in the vise were his. The loss of personal control and critical understanding tipped the very Earth on its axis.

"For God's sake, someone please help me!" he screamed at the door. "Please!"

The shrill cry seemed to mock him as it bounced back and forth off the walls of the empty room.

No one was listening, or no one gave a damn.

Chapter Seventeen

His Steyr in hand, safety off, Ryan ran up the three granite steps under the sign that said 18th Precinct and through the double doorway. Four feet ahead of him, the foyer ended abruptly in a block wall. The building's exterior wall was on his right, so the only path was to the left. He swung the longblaster in that direction and turned down a cramped corridor lit by a flickering bank of ceiling fluorescent lights.

The carnage started just inside the turn. It reminded him of what the enforcers had left behind at the nameless mountain ville.

How many people lay dead in the narrow entry hall, he couldn't even hazard a guess. Detached arms, legs, torsos and heads lay in a sprawling, gory jumble on the floor—creating a bottleneck of the slaughtered. Some were in black uniform; others in civilian clothes. Some of the dead hands still clutched blasters, the slides locked back on empty mags. Some of the victims looked male; others were obviously female. Once enforcers commenced their chilling, they stopped only when they ran out of victims. Up to the border with the acoustic-tile drop ceiling, the grimy walls—and the posters pinned on them—were splattered with blood and other bodily fluids.

Although the decapitated heads could be avoided

or nudged aside with the toe of a boot, there was no way to advance past the entrance without stepping on a severed limb or two.

The heavy glass doors to the station proper lay in huge, crazed sheets on the floor beneath their emptied frames—this was the barrier that had sealed the victims' fates. With locked doors to their backs, they had nowhere to run. Wherever Ryan placed his boot soles, fractured glass crunched under his weight. Thankfully, the body-part carpet stopped at the station's inner doorway.

What Ryan saw instead was clear evidence of a fighting retreat. Spent blaster casings littered the scarred tile floor. Hundreds of them. The walls were pocked with sideways bullet holes from ricochets off armored hide. The floor farther down the hall, as far as he could see, was dotted with more casings. It looked as if the precinct's defenders had fallen back room by room from a wave of enforcers.

Were they acting in desperation? Panic? Or were they trying to lure the attackers into a trap? Did they have a contingency plan? Maybe a cross-fire or massed kill zone deeper inside the building?

Neither was a good idea in this situation. Any kind of trap could backfire if the things being targeted didn't stay trapped. Bullet impacts could keep enforcers at a distance for a while, but when the firing stopped, when the ammo finally ran out, there'd be a one-way ticket on the last train west.

Good strategy or not, the spent brass the defenders had left behind was like that trail of bread crumbs Vee had talked about. He figured it would lead straight to the monsters they were chasing.

Jak leapfrogged ahead down the hall, Colt Python in his right hand and a thermite gren in his left. As he passed Ryan, he gave him a rare grin. The albino enjoyed being on the short end of a lopsided fight. What others took for hopeless odds against superior strength, Jak saw as an opportunity to prove just what a hellscape badass he was. They had no other choice than to go for it. They couldn't get to the vulnerable Magus without first taking on his almost invulnerable minions. In Ryan's opinion, planning for an attack on an unrecced location, against an enemy that just wouldn't die, was a waste of precious time. Surprise was their only hole card—surprise and thermite.

The hallway and the rooms along it on either side were free of corpses and body parts. The defenders had to have been retreating quickly, or there would have been casualties. It worried him that the sounds of shooting inside the building had stopped. That meant either the survivors had barricaded themselves someplace the enforcers couldn't reach—although considering the bastards' strength that was a temporary solution at best—or there were no survivors left. Either the big battle was over and the defenders had lost or they hadn't sprung their trap yet.

Since this was the fourth in a series of similar attacks, it was also possible they'd had prior warning and a few minutes to gather their forces. They could have had a rear escape route set up. There was no telling whether the enforcers had gone to the trouble of covering all the exits before they began the assault. If all they wanted was the guns, they wouldn't care about people getting away.

Autofire clattered on the floor above them. A short

burst brought down a rain of dust from the acoustic-tile ceiling, then another burst and another dust fall.

Apparently not everyone had left.

It wasn't the massed, multiblaster trap he had been anticipating, and most likely, it wasn't one of the enforcers cutting loose. Blasters were not their preferred style. The shooting rattled again, stopped abruptly. Heavy footsteps thudded overhead, and then a piercing squeal rang out. That didn't last long, either.

After a pause the ceiling began to creak and groan. Something really big was lumbering around up there. Something with four-toed feet, he guessed. It seemed pretty clear the shooter upstairs had been a straggler, maybe separated from the rest of the defenders by the initial attack.

"You've got to locate the armory where the blasters are stored," he told the others. "That's where Magus is headed. Keep your thermite grens handy, and don't stand too close when you toss them. Remember how hot these warty bastards burn."

After their trip through the entry hall, he didn't feel the need to remind the others to stay focused and on triple red. A sign above a closed door on the left said Stairs and below the letters was a zigzag symbol representing steps. He reached out for the doorknob.

"Ryan, wait!" Krysty said.

"I'll take care of the one upstairs," he told her. "I don't want it coming up from behind us when we're occupied with its relatives."

"How do you know there's only one?" Krysty asked.

"Trying to think positive," he said with a smile. "I'll catch up with you when I'm done."

"Don't make me come get you, lover."

Ryan winked at her, then pushed into the stairwell and began to climb, his longblaster angled up for a quick shot at the landing above if necessary. The job he had in mind had to be done. If they were going to survive, their rear had to be protected. Facing an enforcer alone wasn't something he could let one of the others do.

The shaft was dimly lit, but he could see scattered wet spots on the concrete steps where drips of enforcer sweat had fallen. The odor of the secretion in the enclosed space made him grimace. He wondered, and not for the first time, how the bastard muties could stand themselves.

At the top of the landing, he pulled back the door, which opened onto a large room. He found the light switch on the wall and flipped it. Banks of fluorescents winked on one by one, revealing a couple of dozen gray metal desks, all of them piled with papers and file folders. Ryan scanned the room over the scope of his shouldered longblaster. Nothing moved. The room looked deserted.

He sidestepped the rows of desks, pointing his weapon as he looked down the aisles between them. There was no sign of bodies or shell casings on the black-and-white-checkerboard linoleum floor.

There were drips, however. They showed up better on the black squares of tile than the white. They led beyond the large room to a connecting hallway so narrow he could almost span it with extended arms. It was as tight as the entry corridor downstairs, and just as potentially deadly. If the enforcer decided to bull-rush him, there wasn't much space to maneuver.

The rooms off the corridor to the left were all dark.

The ones on the other side had windows that over-looked the bonfire on the street out front. In the danc-ing light he could see single desks and chairs, filing cabinets and bookcases. The glass itself reflected leap-ing orange flames.

On the floor ahead of him on the right, he saw a scatter of spent brass. Moving quietly, he slipped through the doorway into a room that reeked of burned cordite and spilled blood.

This has to be the place, he thought as he searched for targets with his longblaster.

Then the floor underfoot began to shiver and vi-brate as if it was being dragged whole over a patch of rough ground. It was a grinding, undulating motion, an earthquake confined to the space of a twelve-by-twelve room. Bright points of light swam before his eye, like flurries of sparks from the raging fires outside, but the room's large window was closed and the sparks were falling between him and the exterior wall. He fought back a wave of nausea as his vision blurred.

Something big was hunkered on the floor in front of the desk. It was making a grunting noise. He put his sights on it immediately but didn't light it up because he couldn't identify what it was. Then his sight cleared.

An enforcer had hold of a downed man's arm and was twisting it around and around on the shoulder joint, in a way it was never intended to move, like wringing out a wet sock. With an audible snap, the tendons and sin-ews broke and the limb came free of its socket. The en-forcer tossed the arm aside and set to work on the head.

Ryan held the Steyr aimed at the creature as it turned to look his direction.

The enforcer made no move to attack. It looked

right at him, then as if his presence didn't matter, it resumed the activity, putting a scaly foot on the chest for leverage, then twisting the head clockwise by its chin. When the chin rotated past the shoulder, the supporting neck made a loud crack. The creature continued to twist, turning the head around and around until the skin and connecting tissue snapped. When the object finally came free in its hands, it grunted in satisfaction. A torrent of blood poured from the head's stump onto the unmoving torso.

A preoccupied monster wasn't what Ryan had expected.

As he laid the crosshairs on its knobby head, the scope's sight picture blurred. The grinding sound returned with a shower of sparks. Everything suddenly lurched, including his stomach. He had to blink to refocus and clear his head. They had shot enforcers pretty much everywhere, without effect. Everywhere but the eye. Ryan figured to give that a try first, on the chance there might be a fissure or weak spot behind it that connected optic nerves to the brain, like in a regular skull.

The Steyr bucked and roared deafeningly in the little room.

In the next instant, everything in his range of vision went out of focus, swimming so violently that Ryan was sure he was going to throw up. Then just as quickly, it snapped back into hard focus.

Nothing happened.

The distance to target had been less than five feet. It was fish-in-barrel range. He knew the round had discharged because his ears were ringing from the sound. Even if the slug had missed the eye socket, even if it had glanced off the brow ridge, the impact of a 175 grain slug should have at the very least snapped back the enforcer's head.

Nothing had happened.

That wasn't true, he realized as he worked the bolt and ejected the smoking hull.

The bullet had disappeared.

Somewhere between muzzle and target, in a span of less than sixty inches, the round had ceased to exist. So had the blurring and the sparks and the grinding sound. The entire room and contents jumped into such detailed focus that it made the memory of what it had been like all the more jarring.

It was as if a veil had been lifted. The light cast by the fires on the street became twice as bright.

The enforcer looked at him again, and this time its yellow eyes slitted with delight. It dropped the head, which made a hollow thunk when it hit the floor, and rose to its full height.

Ryan locked down the bolt on a fresh cartridge, aimed at the eye and fired just as the creature started to move. This time as the longblaster boomed and bucked into his shoulder, the enforcer's head snapped back hard, the bullet zinged off its skull, and slammed into the wall to his left.

Before the creature could recover he fired again. Same aimpoint.

At impact, the knobby head tipped back, the chin tipped up. To keep its balance the enforcer took a stagger step backward, flapping its arms.

Cycling the action, Ryan advanced and fired, forcing the monster to step back and flail or fall on its knobby, double-wide butt.

With a goal in mind, he shot the enforcer square in

the head again and again. Trying for the eye wasn't necessary. The bullets' impacts were like sledgehammer blows to its skull, rocking it back on its heels. The 7.62 mm slugs drove the monster in reverse, shaking the window glass. Through it Ryan could see flames of the burning wrecks outside. He knew he had to keep shooting; he couldn't stop to reach for the frag gren in his pocket. Under the circumstances, it would have been suicide anyway, and there was no guarantee a dose of hot shrap would stop the bastard.

Despite his frenzy of rapid discharge, Ryan kept track of rounds fired.

When he hit the monster in the head for the tenth time, emptying the Steyr's mag, the enforcer's heels hit the wall and its broad back slammed against the window, cracking the glass. The enforcer caught its balance just short of falling out and stood there teetering, windmilling its arms.

With no rounds left, Ryan did the only thing he could think of. He dropped the Steyr and threw his full body weight behind a shoulder strike into the middle of the creature's chest. Under any other conditions, he wouldn't have had the mass or momentum to budge it, but the creature was already off balance. The perfectly timed blow nudged it past the tipping point; the glass behind it shattered. The window frame exploded, and the enforcer toppled out into empty air.

The follow-through, so essential in getting the most power out of the strike, left Ryan leaning forward and well within the creature's reach.

The enforcer's taloned hand grabbed hold of Ryan's wrist, and as it fell backward over the sill, it jerked him off his feet, headfirst through the emptied frame. A wave of blistering heat slammed his face, and locked together, they dropped into the leaping wall of flames.

RICKY MORALES HAD to admit he was feeling a little light in the knees and short of breath as he followed the companions down the police station hall. Who wouldn't be after stepping on a path of severed limbs? Not that he needed further evidence their current opponent was nearly invincible and capable of inhuman violence. He was determined to make a better showing with his .45 ACP De Lisle carbine this time. He had ten shots in the mag, and no matter what else happened in the next few minutes, he was going to burn them all. He didn't want Vee to think he was still just a boy. Or worse, a coward. Because he was neither.

He idolized J.B., but he wasn't happy about the teasing he'd suffered in the redoubt, undermining his machismo and maturity in front of everyone. He didn't like that Mildred, who he deeply respected as a fighter, had felt the need to step in and defend him. He couldn't help freezing up in front of that elevator, though. He had never seen a creature, couldn't even imagine a creature, so strong that that many bullets wouldn't slow it down.

They moved quickly down the corridor, with Jak on point about thirty feet ahead, ducking in and out of rooms on the right and left. The companions advanced like a well-oiled machine. A killing machine.

The beautiful Vee fit right in, as if she'd been part of their crew for years. She didn't need to be told anything; she already knew what was expected of her. She glided along like a cat, light and fast on her feet. Not a kitty cat, though. Kitty cats didn't carry massive gold blasters like that. Marked with stripes like *el tigre de Bengala*, the .44 Magnum weapon she held braced in both hands shouted predator.

Eat you alive.

He could see Vee was not afraid of anything that ran, flew, slithered or swam. She trusted her blaster and her skill with it. Ricky found that very, very sexy. This woman from the past was no shy *mamacita*. She was a natural-born killer.

She was also one of the most gorgeous women he had ever seen. Her beauty went far deeper than her features and body, although they were very attractive to him. What he found even more magnetic was her self-confidence and sense of humor, even as they hurried toward the yawning gates of hell. If Ricky could have made up the perfect woman in his mind—and he had spent considerable time trying to do just that—that woman was Veronica Currant.

Doc hovered around her as they leapfrogged down the hall, speaking in low tones almost nonstop. It looked as if he was running interference, as if he was trying to be a noble knight—a long-legged, scarecrow-skinny knight. Vee didn't need a protector; everything about her said she could take care of herself and then some. Doc was openly hitting on her.

What could an old guy like Doc offer a gloriously vibrant young woman such as Vee? Boring talk and strange manners? An ancient blaster and an even older sword stick? And what about the crazy times when he rambled, talking to dead people and making no sense? The times when Doc acted like a jolt head on a two-week binge?

His teeth were his most attractive feature; he did

have an impressive set. As far as Ricky could see, they were his only attractive feature. Doc couldn't offer Vee youth and vitality. He couldn't give her babies or a lifetime of companionship.

Whether he realized it or not, at that moment, a plan was already taking shape in Ricky's mind.

As if turned on by a switch, automatic blasterfire exploded from the floor directly below them. A surge of adrenaline made Ricky's face burn and his fingers tingle. He couldn't tell how many blasters were touching off. From the volume, there could easily have been twenty or more, all firing at once.

What they were firing at was no mystery.

"This way!" Jak shouted back at them.

The sound of their boots slapping the linoleum were lost in the wall of noise coming up through the floor. It shook the walls.

Jak found a stairwell, and they triple-timed down it. The sounds of pitched battle grew louder and louder. When they hit the next level and burst through the doorway, the sustained clatter was earsplitting. A dead white hand waved them onward.

What with running and the bodies blocking his view, it was difficult for Ricky to make out what was ahead of them. What they were doing seemed loco—charging to meet horrible deaths—but strangely enough, it was also incredibly exhilarating. A terrible, private moment loomed for each of them, and yet they were embracing it with open arms and eyes wide open

By the time they reached the far corner of the basement floor, the full-auto, multiweapon, blastershot overlap had begun to peter out. Like a wag running out of fuel and sputtering haltingly to a dead stop, the clatter dwindled from twenty blasters to five, then one.

The screeches of terror and pain started well before the last blaster fired its last shot.

The albino took them down yet another flight of steps at the end of the hall. Below them was a short landing, and a thick steel door stood ajar. Blaster smoke boiled out of the opening. Painted on the wall above it was the word *armory*.

Armería, Ricky thought. The place where blasters were stored.

The screaming from the doorway made his skin crawl and his fingers tighten on the De Lisle's grip. It sounded as if it was coming from the bottom of a very deep well.

J.B. signaled for them to move down the stairs in pairs.

With Mildred on his right, Ricky stepped over the threshold, into the caustic cloud, which burned his eyes, the inside of his nose and the back of his throat. The fluorescent lights overhead were dim and flickering. Most had been shot out by flying ricochets. He couldn't see the back of the room for the roiling smoke, but there was a second staircase on this side; he could make out the doorway and first few steps. It was a mirror image of the one they had used and ran perpendicular to it.

Through tearing eyes, he could just make out a row of wide figures in purple hoodies. They were hunched with their backs to the door, and their arms were moving in a frenzy. Over what, he couldn't quite see. If one of the creatures had very nearly killed them all, how many were they facing now? Six? Seven?

When he first heard the grinding rumble and felt
it vibrate deep in his gut, he thought it was enforcers
growling in a chorus. But it didn't sound like any noise
an animal could make, not even a double-wide. It was
sharper, more mechanical, metallic, like a shovelful of
rocks tossed in the world's biggest spinning gearbox.
Tiny shooting stars passed before his eyes, and his view
of the enforcers became even more blurred. The shifting curtain of view, the grinding noise and breathing
the dense smoke made him dizzy, as if he was simultaneously suffocating and about to lose his balance.

When the grinding stopped, Ricky wiped his eyes
with his free hand. Where was Magus, the one they
had put their lives on the line to kill? He searched the
smoke for a sign of the half man/half machine, but the
enforcers' bulk blocked his view of the room's interior.

When he glanced over at Vee, she had a shoulder
braced against the wall and was looking down the
sights of her weapon.

Then, cutting through the human screams, from behind the bodies of the monsters came a peal of grating, metal-on-metal laughter. Magus was enjoying the
show, watching front-row center as the victims were
dismembered.

The few defenders still alive were valiantly swinging their emptied M-16s like clubs. All they were doing
was fanning the smoke.

Ricky took aim with the De Lisle, uncertain what
else to do.

J.B. put his hand on the barrel and firmly forced it
down. "No," he said softly.

"But…" Ricky protested.

J.B. shook his head.

Ricky saw the fury in the eyes behind the smeared lenses. He knew what that meant. It was too late. There was no way to save the men in black. Not with the enforcers positioned between them. The plan was to burn up the monsters with the red grens. That was the only way they could be chilled, the only way the companions would survive this fight. Everything else in the windowless, smoke-filled room was going to perish, one way or another.

Was being torn apart by powerful hands a cleaner death than being burned alive? Who was to say?

And ten seconds after the fact, did it really matter to anyone involved?

The youth thought he had seen some triple-hard things in the hellscape, but watching fellow humans torn limb from limb and being unable to do anything to stop it was by far the worst experience of his young life. Worse than losing his beloved sister, Yami, to the slavers.

Most of the victims were past caring, their parts cast aside like garbage; and the creatures pulling them to pieces were so engrossed in the fun they didn't seem to notice that they had acquired a speechless audience.

Everything around him began to blur and grind again. Spots of light fell through his field of vision, then vanished like tiny meteorites burning up in the atmosphere. His stomach lurched. The screams of the still-living victims being murdered not thirty feet away seemed distorted by great distance and depth, as if they were welling up from the bowels of earth.

After a few seconds, the disturbing sensations passed.

"Hey! You stinking lizard butts!" Krysty yelled.

The shout resounded in the small room.

The enforcers didn't look up from their butchering, didn't turn; they paid no attention. It was as if they had all gone deaf.

Krysty waved her arms overhead and stamped her foot, then shouted the same epithet a second time.

One of the creatures dropped a severed arm and appeared to look their way but didn't react to their presence. As if it had gone blind as well as deaf.

"What the nukin' hell!" J.B. exclaimed.

"Why don't they see us?" Mildred asked.

"Why don't they hear us?" Doc said.

"What we have here," Vee said, "is a failure to communicate."

The grinding, the blurring, the shooting stars returned with a vengeance. Ricky tasted vomit in the back of his throat.

With no warning, Vee touched off the Desert Eagle. Three feet of yellow flame erupted from the muzzle, with a tremendous, rocking boom. Ricky watched as she rode the recoil wave like a sec man shooting a 9 mm blaster. Only it wasn't a 9 mm blaster. With her double grip, Vee strangled the muzzle climb of the big blaster; it rose less than four inches. The cycling action spit the spent hull high in the air.

But the 660 grain bullet she had fired seemed to go nowhere. It had no effect on targets downrange. As if she was shooting blanks.

"Son of a bi—" Ricky began.

Then the screen of pretty sparks fell from his eyes. The grinding and nausea stopped. His vision snapped back into sharp focus, and the screams of the dying men were suddenly louder and more distinct.

Across the room the enforcers whirled, blinking their eyes in surprise as if they had just been startled out of a lizard nap.

In the next instant Ricky saw something smaller dashing behind the shoulder-to-shoulder wall of knobby bodies, beelining for the perpendicular staircase with a pair of enforcers on either side. As the trio hit the stairs, he glimpsed something shiny on the treads, a silver shoe?

No, it was a metal foot.

"Don't let the bucket of bolts get away!" J.B. shouted.

The problem was, there were four unhappy enforcers between them and their quarry.

"Gren!" Krysty shouted as she rolled a sputtering thermite explosive across the floor.

On cue, the companions turned tail. They hit the doorway, running full tilt, and took the steps three at a time. Ricky slowed just enough to let Krysty and Vee shoot past him.

At his back he heard the whoosh of the red gren igniting. Before he could suck in another breath, the staircase rocked and a concussion wave and fireball slammed him face-first onto the top step. A blinding white light exploded inside his head, then everything went black. He came to as he was being dragged through the doorway by the back collar of his coat.

"You okay Ricky?" Vee said as she gently rolled him over.

"Santa mierda! Chica, eres estupenda!" he said.

The beautiful Vee had just saved his life.

EVEN TOPPLING BACKWARD and off balance, with one hand the enforcer had the strength to lift Ryan off his feet and vault him through the air. As he cleared the window frame, Ryan was sure he was going to fall into the blaze below, but the power of the jerk and the snap at the end of it cost the enforcer its grip on his wrist and whiplashed Ryan high over the flames. He rode his forward momentum until the last possible second, then cut a slow somersault. He landed on the balls of his feet three yards past the edge of the lake of burning fuel. When he touched down, he tucked his head and shoulder rolled, which lessened the sting of impact. Behind him, three hundred pounds of dead, falling enforcer crashed through the already weakened top of the burning van. Ryan knew what was going to happen next. Coming to his feet, he cleared the SIG-Sauer from its holster and high-kicked for cover across the street.

He never made it to the other side.

The blast from the enforcer's explosive combustion sent him sliding belly down on the asphalt and the blaster skidding away on the wet street into the gutter. Flaming wag wreckage went flying in a wide ring, smashing all the precinct's ground-floor windows. The surge of heat ignited the building's interior.

It took a couple of seconds for Ryan to realize he was on fire, too. He rolled in the street until he had snuffed out the flames on the back of his shirt.

He was still on the ground when something deep inside the building blew up. The explosion was muffled by the surrounding structure, but the street rippled from the shock wave, and the glass in the facing windows in the top three stories shattered and cascaded to the sidewalk.

His companions were still inside, he thought. Fireblast, they're all still inside!

As he pushed to his feet, three figures raced out of the building's left-hand street entrance, two large, one small.

Not the companions.

They were hooded in purple satin. The big ones were enforcers for sure. Nothing else was that wide. What the small one was, he couldn't tell. In a dead sprint, the trio dashed past the burning wreckage. They were headed straight for him.

Ryan looked back for his handblaster. The SIG lay twenty-five feet away, resting up against the curb.

Nuke me, he thought. This is it, this is the last train west.

Unarmed except for his panga, he was facing not one but two enforcers. He didn't have a chance in hell.

He half turned to shield what he was doing from the oncoming monsters, then drew the long sharp blade from its sheath, holding it out of sight, along-side his thigh. He wasn't sure what, if anything, an edged weapon would do to that knobby hide, but he was going down swinging.

The trio quickly closed the distance. He just stood there and let them come to him. Their racing footfalls beat a strange, two-toned rhythm on the street. Slap, slap, slap, clank, slap, clank.

When they were five yards away, the enforcers peeled away from the little guy to bracket him.

Ryan relaxed for a second, then, to the soles of his feet, he coiled his body to strike. He knew his first blow might be his last.

"No!" a grating metallic voice said. "No time for that!"

The enforcers changed course at once, veering away from him.

As the little guy ran past, Ryan saw his face in the glow of the bonfire; likewise it saw his. The interaction between them lasted no more than a fraction of a second, and the recognition was Ryan's alone. It was Magus under the purple hood, of that he had no doubt, only Magus with more flesh and less stainless-steel on its face. One of Magus's eyes was brown and looked human; it was made of tissue not metal—it could have even been original equipment. The cyborg didn't stop, didn't turn to look back. It kept on running, as if Ryan was a stranger not worth the trouble of chilling.

Running.

Magus was running.

Ryan cranked his head around to watch the trio race toward the streetlight-illuminated line of tall, dark trees a couple of blocks away. No hitch in its stride, Magus was keeping pace with his three-hundred-pound play-mates.

The one-eyed man stood there dumbstruck by what he was seeing, and by what just *hadn't* happened. Magus had gone from a familiar, limping wreck to a lithe sprinter. Had it been refitted with a new set of legs? A new tranny? When and where had the startling improvements been made? And what about the face? The normal human eye? Until that startling moment Steel Eyes's physical condition had always seemed to be going the other direction: from bad to worse.

Just as puzzling to Ryan was Magus seeing but not recognizing him. In the recent past they had faced off in Bullard ville at the carny of death and again on Magus's gladiator island. Ryan was sure he and the companions had made an impression in both encounters because they had turned the tables and spoiled Steel Eyes's grotesque fun. Then they'd had the audacity to hunt it down and had come close to chilling it. No one in Deathlands had challenged Magus like that and lived—except them. There was no doubt the cyborg knew Cawdor on sight and wished him to die in the most agonizing way possible.

The sound of running feet made him look back over his shoulder at the precinct. When he saw his companions coming toward him, a wave of relief swept over him. All of them had survived the enforcers and the explosion, and the newcomer Vee had made it through, as well.

Krysty threw her arms around his neck and gave him a powerful hug. J.B. held out his Steyr.

"I think this belongs to you," J.B. said. "You need to be more careful where you leave it."

"Funny man," Ryan replied as he accepted the weapon.

"We took out the enforcers, but Magus got away," Mildred told him.

"Yeah, I figured that when it ran by me."

"Where corpse?" Jak asked, scanning the street.

Ryan stepped over to the curb and picked up his SIG. "Had no blaster," he said as he examined the weapon for damage and found none. "Long story, but I couldn't take the shot. Magus and two enforcers ran in that direction, heading for that line of trees."

"That's Central Park," Vee told him.

"They've got a good lead on us already," Ryan said. "We'll never catch up to them on foot."

"If Magus only has two bodyguards at present,"

Doc said, "this may be the only chance we have to do what has to be done."

"Let's roll, then," Vee suggested.

They ran back to the EMT truck and piled in, front and rear. Vee dropped the wag into gear and stomped the accelerator, spinning the heavy rig's back wheels. As the tires bit in, the truck shot forward with a sickening lurch. Ryan had to grab a handhold overhead or be thrown backward, head over heels, all the way to the rear doors.

Vee hit the high beams after they passed the first block. They lit up the empty street, the empty cross street and the wall of big trees beyond, which was coming up fast. There was no sign of their quarry anywhere.

"They really covered a lot of ground, didn't they?" Krysty said from the front passenger seat. She was practically shouting to be heard over the roar of the engine. "Were the enforcers carrying Magus?"

"Like a fifty-pound bag of shit?" J.B. added.

"No," Ryan said. "Magus was on foot, too. And hauling ass."

"Magus?" Mildred asked over his shoulder.

"It was stranger than strange," Ryan said. "Magus ran like a jackrabbit."

"That is not possible," Doc argued. "Magus is horribly crippled and has been since the day we first crossed paths."

"That's what I thought, too, until I saw it happening," Ryan said. "I'm telling you I saw it."

Without slowing, Vee blasted across the perpendicular street, then jumped the curb to the sidewalk bordering the park. For a second, they were airborne, all four wheels off the ground. They landed with a crash on the far edge of the sidewalk. The front tires hit first, then the back ones slammed down even harder. The impact staggered Ryan; it also opened the rear compartment's cabinet doors and drawers and sent the contents flying every which way.

"Nukin' hell, woman," J.B. bellowed, "are you tryin' to chill us back here?"

"Sorry," Vee said. "Did you break a nail?"

Then she cut the truck a hard left, its four wheels sliding across a wide stretch of wet lawn and onto a walking trail barely wide enough for the wag. With paved ground under the vehicle, again she put serious pedal to metal.

"They could have just as easily gone right," Krysty said as the truck slingshot-accelerated down the gently curving path. "Why did you turn *this* way?"

"Because *those* aren't joggers," Vee said, taking a hand off the wheel to point with her finger.

At the extreme limit of their range, the high beams picked up three figures running ahead.

From the shrill scream of its engine, Ryan guessed the wag couldn't go any faster. That was probably a good thing, because they were already doing better than one hundred miles an hour on a narrow path designed for pedestrian traffic. The stately trees on either side of them blurred into a wall of solid black as they rapidly gained on their targets.

"Run down the nukin' bastards!" J.B. shouted.

"I think you are on to something there, John Barrymore," Doc chimed in. "Three birds with one very heavy and fast-moving stone."

Ryan had no problem with squashing the enforcers

and their master. Quick and messy worked just fine for
him if they could chill them all in one go.

Vee seemed okay with the idea, too, but before she
could close the distance—and the deal—the trio crossed
a two-lane street ahead and took off down another path
that bordered what looked like a small pond or reservoir.

"Hang on!" she shouted.

By now Ryan knew better than to ignore his driver's warning. He grabbed a handhold as the wag left
the path, flew off the curb, crashed onto the street and,
an instant later, jumped the curb opposite, again going
four-wheels airborne. They came down hard and at high
speed. If Vee touched the brakes once they'd landed,
he didn't feel it; when they slammed down the second
time, she locked them up good, stomping on the pedal
with both feet and pulling up on the emergency brake
to keep the truck from skidding off the path and going
headfirst into the lake.

It was a memorable moment, for sure.

The violence of the final swerve cost Ryan his grip.
He flew across the compartment and ended up in a
tangled heap with J.B., Doc, Mildred, Ricky and Jak,
on top of the bound and gagged paramedic.

Feathering the emergency brake and accelerator,
Vee somehow regained control of the wag and got them
pointed in the right direction. Ryan regained his feet
just in time to see the high beams light up their quarry
ducking to the right, off the walking path, away from
the shoreline, and disappearing into a dark, thick stand
of park trees.

Vee roared across the lawn and skidded to a stop beside the edge of the forest. The trunks were too closely
spaced for her to enter and follow with the truck.

"How big is this grove?" Ryan asked her.

"Pretty big. Maybe an acre. It's longer than it's wide."

"Can you drive this wag around to the other side of it?"

"Sure, no problem," Vee said.

As she started to pull away, he put a hand on her shoulder and stopped her.

"No, no, we're going to split up first," he said. "Jak, J.B., Ricky, you're coming with me. Grab those." He pointed to flashlights on the floor that had jumped out of the cabinets along with assorted first-aid and medical gear.

"Everybody else rides to the far side with Vee," he continued. "Use this wag for cover, and set up an ambush there. If we're lucky, the four of us can drive them out of the woods right into your guns. Watch where you're shooting, though. Make sure you have clear targets and background."

"What if they won't come out?" Mildred said.

"Then I guess we'll have to fight the bastards in the trees," Ryan said.

"And the dark," J.B. added.

As Ryan hopped down from the rear compartment, Vee cheerfully called out to his back, "Hey, running them down would have been way too easy anyway."

Chapter Eighteen

Leaning against the limo's front fender, arms folded across his chest, Angelo McCreedy stared down at the spit-shined toes of his black uniform shoes. It appeared that God Almighty had had other, more pressing concerns than answering his too-little-too-late prayers.

Though he had strained his brain attempting to telepathically transmit a convincing plea for mercy, no lightning bolt arced down from heaven to free him from his homicidal, crocodile-headed captors and their insane, half-metal leader. A Greater Power hadn't reached out to confuse the minds and speech of his enemies; they hadn't fallen into fighting among themselves like the builders of the Tower of Babel—allowing him to slip quietly away.

Simply put, nothing the least bit biblical had happened—except of course the unthinkable slaughter in the police station, which was like a George Romero version of Revelation.

McCreedy's last desperate hope had vanished. He wasn't going to escape. He wasn't going to survive.

If the purple hoodies didn't tear his head from his neck, the NYPD would shoot it off when they finally closed their net and sent in the SWAT team. He had assisted in a horrible massacre of their fellow officers. He had provided perpetrators with luxurious transportation to and from the crime. In the eyes of the metropolitan police, he would be as guilty of the crimes committed as the purple hoodies. No way would they let him get out a word of explanation before triggers were pulled. And even if they did let him speak, who would believe what he had to say?

No, there was only one way this mass-murder spree was going to end: with more flying bullets than he could count. Since his captors had proved themselves immune to alloys of lead, that problem was entirely his. He saw himself caught in the middle of the fray between cops and monsters, shot a hundred or more times, doing the Bonnie-and-Clyde shimmy and shake.

He had followed the little one's directions back to the Village and the underground parking garage, where they had dropped off the poor guy with the ruby birthmark. This time he had been ordered to stay by the limo with one of the crocodile people while the little guy and the other monsters went inside.

He hadn't asked how long they would be. It would have been a waste of breath. And every breath he took from now on was precious to him.

In the distance he heard explosions and long strings of rapid gunfire. The city was under siege. At this point who was responsible was no mystery.

Then a trio of cop cars with sirens screaming and lights flashing roared past the building and on down the street. They were driving in such close formation that it looked as if the first car was towing the other two. Hope resurfaced to the beat of his pounding heart. If he could separate himself even a little bit from his lone captor, if he could get the attention of a passing squad car...

McCreedy tried to glanced surreptitiously over at the purple hoodie who was guarding him. But the hoodie caught his movement and glanced back.

The expression in the yellow eyes seemed to say, "Please, just try to run away. Pretty please."

THROUGH THE CURTAIN of distortion and the accompanying grinding sound, James Nudelman watched as the reptilians came and went on the other side of the room. He couldn't tell if they were the same monsters coming and going; they all looked identical to him. There was no sign of the littlest one, though. The creatures took away a prisoner; they brought in a new one. They didn't say word. Some of the captives struggled in their grasp; others were tossed, as limp as dish rags, into their cramped cells. Some yelled for help; others were mute, almost catatonic with horror.

Though the screaming and echoes of screaming continued in the long concrete room, it had become just a highly irritating background noise. The initial impact had been all about a sense of empathy—a human connection and a shared plight. But he couldn't sustain compassion for people who refused to recognize his existence. The fact that he was alone in this had sunk home.

Perhaps because he had finally lost his voice, Dr. Ransom had stopped yelling and was curled in a fetal ball on the floor of his cage with both hands cupped over his face, covering his eyes. Nudelman had given up trying to get his attention. It was a waste of effort.

Apparently the brain surgeon was brain damaged. How was that for irony?

Then the room's lone door opened, and a purple

entourage swept in, led by the limping little guy. He hadn't seen it walk for any distance before that moment. It shambled along unevenly, alarmingly, not quite dragging the left leg, but there was a lift and roll to the hip on that side as it swung, then planted the artificial metal foot. When it put down its weight, there was an accompanying upward thrust of the bent-at-the-elbow opposite arm to maintain balance. The foot made a sharp, clanking sound on the concrete.

When the entourage walked right up to the door of his cage, Nudelman realized he was being singled out and took it for a bad sign.

Through a gap between the wide hips in black track pants, he could see Dr. Ransom lying on the floor of his cage. The neurosurgeon hadn't budged from the fetal ball. Even though the newcomers were impossible to miss, like a herd of rhinos, he didn't seem to notice them, either. So perhaps what Nudelman had taken as a personal slight wasn't that after all. It appeared he wasn't the only living creature Ransom couldn't see or hear.

The first thing the little guy did was address its lumbering minions. In a voice like a blender grating ice cubes, it said, "Stay on this side of the room. Do not go near the other side of the room. Do not even look at the other side of the room. I know you glanced at it coming in. That was only natural, and no harm was done. But it is not what you think it is. It is dangerous beyond your ability to understand. We are at a critical juncture in this mission. You must follow my orders to the letter."

Though the reptilians were huge, alien and terrifying, and Nudelman sensed them capable of bottomless violence, they seemed meek and docile in the little guy's presence. It wasn't fear—more like a calming effect. Their foreshortened crocodile faces had a limited range of expression because of the thickness and toughness of the hide—and perhaps the rigidity and morphology of what lay beneath—but they shot sidelong looks at one another, tongues darting in and out between rows of very sharp teeth. None of them so much as peeked at the other side of the room. Their strange-looking feet remained rooted to the concrete floor.

To Nudelman it seemed a very odd thing for the little guy to order.

What harm was there in looking across the room? And what on the other side was so dangerous? To him that area looked pretty much the same as his, with the exception of the blurring and spots that divided them. When he looked around his half, the visual anomalies weren't there. If the captives on the other side could see them, too, and felt and heard the grinding, he had no clue.

Telling a human not to look at something would only arouse a deeper curiosity, witness the lesson of Lot and his daughters leaving Sodom. Perhaps the reptilians had no curiosity to arouse. But when he thought about it, even chameleons had a spirit of inquiry. It was bred in the bone of all living things.

"It's time to go," the little guy told him in that awful voice of doom.

He found it difficult to hold the creature's gaze. The way its steel retinas whirred as they opened and shut, like a pair of autofocus camera lenses, was very disturbing. And yet it was even harder to look away.

"Go where?" Nudelman asked.

"The future."

Two words that meant nothing to him.

"I don't understand…"

"You're a whitecoat. You already have the necessary theoretical background, so I will cut to the chase. I am called Magus. I have come from the near future to pick up a few things that aren't available there. Your expertise being one of them. I've been here many times before on similar missions. You have a lovely city."

"Time travel? You've got to be kidding."

"Trust me, Dr. Nudelman, I'm not kidding."

"Time travel is impossible," he protested. "It's been calculated that to make a single jump forward or back in time would take the entire energy output of the sun. So after a single journey was completed, the sun would go cold, and every planet in the solar system would look like dead, frozen balls of rock.

"The calculations are wrong, I assure you. I am living proof of that."

"And you built this time machine?"

"Not really. Let's say I just stumbled onto it in my travels. And it's more of a time *hole* or *tunnel* than a time machine. It exists as a single, fixed corridor, accessible in both directions, future to past, past to future. It only has one entrance and exit in the future, roughly one hundred years from now, and one entrance and exit in the past, located in New York City on January 19, 2001. That's why I've visited you here and now so many times. But for all I know, there may be other time tunnels."

"Why that date and this place?"

"You would have to ask the people who designed and built it. But I'm afraid they are all long dead. They didn't leave behind an operation manual. And current fixed settings could be the result of the control machinery succumbing to the age of its components, or accidental damage."

Nudelman sagged as his mind tried to create a web of logic that could contain all of what he had just been told. Objectively, it was one absurd proposition heaped upon another, leading to an inevitably absurd conclusion. Subjectively, he was staring at a face that he knew could not possibly exist in his own time. He kept as up-to-date as anyone on the latest developments in nanotech and bioengineering. It was his profession and his life's passion. If that unnatural melding of flesh and metal was real and not a hallucination brought on by prolonged exposure to pee-battery chemicals, it hadn't been perfected yet.

He decided to try another tack that might lead to valuable information or at least settle growing concerns about his own sanity.

"Mr. Magus, why can't the people over there see and hear me?" he said. "And what is that grinding noise I keep hearing?"

"Don't worry about that," Magus told him. "Worry about what you're going to do for me."

"And what exactly is that?"

"You're going to perfect your urine-powered battery for me and then integrate and incorporate that power supply into my existing biological and mechanical systems. We'll start small at first, working with the ancillary subsystems, then gradually expand to the macrolevel. My kidneys are fully functional, so a urine source shouldn't be a problem."

"You could always import it," Nudelman said. "That's what I had to do."

"My sec men and slaves will meet all your experimental needs," Magus said. "My primary goal is developing an integral power source. It's very inconvenient to have to plug myself in and wait for the charge to build. An internal, self-sustaining power supply would make me independent. Biological and mechanical systems could be fueled simultaneously and with the same organics. I would eat and drink as I normally do, and when I urinated, it would power my servos. The two types of system, biological and mechanical, would mesh seamlessly. And if my existing human biology continues to fail, I can install inanimate replacement parts and additional urine-powered batteries to run them."

A light went on in Nudelman's head. Maybe there was a graceful way out of this after all, he thought. He chose his words as if his life depended on it—because it surely did.

"The urine-powered battery concept is still in the early experimental stages," he said. "You saw the weight and volume of the equipment in my apartment. Dragging a ton of processing units around behind you isn't much different than plugging into a wall socket or a generator. You're going to be tied down the same either way, unless you and the batteries are always riding around in a semitrailer.

"To be honest, I'm a long way from microminiaturizing the batteries to the point where they could be installed in a human-size body and produce efficient, reliable results. And the lifetime of the existing bulky batteries needs to be extended considerably for them to be worth surgically implanting. Which may ultimately mean finding and using a different chemical medium of pulling energy from pee. In other words, starting over from square one."

Nudelman paused a second to let that sober news sink in, then went on to what he hoped would be a viable alternative and let him off the hook. "Have you considered using a nuclear power source for your internal systems? Or solar, for that matter?"

"I've not only considered those ideas, I've gathered experts to work on developing them. So far, the solar panel hat does not seem promising. In a high wind, the downsides are all too evident. And at this point the risks of radiation leakage and further damage to my biological systems seem insurmountable. You are not the first volunteer, by a long shot. I'm not putting all my eggs in one basket. I want as many options as possible for solving the problem."

"What happens if I come to a dead end?" Nudelman asked. "What if the urine-battery process won't achieve what you're after? If I fail, can I come back here? Can I come back here if I succeed?"

"You're asking what's in it for me? Oh, that's rich."

The sound of Magus's laughter made him recoil.

"You're never coming back here. I'll find other things for you to do."

"What sort of other things?"

"I can always use a talented whitecoat to dig latrines."

Magus smiled on one side of its face only, the human side. It was a smile divided. The metal side was an unmoving mask made of overlapping plates. In a way Nudelman identified with the creature's deformity. They both had faces that shocked and drew unbelieving stares. The scale of Magus's disfigurement made the stain of surface pigment he bore seem trivial, but under the circumstances that realization didn't make him feel any better.

At the back of the pack, one of the crocodilians had half turned to peek over its shoulder at the goings-on across the room. Amid a pulse of grinding racket, on the far side of the curtain of sparks, a new group of its fellow monsters, or maybe the same one, had entered and were stepping up to one of the occupied cages.

So maybe it had curiosity after all.

But it was curiosity without guile.

Magus rounded on the offender immediately—a comical confrontation because of the disparity of size and weight.

"What did I just tell you? You have to fight the pull of your natural impulses. You all do, or this is where and when we die. Focus on this side of the room and the brethren that are in it, or it will all end and you will never be with any of them again. Do you understand?"

When Magus turned back, Nudelman said, "Natural impulses to do what?" The crocodilians looked perfectly capable of tearing an elephant apart with their bare hands and thumb hooks.

"They are a species with strong group bonds and a primal need for group contact. They require a physical and emotional anchor. Without it they are lost. They can't function. For example, they sleep in piles like cats. Big sweating piles."

"That's hard to imagine."

"You don't have to. You're going to witness it first-hand."

"What's so dangerous about the other side of the room?" Nudelman asked. "Are the creatures over there meaner or something? Are they from a different family group? They all look the same to me. I can't tell them apart."

"You ask a lot of questions."

"I am a scientist. It's what I do."

"Get him out of the cage," Magus said.

The door opened and a powerful hand reached in, grabbed him by the neck and hauled him out, into a heap on the floor at the feet of the little guy.

He straightened slowly, for fear of straining something in his back. It felt really good to stand upright. Though not by any means a tall man himself, when he reached his full height, he looked down on the stooped, broken creature that was Magus.

Over the top of the hooded head Nudelman saw Dr. Ransom sitting up in his cell, staring blankly at him.

Nudelman waved both arms and yelled, "Hey!"

Ransom did not respond.

"Are you blind?" he shouted across the room, still wildly waving. "Are you deaf? Hey, asshole, I'm getting the fuck out of here. What are *you* doing?"

The neurosurgeon showed no sign of having seen or heard him.

Nudelman had had enough. Now that he was free, he could present his case for recognition more directly. Stepping nimbly around Magus and his retinue, he started across the room to confront the infuriating man, with the idea in mind of teasing and poking him through the bars. Let the asshole ignore me then!

As he approached the putative barrier that divided the room lengthwise in two, the visual and aural symptoms he had experienced greatly intensified. Individual specks of light became meteor showers, and the blur-

ring was like looking through a sheeting waterfall. The
closer he got to Ransom, the less clearly he could see
the man and the louder the grinding became—until he
vibrated to it, head to foot, as if he was being dragged
at high speed over broken ground. Or standing next
to the roaring engine of a 747. The sensory overload
nearly doubled him over with waves of nausea.

Before he could take another step, Magus clapped
a steel-clawed hand on his shoulder from behind and
squeezed.

Whatever combination of servo motors were power-
ing those inhuman fingers, it produced enough pounds
per square inch to crush igneous rock. In this case it
was crushing something much less challenging—his
nerves, tendons and bone. The pain that shot through
his arm and back made him shriek and dropped him
hard to his knees on the concrete.

"No means no," the metallic voice said into his ear.

It was like something that might be said to a small,
misbehaving child. Or a naughty pet.

Nudelman slipped from knees to belly on the floor
and groveled there. The excruciating, nonstop pain
made him shameless. He slapped his free hand on the
concrete like a wrestler saying "Uncle!" Apparently
Magus was not a fan of the World Wrestling Federa-
tion, because the steel fingers did not relent. Tears ran
down Nudelman's face as he begged in vain to be re-
leased from the pressure.

Any illusion that Magus was some kind of poor
crippled and defenseless creature went out the window. Any illusion that he and Magus were in some kind
of symbiotic, scientist-sponsor relationship was gone,
as well. The real pecking order had been established.

James Nudelman was neither more favored nor more valuable than the lizard boys decked out in purple satin; like them he was just another squirmy dog that when kicked failed to bite.

Chapter Nineteen

Lieutenant Zach Nathaniel stared at the strange machine planted smack-dab in the middle of an utterly trashed Greenwich Village apartment. ESU leader, Thomas Holmes, stood by his side, in an all-black combat outfit, bristling with holstered and shoulder-slung weapons and communications gear.

"That door looks like something off a fucking submarine," Holmes said.

It did. That was exactly what it looked like. It had the same kind of airtight and watertight, hermetic seal and locking wheel, and a six-inch-thick porthole window.

The rest of it they had been denied access to.

From the far side of the crime-scene tape, Nathaniel could see through the open door that the floor was made up of metal plates. They were smooth and looked shiny. He could also see the inside of a matching door at the other end of the chamber.

NYPD bomb techs in their padded suits and helmets were the only ones who'd entered it. They could find no evidence of explosives, and there was residual radiation that had no apparent source of origin. They couldn't figure out what the unit was or who had made it. Their guesses fell in line with Nathaniel's, which were based on the obvious features.

It was some kind of killing chamber. Like a gas chamber.

Or a prison cell.

According to the CSI techs who'd examined the outside surface, above and below the floor, it was a single unit, apparently one-piece. There were no joins or welds. The estimated weight was astronomical. It was far too large and too heavy to have been carried up the narrow stairs and deposited in the living room. Only a crane could have put it where it was. And the chamber would have needed to be lowered into position down through the roof. But that was impossible, as well, because there were levels above, which prohibited dropping it through those living room ceilings and floors. Using a crane to swing it in through the front of the apartment would have required taking out two of the front windows and an intervening section of the weight-bearing wall.

Within an hour of the device's discovery, federal authorities had ordered NYPD to seal it off and stand down. The department was waiting for a team of top scientists from DC to arrive on scene and suss it out, but that had been delayed. In the wake of the violent attacks around the city, all flights had been diverted from the two main airports until further notice. At last word, the scientists were leaving shortly, by military helicopter from Langley.

Holmes had screwed up, big time. Before their dynamic entry into the office building, his ESU crew should have identified the small, hidden elevator and its exit on the alley. But they hadn't. An oversight in the heat of battle. Shit happened. There was no confirmation that the perps had used it, but it was the only way they could have gotten out.

Unless he somehow made it right in the aftermath, Holmes's career was toast. And his wasn't the only head on the block. There had been random mass-murder attacks all over the city, and NYPD had no one in custody. Four well-defended precincts had been taken down with enormous casualties, their armories looted of automatic weapons and ammunition.

In the wake of events the harried, out-of-his-depth mayor had been forced to give a second, far-less-rosy press conference to local and national media. The last thing he'd said to Nathaniel on the way to the podium was "*Do* something!"

Apparently the mayor didn't care what that something was. The operative term was *do*. Of course, if the something didn't turn out to be a solution to the problem, all holy hell would come down.

Nathaniel had already made a decision, and the pieces were quickly falling into place outside. His strategy would either end the crisis and be a rocket booster to One Police Plaza or his career in law enforcement would be just as dead and buried as that of the man standing next to him. The plan was based on an analysis of all the events, all the current information, and also on a gut feeling he had.

Shortly after the scene had been locked down, he had interviewed the survivors of the first precinct attack, the few who weren't immobilized by shock. They all told the same story: scary-strong men in hoods, immune to bullets, on a senseless murder-and-mayhem rampage, dishing out a level of violence unheard of.

The CCTV footage of that precinct attack was unwatchable for more than twenty seconds; only the CSI analysts and pathologists could stomach the sight of it. Officers and civilians had been literally torn limb from limb while they were still alive. The crime scenes at that precinct house and the other three would be tied up for weeks while the experts sorted out what had happened and to whom.

Nathaniel knew that what the video showed was not possible outside a CG movie special-effects lab. To pull off arms and legs and heads like that would take superhuman strength.

They also had CCTV of the Plissken crew entering the Eighteenth Precinct after the attack was well underway, once again following in the footsteps of the purple gang. The video showed them stepping over body parts and doing a room-to-room search of the ground floor—for what wasn't clear. But they hadn't been targeting the officers and staff still alive in the rooms. They'd looked and moved on.

In the armory, things had changed. The leggy redhead had tossed what Ballistics had identified as an M201A1 thermite grenade, which had resulted in a powerful explosion that had killed the last surviving officers and the purple hoodies who'd been trying to rip them apart. The armory camera had died in the fireball, as well.

From the video Nathaniel couldn't tell if the redhead's target had been the cops or the purple hoodies. If one or the other was collateral damage. The shock wave from the blast had knocked out the building's other cameras, too, so they didn't know if the Plissken gang had survived, or if they had, what direction they had gone.

The city was on total lockdown except for police and emergency vehicles. A twenty-four-hour curfew was in place. Anyone caught on street without proper credentials, day or night, would be arrested and/or shot. In other words, Manhattan was now under martial law. That was the news the beleaguered mayor had delivered to a national audience.

Trying to make sense of what the perps had seized—first, medical and technical specialists taken prisoner, then full-auto guns and ammo looted—was an exercise in futility. So was trying to figure out why they didn't drop when hit by bullets point-blank. In the end it didn't matter what kind of body armor they were wearing or what the hell they had stolen; all that mattered was what they planned to do with it. After sifting through every scrap of evidence, that was the lieutenant's conclusions.

Obviously the small group of attackers had to have come from somewhere. Probably from outside the city and maybe from out of state. Given the number of individuals involved, they had to have an assembly point, although it didn't have to be on Manhattan. They could have been assigned targets in advance.

From the report of Mrs. Adela Blair, who lived three brownstones down, the initial firefight in the street outside didn't seem to have been planned in the same way as the attacks on the hospitals and precincts. She described two opposing groups: the purple hoodies and the Plissken gang. Each was trying to kill the other; both were using automatic weapons, but the Plisskens had explosives, too. The civilian casualties of the gunfight were bystanders, not designated targets. If the Plisskens were chasing the purples to do them harm, they didn't look like federal law enforcement or spy-agency types on a sanctioned mission. Quantico and Langley had no information on any of them, except for the concealed-carry handgun permit of the frozen and thawed Mildred Wyeth. Was he looking at rival murder and kidnap gangs fighting a turf war in the middle of his city?

If the starting point of the crime spree, the first gunfight, wasn't planned, if it was a consequence of or a reaction to a surprise attack by the Plisskens, then it was conceivable that the purples had originally intended to keep this site secret, do their dirty work elsewhere and return with the spoils to this block, to this apartment and to the machine of unknown function standing before him.

More and more the device seemed to be central to the problem.

What the device was or wasn't was another point of futile speculation. It was a question that couldn't be resolved until after the unit had been examined by government scientists, and even then, they might come up empty. What mattered was that this apartment was where it had all begun. No other apartment in the building was trashed. No other apartment had a strange device in the living room. No other building had a ka-zillion bullet holes in its facade. The logical assumption was that the purple hoodies had first appeared in the same room where he and Holmes stood.

His career hung on a subsequent, less certain leap of logic: that the purple hoodies would eventually return here, either to reclaim the machine or use it in some way to remove themselves and their booty from the island before they could be captured or killed.

Did he really expect them to come back? His gut said, "Yeah, but not with fifty armed police protecting the crime scene."

Because of the way the perps had avoided police patrols and pursuit, Nathaniel guessed they were listening to a police-band radio, and planning their routes of travel accordingly. His first move was to get authority to remove the police presence around the apartment and then to announce the destinations of the reassigned personnel over the radio. The order was a fake, intended to make the perps think the way back was at least temporarily clear. The helicopter surveillance had been called off, rerouted to overfly the other crime scenes. Bevies of squad cars blocking the street had peeled away with sirens blaring, but most of the officers were stationed in the buildings across the way. The ESU vans had hurriedly departed without their personnel. The SWAT units were positioned inside the target building.

From the street it looked as if there was nothing left but the crime-scene tape crisscrossing the building's bullet-pocked entrance. All units responding to crimes in progress.

"Are your spotters in position?" he asked Holmes.

"We have rooftops on all adjacent streets blanketed with snipers, but they're holding positions low profile. Every way in is covered. No one is going to enter this building without our knowing about it well in advance. Once they're in, we're not letting them out, except in body bags."

"No gunfire until we have positively identified the suspects and they are in the kill zone," Nathaniel said. "That means let them get out of their vehicles, let them enter the building. I don't need to tell you about the size of the spotlight on us. The only way to contain what we're going to turn loose on them is within four heavy walls. We open the trap to admit the suspects, then close it with ESU inside. No negotiations. No surrender. At all costs deny them access to the machine in this apartment. It could still be a nuke for all we know."

That possibility seriously raised the stakes for ESU and for him, too. But they all knew what they'd be getting into, and why.

This had ceased to be a murder investigation. This was personal. Brothers and sisters in uniform had died in unspeakable ways.

Thomas Holmes made it clear he felt the same way. There was more than just his shield on the line. "My people are going to end this, Zach," he said. "You can bet your ass on that."

"You've got to keep them reined in tight, even though they want blood," Nathaniel said. "Cold and professional until this is finished. That's how we make it come out the way we want."

Holmes never got a chance to confirm his understanding.

Three things happened almost simultaneously. A bright flash burst through the windows facing the street, brighter than any light Nathaniel had ever seen. It stabbed into his retina like ice picks. The explosion that closely followed was so loud it seemed to be inside his head; he covered his ears, but it was too late. As he dropped to his knees, a rolling shock wave carrying a payload of scoured debris slammed the front of the 150-year-old building, the walls shimmied, the floor undulated and the windows that still held glass imploded. The flying fragments turned his face into a pin cushion.

Nuke strike! he thought. Jesus Christ, we've taken a direct hit!

Chapter Twenty

The enforcer dragged the master's new slave through the building's parking garage. Between cage and stairs leading up, its legs had gone all wobbly at the knee, no longer able to support its insubstantial weight. It didn't bother trying to hold the bound and gagged human upright but pulled him along by the back of the neck, like a bundle of rags, toes scraping across the concrete.

"Put him back in the trunk," the master said, then slipped through the side door of the limo.

The enforcer's brethren followed. Their combined weight made the long wag sag on its springs.

It lifted the parcel up with one hand and dropped it onto the pile of autoblasters. The human moaned through the duct tape around its mouth as it was rolled face-first against the wheel well.

After adjusting the heap of weapons, it slammed down the trunk lid. The black tint of the rear windows obscured its view into the limo. Likewise, those inside had no view out.

The passenger-compartment doors stood open in invitation, but the master hadn't ordered it to join them. Flicking out its tongue, it tasted the scent trails its kin had left behind.

The others hadn't seen what it had seen at the train platform.

If they had, they would have been feeling the same pull. It turned from the rear of the limo and raced back for the long room, bare feet slapping the concrete. If the other brethren had seen what it had, they'd be running alongside. But without the power of speech, it had no way of describing the passengers in the subway train opposite them—the perfect copies of them all, including the two brethren who had died in the street.

It had glimpsed them again across the long room with the cages, through the twinkling lights, beyond the blurred curtain. And the pull had become almost unbearable.

The connection it felt to its own had nothing to do with a shared experience—being hatched from the same clutch of eggs, buried in the same yard-deep hole in damp sand, crawling together upward, into the warm light. It had no memory of its birth or the circumstances surrounding it. It had never seen one of its own kind born. It had only seen them die. It didn't know its father or its mother or if it had either, for that matter. It knew nothing of the history of its parents or the history of its own species. And the capper: it didn't know it was missing anything. It lived only in the present, taking in information, reacting to it.

They were called enforcers by the master, and guardians, too, but they didn't have names of their own. They couldn't have spoken them even if they did; they lacked the physical wherewithal, the proper voice box and musculature to form intelligible words. What they had were odors, scents unique to each and superkeen senses of smell and taste inside nostrils and on the surface of the tongue and interior of the mouth. From the day of their hatching and for their whole lives after that, they had soaked in a stew of each other's dripping sweat. The intricate intermingling of individual scents was a constant reminder that they existed as a sum of parts, that they were not alone, that they belonged to one another.

When a component of the swarming, filial aroma was lost, it felt as if a limb had been struck off; worse, as if a part of their hearts had died. It left a wound that never healed—unlike the wounds created by the softies' blasters. The softies, who stood waiting so patiently to be pulled apart. When it snapped the softies' bones, pulped the warm, pliable flesh, drew forth the slippery things inside them, they stayed broken. Their answering bullets gave it no pain. There was no gushing blood. And the chunks of hide lost to blasterfire were not lost for long. Its divots were already growing back.

It opened the door to the stairs and started down.

It possessed no cunning, except in the sense of anticipating the movement of its intended prey. It didn't see what it was doing as betraying or tricking the master. It didn't fear the consequences of the act, because it couldn't foresee any. Besides, it wasn't afraid of death for itself, only the death of its brethren, which it would suffer over and over with every intake of breath for as long as it lived.

The master did not control the brethren by fear. It controlled because it was the master. It had always been the master. One sniff had told them that. Just like one sniff had told them who they were. The master had always given them purpose and direction. The master understood their needs. Obedience to the master was an automatic response. If the master had said "Get in

the limo" it would have obeyed the command without
question. But the master hadn't said anything.

It was a creature of simple function and operating
parameters: a guardian, an enforcer. Protect this. Kill
that. The twin poles of the possible. It couldn't frame
the concept of an indeterminate or intermediate outcome; it didn't know what a "gray area" was, but it
was in one now.

It reached the bottom of the stairs and ran, all the
way to the long room's entrance. Without hesitation it
opened the door. The machinelike placidity and com-
posure it felt even in the heat of battle was gone. It
could taste the empty place in its heart. A creature that
did not bleed was bleeding.

When it entered the room, the brethren on the other
side of the shifting curtain failed to notice; they were
busy stuffing a squirming white-coated human feet
first into a cage. The two lost ones were there. Alive
again. The why of that was another concept beyond its
ken. At that point nothing short of death could have
stopped it from crossing to the far side of the room,
not even the master's direct command. The yearning
for completion was too strong.

As it stepped up to the barrier, showers of sparks
descended, the floor shifted under its feet, the grinding noise became a roar that shook it to its core. Bits
of newly regrown hide fell away like crusts of dried
mud in a heap around its feet. In response to the sensed
threat, its internal eyelids automatically snapped down.
When it took the next step, passing through the curtain,
the grinding shut off. The blurring and the shooting
stars vanished. Its hide crackled and snapped against
its endoskeleton as if electrically charged.

The first breath it took was a reunion. It had never felt such joy.

The brethren turned from their work to stare; they seemed stunned by its sudden appearance, which was understandable because they had no wounds of their own to heal; on this side of the room, the family was whole, every scent layered in its familiar place.

It wanted nothing more than to get in a pile with its brethren, to sweat and sleep in unconscious bliss. But it suddenly felt a different sort of pull. A pull that had nothing to do with scent memory. It wasn't an interior impulse; it was just the opposite, as if something from the outside was pushing it from behind. Literally *pushing* it. The bare soles of its feet began to slip on the concrete, and the invisible hand at its back kept pressing until it was skiing across the floor, unable to change direction, to stop or slow the acceleration.

It looked up to see a mirror image of itself, its perfect double, not thirty feet away doing the same thing. Arms windmilling for balance, they helplessly slid toward each other like two magnets on a sheet of ice.

As their bodies closed the distance, it saw the shock and terror in its own eyes.

Chapter Twenty-One

Ryan watched the EMT truck's taillights disappear around the far end of the grove. Then he waved the others toward the tree line. "Let's go," he said. "Fan out. Keep noise to a minimum, but move quick as you can. There are a million rat holes out of this stand of woods. We've got to get on their trail fast, Jak, and run them down. The enforcers will protect Magus first and fight second. That means we can drive them ahead of us, make them go where we want. If you see targets, open fire. Don't wait for the rest of us to join in."

"And don't forget to aim for Magus first," J.B. said, pushing his spectacles up the bridge of his nose and screwing down his hat. Take out that walking junk pile, and it's game over."

When they turned on their flashlights, the bright beams didn't penetrate more than a yard past the first row of trees. The grove beyond was as black as pitch.

Ryan put a hand on Ricky's arm. "Stay alert and watch your field of fire," he said. "We're going to be just fine."

The youth nodded, squinting at the light in his face.

On Ryan's signal they filtered into the tree line. Right away the one-eyed man could see it wasn't a natural grove. The trunks were evenly spaced and in staggered rows four feet apart. What that meant was there was no straight course: if they walked between two trees they had a third directly in their path, so they had to detour around it. What with the light bouncing back off the trunks, it was hard to see very far ahead.

Having fanned out in a skirmish line among the trees, they couldn't see one another, only the dancing beams of their flashes. J.B. was on the far side of Jak, who was on Ryan's left; Ricky was on his right. As he advanced, he held the flashlight in his left hand and the Steyr in the right by the pistol grip, safety off, 7.62 mm round under the hammer.

Magus and company didn't have much of a head start on them. They had no lights, and he figured the staggered trees and close spacing would slow their progress. The unnatural layout was a double-edged sword: it made it harder for the enforcers to get to them but also harder to hit the enforcers with bullets or grens.

A shout of triumph rang out to his left.

"Got 'em!" Jak said

"Keep on the trail," Ryan advised. "Let's move it. Let's close on them. Pick up the pace!"

On either side of him pure white flashlight beams bounced wildly up into the branches as they ducked around tree trunks, zigzagging back and forth to stay on course.

Then Ryan caught an odor riding on the winter-night air. Not wet trees or dead leaves. It was unmistakable. Cat piss on steroids.

Ten feet ahead, at the extreme limit of his vision, he caught a glimpse of shiny purple in the beam of his flashlight. Then darkness closed in, and it was gone.

"Dead ahead of me!" he yelled. "Don't let them flank us or double back!"

He couldn't hear the heavy footfalls ahead, because of his own, or the sounds of snapping branches over the noise from the ones he was breaking. The pounding of his heart and the rasp of his breathing blotted out everything else.

From the darkness to the left came the resounding boom of J.B.'s M-4000 scattergun. A high-brass load of double-aught buck slammed into tree trunks.

He only got the one shot off.

"Jak, Ryan, they're coming back your way!" J.B. cried.

The albino's .357 Magnum Colt Python blaster barked twice. Muzzle-flashes lit up the undersides of the branches, and sharp reports echoed through the grove.

They were fighting blind, Ryan thought as he ran, but dammit, they were gaining ground inch by inch. It was just a matter of time…

He fully expected to see the wide backside of an enforcer pop into view ahead of him. Instead what appeared between the trees was the front side, and the enforcer was charging right at him, grazing alternate massive shoulders against the staggered trunks to shorten the distance between them. The glancing impacts dropped a shower of dead leaves and twigs in its wake.

Ryan stopped, shouldered the Steyr, and when the enforcer rounded the next trunk, he fired. The hooded head snapped back. The enforcer staggered sideways a couple of steps before it recovered its balance and kept on coming. The momentary pause gave Ryan time to

dig out a thermite gren and pop the fuse. He threw the
gren but couldn't make it break in a curve around the
trunk. It hit the bark with a thunk and bounced off to
the side, sputtering like a miniature volcano. Three
seconds later, when the full four-thousand-degree heat
blasted forth, the tree burst into flames.

At a safe distance from the conflagration, the enforcer's yellow eyes gleamed at him in the dancing
light.

Ryan realized what Magus had done: divided forces
so it could easily escape. Four humans vs one enforcer
in dense forest was no contest. The companions didn't
stand a chance. They couldn't kill it with bullets, and
they couldn't corner it and take it out with thermite; to
make that option work they'd have to go toe to toe with
the monster and hold the gren up against its ball sack.

Magus's vulnerability was their only strategic advantage. And by now Steel Eyes was putting as much
distance as possible between them.

The De Lisle roared five times in rapid succession as
the enforcer darted around a tree. Five .45 ACP rounds
slapped into the side of the hooded head. Ricky might
as well have blown it kisses.

"Run!" Ryan shouted as he dipped a shoulder and
darted past the enforcer's outstretched hand. "Run for
the far side of the trees. Get out of the woods!"

Slinging the Steyr in midstep, he switched the flashlight to his right hand as he sprinted. They couldn't
stand and fight. Not here. Even though the open space
beyond the grove of trees made the thermite grens just
as worthless, there was still a chance they could outrun the monster.

Or maybe the others in the EMT truck could divert

its attention before it caught up to them. If they could get into the back of the wag or hang on to the sides, they could get safely away.

Close behind them the enforcer crashed through the trees.

Ryan struggled to maintain his pace as he wound around the trunks. He couldn't fall or drop the flashlight.

Doing either meant a horrible death.

As he burst through the last row of trees, an open field stretched out in front of him. The EMT wag was nowhere in sight. J.B., Jak and Ricky joined ranks with him, legs pumping, flashlight beams swirling on the grass ahead.

No one spoke. They needed every breath of air to keep running.

Ryan could hear the enforcer approaching them from behind; it sounded like an oncoming freight train. It was hard to imagine how something that massive could move that fast. Without the tree trunks to slalom around, it was pouring on all the straight-line speed at its disposal.

An angry roar erupted from Ryan's right, out of the pitch darkness. It rapidly grew louder and louder.

Then the high beams of the EMT wag flashed on, flooding the field and the runners in blinding light. It wasn't slowing.

"Oh shit! Oh shit!" J.B. groaned.

One second the enforcer was right on their heels, the next it was gone, swept away.

Metal and glass crashed behind them, and against his back, Ryan felt the whoosh of the wag as it rushed past. As he turned, his flashlight lit up an enormous figure cartwheeling high in the air, presumably hit by the bumper, then the cab roof, then the top of the rear compartment box like a series of steps, each taller than the last.

The taillights of the wag blazed as Vee slammed on the brakes.

The enforcer landed in a stiff heap, forehead and bent knees resting on the ground, arms tucked behind it on either side. Like a tipped-over statue.

The wag's transmission screeched as Vee shifted gears; the white backup lights flashed on and the reverse warning noise began to beep. The rear tires spun on the grass, then the wag picked up speed. When she hit the enforcer the second time, it didn't go flying; it was driven under the back bumper. The back wheel on the right plowed over it, making the wag lurch to the opposite side, then snap back. She kept reversing until she had the prostrate figure in her headlights, then braked and shifted again.

The third time Vee ran over it, she rolled a rear wheel onto the middle of its back and stopped there.

"Santa mierda!" Ricky exclaimed.

The wag's doors opened and everyone inside piled out.

"Wow," Vee said, "that was way more fun than I'd thought it would be."

They trained their flashlights on the still form trapped under the back wheel. There was no sign of blood on it or the grass.

Ryan nudged its head with the toe of his boot. It moved easily back and forth, as if it was no longer connected to the neck bones.

"Is fucker dead?" Jak asked.

"We'd better make sure," Ryan said. "Vee, drive the wag off it and move a safe distance ahead."

When she'd done that, he pulled out another thermite gren, primed it, then set it on the creature's swayback.

"Everybody stand clear," he said.

When the gren flared, so did the enforcer. A towering column of flame lit up the field.

Returning to the EMT wag, Ryan noticed the heavy front bumper had acquired a deep, V-shaped dent in its center and the windshield was cracked at the top—from an impact with flying lizard butt. After they had all climbed in, Ryan leaned into the driver compartment and said, "We'd better put some distance between us and the bonfire in case someone gets curious."

Vee dropped the vehicle into gear and drove back the way she had come, around the end of the grove of trees and onto the pedestrian path. When she reached the shore of the pond, she stopped and turned off the headlights.

"We're never going to find Magus in the dark," Krysty said from the front passenger seat. "What are we going to do now?"

"I still can't get my head around how different ol' Steel Eyes was," Ryan said. "Not only could it run but it had a real, human eye. I don't see how the injuries to Magus's flesh and bone could have been repaired between leaving Deathlands and arriving here. And why didn't it recognize me?"

"You told me it had made more than one trip back to this time and place in the past," Vee said. "Do you have any idea how many trips?"

"Could be dozens, maybe more," Mildred said.

"Like Ryan said, until now it was all just unconfirmed rumors."

"I have an idea," Vee said. "Fair warning, it comes from the plot of one of the early Clanker novels. I had to research time travel to straighten out the author's facts. There's a theory in physics that there are an infinite number of parallel universes, each separated from the others by a kind of insulating, invisible fabric. When Magus makes an incursion into January 19, 2001, it creates a new offshoot of time, a new, separate universe with its own unique arc of destiny. The overlay of so many offshoots in one place and one time could cause them to compress against one another, which in turn could cause friction on the fabric separating them. According to the theory, when the material dividing parallel universes is worn thin or torn away, when the natural separation of proximate timelines ceases to exist, contiguous events become simultaneous and potentially catastrophic."

"Although your command of language is most admirable," Doc said, "I must admit I am not entirely following you, my dear. Perhaps you could expand that a bit?"

"Magus has traveled to the here and now one too many times," she said. "The separation between the new universes that were created on each visit has been destroyed by their sheer number and temporal weight. With barriers removed, those unique offshoots are in the process of coalescing—or have already done so. That's why there is more than one Magus in New York City on this night. That's why multiple attacks are happening all at once. It's the same Magus coming here from different times in your future. The Magus you saw running away wasn't miraculously recovered. It had yet to be injured."

"An earlier version of it then?" Ryan said. "And the reason Magus didn't recognize me on the street was that that particular version of Steel Eyes had never met me before?"

"You got it."

"Dark night!" J.B. said. "This makes my head ache."

"What did you mean by 'catastrophic'?" Mildred asked Vee.

"Again theoretically, when an object, living or otherwise, moves forward or back in time, the act of traveling builds up a store of kinetic energy in its physical mass."

"You mean like a static charge?" Mildred queried.

"Uh, no," Vee answered. "More like a thermonuclear bomb."

No one spoke for a long moment as that sank in.

Then Ryan broke the silence, "I need some time to think this through and come up with a new plan. I'm going to take a walk."

"Don't be too long, lover," Krysty said. "Remember, we're on kind of a short leash here."

WHEN VEE OPENED the truck's driver door, Doc was outside waiting for her. He gallantly offered her his arm. "Would you care to stretch your legs a little, my dear?" he asked.

"Sure, why not," she said.

They started a slow, stately stroll around the still pond. But for the intermittent crackle of gunfire in the distance, it could have been the idyllic setting of a romance novel.

She wasn't concerned about Doc misbehaving with her. He seemed a perfect, dignified gentleman. Besides, she knew how to take care of herself.

He patted her lightly on the arm and said, "Veronica, my dear, I know it is difficult, but you must come to grips with what is about to happen. The nukecaust cannot be ignored in the hopes that it simply goes away. This world is going to end tomorrow, and if you remain here, you will end with it."

Doc stopped and turned to face her. "Come back with us to Deathlands when we leave. You will love the challenge and rawness of the place. I sincerely believe you were born for it."

As they continued to walk, Doc began to tell her about his world and the strange things that inhabited it. He talked at great length and animatedly about the radiation zones. The swamps. The desolate plains. The villes. The barons. The blackhearts. The doomies. The stickies, scalies and cannies. The scagworms and water-bug people. And the hard-nosed Deathlanders, like the companions, who fought every day for survival against long odds and with scant reward for their efforts. He painted her a picture of a poisoned land teetering on the edge of oblivion. Blessed with absolute freedom and very little justice. Where blaster and blade ruled and mercy was far too often a stranger.

"Sure enough," he went on, "the hellscape lacks some of the niceties of the twenty-first century, but those flourishes of culture and technology are going to vanish at high noon tomorrow anyway."

Doc paused in his speech and took a deep breath, seeming to summon his courage. Then he said, "I assure you, Veronica, I am not nearly as old as I look.

When I was time-trawled against my will, it caused a superficial, premature aging. In a strictly chronological sense, in terms of sunrises and sunsets on the planet, I am in my thirties, not that much older than you."

"Gee, Ricky doesn't look his age, either," she said. "He told me he just turned twenty."

She expected Doc to berate the teenager for lying about his age, for he was clearly nowhere near twenty, but instead he said, "I think you are a remarkable young woman."

She suddenly knew where the conversation was headed. It was a turn she intended to cut off before it picked up speed.

"You're not really going to propose to me, are you, Doc?" she said incredulously. "You've known me for all of six hours."

"Not a proposal of marriage, but to propose that you accompany us back to the future, where we could have the time to get to know each other better. The world is going to end tomorrow. There is precious little time left to get acquainted."

"I think we should go back now," she said with finality. Then it was her turn to pat him gently on the arm. "After all, we still have a homicidal, time-traveling cyborg to chill…"

Doc looked at her and laughed, and the uncomfortable tension of the moment dissipated. "Yes, indeed, chill. You are a quick study, my dear."

As RYAN CLIMBED back into the rear of the truck, the others were all there, hunched over and listening to the chatter on the radio. He could tell from the body language something had happened. "What is it?" he said.

"Vee says the cops have just been pulled off her apartment," Mildred told him.

Krysty craned her head around from the passenger seat and smiled up at him. "The way home is clear, lover," she said.

"You're sure?"

"They've already started to pull their forces out," Vee said. "Sounds like they're relocating manpower to reinforce precincts that may still come under siege."

"That's our cue, Ryan," Krysty said. "Our ticket out."

"In this truck we can pull right up to the front of my building," Vee stated. "Lights and siren are the perfect cover. If any cops are left behind, they'll think we're picking up the bodies from earlier in the day."

"What do you think, Ryan?" Mildred asked. "Are we all on the same page here?"

"Yeah, only I figured we'd have to fight our way in to reach the unit," he said. "It's clear we'll never catch Magus now, and even if we do, we can't catch every version of it. My plan was for us to return to the time hole and get the heck out. The sooner the better."

"We still have enforcers to deal with at the other end of the pipe," J.B. said. "A lot of enforcers."

"We'll just have to take our chances with that," Ryan said.

"At least we *have* a chance that way, J.B.," Mildred said. "If we stay here, we've got nothing."

"The only way to destroy our Magus, the most recent version, once and for all," Ryan said, "is to trap it here in the past. We can do that by closing the Deathlands end of the time hole."

"Let Magus learn firsthand what hell on Earth is all about," Mildred asked.

In the next instant everything went white, the details of the truck interior vanished. Before his eye could recover from the blast of superintense light, a terrible explosion followed—the loudest boom he had ever heard. Two heartbeats later a shock wave jolted the vehicle on its springs, then it was slammed by a blast of hurricane-force wind. Through the windshield to the south, beyond the end of the park's darkness, an immense orange fireball blossomed. As the companions watched spellbound, from its roiling apex, a churning, dark mushroom cloud rose.

"My friends, it appears Armageddon has come a day early," Doc said.

Chapter Twenty-Two

The little one was leaning through the limo's privacy window, intent on hearing the latest bulletin coming over the police-band radio. Trapped in the driver's seat, McCreedy nearly gagged at the smell of its head. Pus and machine oil. Putrefaction and lubrication.

From what he could gather from the radio, cops were moving all personnel from a location in the Village to put out fires raging elsewhere in the city. The address meant nothing to him, but it got the little one very excited.

"Write down that address," it snapped.

"Sure." McCreedy took a pad and pen down from behind the sun visor and made a note.

As he was putting it back, the little one said, "We must go there at once. There must be no delays. Take the fastest possible route. Do you understand?"

"Not a problem," McCreedy said. He looked up into the rearview mirror and winced at the nightmare visage staring back at him. "Do you want to leave the other one behind?" he asked. "It closed the trunk lid, like, three minutes ago."

The littlest monster's face sagged before his eyes; to be accurate, only half of it sagged because the rest of it was metal. And that wasn't the worst of it. The fan blades of its retinas opened as big as cherry pits.

"Shouldn't someone get out and check to see what's happened?" he said, trying to be helpful.

"No, you imbecile!" the grating voice roared in his ear. "It's too late for that! Drive. Drive! If you want to live, drive as fast as you can!"

"Where?"

"It doesn't matter! Away from here. Get us away from here!"

Before the side doors slammed shut, McCreedy already had the heavy car in motion. If the little half-metal bastard wanted fast, he'd give it fast. He cut a tire-squealing turn and rocketed out of the parking garage. The streets were empty, reminding him of scenes from that black-and-white Gregory Peck movie about the end of the world, *On the Beach*. They were that grim and that empty.

He headed south, down the center line of a six-lane street. He had the gas pedal mashed against the fire wall; the big-block V-8 was at redline. Given the extreme load it was carrying, even on flat ground and the long straightaway, the limo strained to make ninety.

Behind them something flashed. It flashed so bright that it blasted through the black-tinted glass. Startled, McCreedy began to oversteer but caught himself and recovered. In the back, the little one let out a long, unbroken yell. A deafening explosion rolled over the vehicle. Then a shock wave slammed into its rear. On both sides of the street, huge ground-level plate-glass windows imploded one after another, like falling dominoes.

For a sickening instant the back wheels lifted high off the ground, spinning madly, even as the front end nosed down. Through the windshield, all McCreedy could see was pavement. Drive wheels lost, with ninety miles an hour of forward momentum, he was sure the long car was going to posthole, auger in nose first, then flip end over end. As a gale-force wind swept over them, bearing a seething mass of debris, the limo's rear end came crashing down. His purple-hooded cargo hit the ceiling, then the floor. For a terrifying moment he had no control of the vehicle. It started to slew sideways. Instead of twisting the steering wheel, he let the limo find its own track.

As they straightened, the little one screamed at him from the rear compartment, "Don't slow down! Don't slow down!"

McCreedy took a quick peek at his side mirror. Something unthinkable was rising in a huge ball of fire from the heart of Manhattan.

"Not a problem!" he shouted back.

Chapter Twenty-Three

Lieutenant Nathaniel sat on the apartment floor surrounded by trashed possessions and broken glass. Groggily he took stock of his injuries. He was stunned but not blinded. His ears were ringing some, but he wasn't deafened—he could hear a squalling symphony of car alarms set off by the explosion. When he touched his face, he felt the hard, sharp ends of bits of glass sticking out of his skin. Touching them hurt, so he stopped doing that. The facial wounds were bleeding, and the blood dripped off his chin and down the front of his NYPD windbreaker, onto the debris between his legs. He wasn't seriously wounded. The fragments in his face could wait to be removed.

After he stood up, with his hand flat against the wall, he braced himself and helped Lieutenant Holmes to his feet. "You okay?" he said.

The ESU leader's mouth was bleeding. "Holy shit," he said, "was that what I think it was?" Blood had painted his teeth pink. He hawked and spit a bright red gob on the floor.

"Whatever it was," Nathaniel replied, "there are others on duty who can deal with it. That's not our problem. Our problem is bringing down those responsible. The explosion doesn't change that. It doesn't change our game plan, either. They left something important behind, and they'll be back, you can bet on it."

The apartment door opened and three ESU officers entered with sidearms drawn. They looked with concern at their commanders.

"Are either of you hurt?" one of them asked.

"No, just superficial cuts," Nathaniel replied.

"I'm fine," Holmes said. "What about the others down the hall?"

"We got off easy, sir. The front of the building took the brunt of it. Baxter had a fall on the stairs, but he's okay."

Nathaniel was relieved they didn't need to call in an EMT bus, because he didn't want to see another NYPD officer hurt this day, and because the presence of a unit on the street could alert the perps that officers were down and that they were walking into a trap.

"Do you know what hit us, sir?"

"A real big bomb, son," Holmes said with a straight face.

"Probably set off by the terrorist perps we're hunting," Nathaniel added. "We've got to stop the bastards before they reach this room. That is imperative. Everything depends on it. Stop them at all costs. I don't care if you have to bring down the building to do it. What we have here might be a second nuclear bomb."

The ESU officer looked at the device and frowned. "But if the building goes down, won't it blow up?"

"Guess we'll find out, won't we?" Nathaniel stated.

"If it's another bomb," Holmes said, "it'll blow up for sure if they get their hands on it. Are we clear?"

"Yes, sir. Crystal."

It was a shoot-to-kill order. No prisoners.

"You three, back in position, then," Holmes said.

Nathaniel stepped over to the emptied window. The street below looked like a war zone after a blitz attack.

"Get on the horn and get us a casualty report," Nathaniel said. "Make sure all the rooftop lookouts are still on-station and ready for action."

Before the ESU leader could key his com unit a message from a rooftop came through their earpieces.

"We have a target in sight. Closing fast. Black stretch limo. No visual on occupants."

McCREEDY CHECKED HIS side mirror for the fiftieth time—it had become like a nervous tic—and saw only black sky behind them. After the initial, dome-shaped fireball had burned itself out, the mushroom cloud had been swallowed up by the January night. His ears felt as if they were stuffed with cotton, and when the little one spoke, it sounded as though they were both underwater. He had the Village address written down, so it didn't matter if he didn't catch everything that was said. He knew where he was going.

And there was no one to stop him from getting there.

The police seemed to have gone underground.

It was a short trip with no traffic. He made rolling stops through the red signals. When he turned down the street the address was on, most of the streetlights were out and there were only a couple of lights on in the rows of brownstones. The limo's headlights lit up burned-out cars, buildings without window glass, miles of crime-scene tape and drifts of miscellaneous litter. It looked like any street in South Bronx; only it wasn't South Bronx—it was Manhattan.

A steel claw hand reached through the privacy

screen and clutched his shoulder. Even through the padding of his uniform jacket, the squeeze was so hard it made him squirm and shut his eyes.

Faintly, as if from down a long, empty tunnel, a metallic voice said, "Stop here."

McCreedy double-parked beside a pair of burned-out wrecks at the curb.

The little one turned to the five monsters stinking up the passenger compartment's surround of white leather couches. "No matter what the radio said, there may be an ambush waiting for us. I want you to search all the buildings on this street, starting with that one."

A metal finger pointed at an entrance crisscrossed with yellow plastic tape.

"If you find any humans hiding inside, kill them. And when you're done with that, move on to the other buildings."

As the big boys in purple piled out of the limo, the little one turned to McCreedy and said, "Their species has evolved a highly refined olfactory sense. They can smell humans a mile away."

He needed no explanation of what they did to humans after they found them.

STANDING IN THE darkened room, Nathaniel edged around the side of the tall windowsill, watching the stretch limo through an infrared spotting scope as it stopped in the middle of the street.

The murdering bastards were riding in style.

Behind him, Holmes spoke softly into his com link microphone, giving the order to the snipers on rooftops across the street to move forward and assume firing positions. "Brothers and sisters may be in the line of fire but out of sight," he said. "Make sure of your shot angles and background."

Having seen what little effect 5.56 mm bullets had on them, Holmes had pulled out the big guns, literally. All four of the precinct's M82 Barretts were lined up on the opposite rooftops. If used on human beings, fifty-caliber weapons were in violation of the Geneva Convention; they were officially designated as anti-materiel.

Truckstoppers, in other words.

From what Nathaniel had seen, the perps were trucks. And for sure they needed stopping.

"Maybe you'd better stay back, out of the line of fire," the ESU leader said. "Let my people handle it."

"Come in after you've wrapped it up in a bow?" Nathaniel said. "Not fucking likely, Holmes."

They left the trashed apartment and its strange contraption and joined the ESU officers waiting in another apartment just down the hall. Because its windows weren't visible from the street, all the lights were blazing. The SWAT team was lined up in preparation for the assault. A second unit was in position on the ground floor. Their Plan A was to trap the perps on the marble staircase. They had minicams set up so they could see the kill zone and its approaches and synchronize the two prongs of the attack. Once all the perps were on the stairs, they would spring the trap from above and below. The walls would backstop the torrent of bullets, and there was nowhere to run.

"One more time, team," Holmes said. "If necessary you have the green light to use the fragmentation grenades you've been issued to bring down these suspects. *Necessary* is the operative word. That means all other options have been exhausted. And be damned sure no one else is in range when you pull the pin."

The use of antipersonnel explosives on criminal suspects was in no way SOP for the Metropolitan Police. Not even as a last resort. The negative publicity for a militarized law-enforcement unit aside, there was too much risk of injury to bystanders. When a grenade blew, the flying shrapnel had no brain aiming it. The top brass at One Police Plaza had seen the video feeds of the attacks on the precincts; they knew what they were up against and had decided to let the dogs out— the dogs of war.

A voice crackled in Nathaniel's earpiece. It was a spotter on a rooftop around the corner.

"Confirm five targets now exiting suspect vehicle," the officer said. "They are crossing the sidewalk and approaching your entrance. I see no sign of weapons, just empty hands."

Nathaniel had seen what they could do with empty hands; they all had. The images were burned into their brains. They were past the point of no return. Nothing could stop the trap closing. It was all downhill, like an avalanche.

Holmes gave a curt final order for silence on the com network. No verbal commands but his, no talking unless he requested specific information or had determined the mission was complete.

Because the ground-floor entrance's door was already broken down, the only thing keeping out the perps was a few yards of yellow plastic tape.

He couldn't hear footfalls from the story below but saw, watching over an ESU tech's shoulder, stout figures appear on his laptop screen. In the eerie, green-tinted, infrared minicam picture, they looked menacing, powerful, merciless and not entirely human. Nathaniel felt a wave of pure hate sweep over him. He didn't know what they were and didn't care. He just wanted them smeared in tiny pieces on floor, walls and ceiling.

He did notice that the littlest perp was missing. What that absence meant he had no idea. And it was too late to do anything about it anyway. He removed his com earpiece and let it dangle on its cord. Then he thumbed in a pair of ballistic earplugs. What was going to happen next was going to be loud.

The five hooded perps crossed the glass-strewed foyer, looked up the flight of marble steps and paused. Nathaniel watched as they tasted the air with long, ribbonlike tongues. Not even close to human.

Just when the jaws of the trap were about to slam shut, everything turned to shit.

Instead of climbing up the stairs, the suspects turned away from them and headed for the apartments along the ground-floor hallway.

Holmes didn't have to warn the team on that floor of the sudden change in direction. They were all watching the same video feed. The downstairs hall wasn't nearly as neat a kill zone as the staircase. It had some real drawbacks, but they had gone over that possibility along with several others and had a contingency plan in place. Before the engagement commenced, they had to be in position to back up the ESU team on the floor below.

Holmes growled one word into his headset. "Go!"

On that order the first man in line swung open the apartment door, and the men behind him stormed past, racing down the dark hall toward the top of the staircase. Holmes and Nathaniel brought up the rear.

Before they reached the stairs, automatic gunfire erupted from below. And there were screams sandwiched between the long bursts; Nathaniel was sure of it. Holmes hit the room's lights, and the stairs and hall below came into view. Because it was a cross-fire ambush, they couldn't rely on their night-vision goggles to separate targets from fellow officers.

By the time the first officers reached the bottom of the stairs, the corridor where they had hoped to trap the perps was empty except for two bodies in black. Looking down the hall from a position just below the landing, Nathaniel could see dark blood still pulsing from the neck stumps, spraying the foot of the white wall. The heads were nowhere in sight. Gunfire and screaming continued, also out of sight.

One reason the lower hallway had been a second choice of kill zone was because of the doors to the apartments on either side. Unlike the stairway, the perps had flat ground to run on and a choice of places to scatter to. Given the direction of the screams and shooting, though, they had gone straight into the apartment after the second unit of ESU.

Then the shooting stopped, and there was only screaming.

The sound of it made Nathaniel's skin crawl.

Because he was at the back of the pack of wide-shouldered men in body armor, some carrying riot shields, when he reached the ground floor he couldn't see very far ahead, and what he could see kept getting blocked by bobbing black helmets. He kept shuffling forward as the SWAT unit filled the hall and moved toward the breached doorway on the left. As the line of men continued to advance, he assumed officers were pouring into the target apartment. Gunfire roared again, an unbroken torrent of it, confirming that assumption. The noise rattled inside his head, despite the ballistic plugs he wore.

The men in front of him kept advancing steadily, which was reassuring. In his mind he envisioned them overwhelming the five perps with sheer numbers and firepower. The clatter of automatic weapons continued unabated, hundreds of rounds ripping off. Were the perps already down? Was ESU taking turns emptying their mags into the fallen bastards' heads until they turned to a puddle of red mush?

Nathaniel had no idea how far-to-shit things could go until the shooting at the other end of the hallway abruptly stopped. There was a piercing scream. Then two. Then three. All at once. A second later a handful of the men in the corridor closest to the target doorway turned tail. Not all, but enough.

They reversed course 180 degrees and started to run, knocking the men in front of them out of the way.

Holmes tried to hold them back with his bare hands but couldn't. They wouldn't stop. Their eyes were wild with panic. And they were in full retreat mode, charging three abreast.

Along with Holmes, Nathaniel found himself forced to back up to the foot of the stairs.

As the stampede swept past them and out the front door, something bounced out from between their running feet. Something dark. It rolled erratically, like a lopsided volley ball, and came to rest against the wall.

It wasn't a volley ball.

It was a head.

And it looked as if it was still screaming.

From down the hallway, someone shouted, "Fire in the hole!"

Chapter Twenty-Four

When the shooting started, Magus let out a smug little laugh. As he suspected, his adversaries were hardly worth that title. So predictable. The radio call had been a fake, the bait for an ill-advised trap.

He leaned toward the limo's privacy window and addressed the driver. "I want you to get out now," he said. "And then open the trunk."

There was fear in the man's eyes as he looked up in the rearview mirror. Would he obey or wouldn't he? Which did he fear the most? The thundering roar of full-auto blasters or the steel hand that could break rock so close to his neck?

The driver made the right choice, the wise choice. He opened his door and got out. Magus exited, too, then waved the man around to the limo's popped trunk lid.

Magus guessed that snipers were in position on the rooftops across the street and that their longblasters were already aimed down at them. A simple trap designed by simple people. When the riflemen didn't immediately open fire, Magus knew they had no green light and the person who could give the command to turn them loose on targets in the street was probably tied up in the ferocious battle with enforcers.

Magus leaned over the man huddled in a corner of

the trunk. "If you struggle, I will crush your wind-pipe," he told him.

Then to the driver he said, "Get him out of there. He's coming with me. Take off the gag, but leave his wrists tied."

When the driver pulled Nudelman over the bumper, Magus reached into the trunk and took out one of the M-16s. He dropped the magazine into his hand, then tapped its bottom against the steel plate on the side of his head. The weight and the sound—solid not hollow—told him it was full up. The rest of the stolen blasters he had to write off as the cost of doing business. There was no one to carry them all, with the enforcers handling another task, and they didn't matter in the long run. What was locked in Nudelman's brain was worth far more to him than a couple of dozen pre-dark blasters.

"Follow me," Magus told the driver and the hostage, whose wrists were still bound. "If either of you try to escape, I will shoot you down."

The din of blasterfire from inside the building suddenly stopped and screaming could be heard. Shrill and seesawing, it sounded like a cat fight. Magus limped up onto the sidewalk, past a charred tree, then down the steps of the basement apartment of the brownstone next door.

He wasn't concerned about the snipers reporting his movements to their superiors or leaving their posts to hunt him down. They were number two on the enforcers' to-do list. And even if they did sound an alert, he planned to be long gone before the cavalry arrived.

Magus opened the door's lock with a key from his hoodie's pouch pocket. He made the driver and

Nudelman enter ahead of him. The dark apartment was empty, stripped of furnishings. There was nothing to trip over, but Magus turned on the lights anyway. For any number of reasons, illumination didn't matter.

The other apartments in the building were empty, too. No one lived there. Except for the mysterious balladeer, of course. That had been a rumor Magus had started through one of the unwitting human minions. He had found it most amusing. And the perfect cover for strange goings-on inside.

The first clue that something had gone amiss on this time jump was the alarming shift in the terminus of the exit hole. It had moved approximately seventy feet to the north from its normal position in the second-floor apartment *next door*. That apartment was where the time hole had always spit them out before. That's why Magus had purchased the entire building and left it empty.

"Stop there," he told the two men. He opened a closet door, touched a catch inside the jamb and the back of the enclosure swung inward, revealing wooden steps leading up. As part of "Bob Dylan's" remodel, he had installed a hidden passage that led from the basement apartment to its counterpart on the second floor, the time hole's terminus.

Magus turned on the stairway lights, then ushered the men up ahead of him. They climbed quickly past one landing; the top of the next ended in what looked like a blank wall. Again, a touch on a catch and the wall popped inward. They faced the back of another closet door.

There was noise coming from the other side. Magus put his surviving human ear against the door in order

to hear better. One individual was talking in a grating, metallic voice.

His own voice.

The second clue that something had gone seriously
awry had been the apparition on the opposite metro
train at the West Fourth Street station. Because his
comp-enhanced brain could recall in great detail every
transit he'd ever made to the past, every route taken
and the timing of the same, he'd known there was the
remote chance of a near crossing of paths on that particular subway platform at that time of day. Under different circumstances, he would have avoided it like the
plague, but they'd been taking fire at the time from
Cawdor and his cohorts.

Sure enough, the unlikely had happened.

Two identical ships had passed in the night.

That meant the erosion of temporal barriers and its
anticipated consequence was no longer simply a theoretical possibility. The distinctly separate action lines
of adjoining, parallel universes had merged to the point
that from the present universe one, the others had become visible and real.

Too much monkey business in one time and place;
that was on him.

From the moment he'd set foot in the past, he had
always known there was a chance of such a thing happening, but he hadn't expected it to come without warning. There was no going back, no reset button after the
delamination of universes on January 19, 2001, had
begun. The temporal traffic jam he had created was
now a permanent fixture of the time hole's jumping-off
point, as were the event and timeline mergers.

The only way he could ever safely return to loot the

past again was if he could recalibrate the time-hole controls, arrive, say, a day or two earlier—or a month. There was no point to arriving the day *after* Armageddon. He hadn't tried to adjust the controls before because it had seemed unnecessary—there was plenty of plenty on the date in question—and misguided tinkering risked destroying the link altogether.

To accomplish the recalibration he had to get back to Deathlands and quickly, because the year 2001 was about to come to a violent and premature close.

The other end of the time hole remained fixed positionally in the desert redoubt but not temporally. He had used this route to the same point in the past many times. The only variation that existed in the New York past was the time of day he chose to *leave* for the hellscape—something he had been very careful not to duplicate.

Magus opened the closet door and limped into a brightly lit room with the M-16 held hip high. Through the rain of falling sparks he could see the time-travel unit. It was sitting right where it was supposed to be, which was understandable as he was looking through a blurred curtain into the past. Next to it was the room's only other furnishing: a silver boom box.

The occupants of the room didn't notice the door opening or three people stepping in with them. They were unaware of the grinding noise, too. Magus's present viewpoint was like a one-way mirror. He could see the past, but the past couldn't see him because it was still intact; it had a separate beginning, middle and end. Only when the failing barriers were breached did all events and beings and timelines fully merge, like two connected soap bubbles becoming one.

Eight enforcers were loading oblong crates through the time unit's door, overseen by a carbon-copy Magus. He presumed they had used the same entrance he had, because apparently no one on this side of time—meaning the police—had seen them enter.

No, not a carbon copy, he corrected himself. It was the *same* Magus. He was looking at himself. A disorienting perspective. Because he had already lived the next few months back in Deathlands, he knew what was going to happen and the other version of himself didn't. To the earlier Magus, the future was still a surprise.

He had always thought of himself as taller, too.

A man in a lab coat with bound hands sat on the floor beside the time unit. Magus recognized the electrical engineer he had taken prisoner a while back. The matériel being moved into the unit was equipment and construction parts taken from his university lab. The whitecoat's subsequent rewiring of circuitry had given Magus full command and improved function of his right hand.

From that kidnapping, he could easily calculate the date and time of his earlier version's upcoming return to Deathlands. As he had hoped, the arrival in the hellscape wasn't too far in the past—only eight months. Not too long a lifespan to live all over again.

And eight months would give him ample time to prepare a proper welcoming committee for Cawdor and his compatriots in the redoubt, should they escape the fires of nukeday and manage to jump back to their own time. This was a golden opportunity to end their interference once and for all and to pull off the ultimate, soul-crushing surprise. Either way, he would be rid of them forever.

There was just one intervening obstacle: another Magus already existed in the target timeline. He was looking at him. The explosion he had just survived was ample evidence of what happened when one time-traveling being made physical contact with an identical counterpart. He had no doubt that's what had happened back at the storage site—the need for touching was hardwired into enforcers, a fundamental urge. Nature abhorred a vacuum, but what it abhorred even more was double occupancy: two versions of the same entity in the same space and time.

Magus found himself strangely elated at the prospect of the unthinkable thing he was about to do.

When the adjacent universes ground together in the small, Victorian living room, it sounded like a bulldozer shovel blade scraping across concrete. Standing well back from the blurry curtain and spark shower, Magus flipped the M-16's charging handle, dropped the safety and, from the hip, fired a single shot in the direction of the anomaly. The report shook the room, the hull leaped from the ejector port, but the bullet never made it to the other side. It vanished somewhere in the seam between tightly pressed realities. Like shattering glass, the visual and aural effects fell away, leaving the living room and two universes undivided.

When the curtain dropped, Magus and his captives became visible to the enforcers, who took a step toward them, automatically moving to defend their master. They stopped in their tracks when they realized who had appeared before them. Long tongues flicked out between pointy teeth and nostrils flared as they tasted the air.

The metal jaw of Magus-from-the-past dropped when he saw his double; it dropped even lower when he took in the longblaster. As his steel eyes tightened their focus, they made a low, whirring sound. Then a figurative light went on behind them.

Magus-from-the-present admired his former self's critical intelligence. It had taken only a second to realize what was about to happen and why.

"Kill it!" earlier Magus cried.

"You can't kill the master," Magus told his knobby minions.

"Kill it quick!"

"Not the master."

The enforcers looked at Magus. Then they looked at his doppelgänger. Both smelled and tasted the same, because they were the same. Hooded heads swung back and forth as they tried to unravel the mystery. Meanwhile they were rooted to the floor. Clearly they didn't know which version to follow.

Magus put a merciful end to their dilemma. And to himself.

He shouldered the M-16 and aimed at Magus-from-the-past's head. It was interesting and gratifying to see how his other self reacted to impending death. Not with protests or whimpering, not with a desperate attempt to flee. His former incarnation tapped a steely fingertip on the still-human part of his temple as if to say "Put it right here, pal."

And Magus did just that. The M-16 bucked hard into his shoulder, making the side of his face capable of doing it wince. A wet slurry of brains, shattered circuit boards, skull bone and the flattened, through-and-through 5.56 mm round smacked into the wide chest of the enforcer standing behind him.

Magus watched the familiar knees buckle and a lifeless corpse crumple to the floor.

For good measure he leaned over and put two more point-blank shots into the nonmetal part of the skull.

The enforcers stood frozen, unable to grasp what had just happened.

"Continue loading the gear," Magus told them. "And when you're finished put these two in the unit with the third captive."

The familiar command from the familiar voice set them at ease. They obeyed him without hesitation.

"Why me?" the driver asked in a voice breaking with emotion. "Why are you taking me? I've done everything for you that I can. Why don't you just let me go now."

"I don't think so."

"I'm not a doctor or a scientist. What good am I to you where you're going?"

"Spare parts," Magus said.

The driver's face went pale. He opened his mouth but no sound came forth.

Dr. Nudelman chose that moment to speak up. "The one you killed looks just like you," he said.

"No, it *was* me. I just killed myself."

"Avoiding a time-paradox crisis?"

Magus smirked with half his face. One of the bonuses to kidnapping predark whitecoats was that they made interesting conversationalists. A Deathlander wouldn't know a time paradox from a bag of rocks.

"Obviously," he said. "And now there is only one of me in this little corner of the universes."

Nudelman nodded toward the enforcers. "Who are they, then?"

"They are themselves, the same creatures you have already met, only as they existed eight months in the past."

"What happened to the ones who kidnapped me?"

"They're out in the world, doing my bidding."

"That raises the possibility of another critical paradox. The two groups could cross each other's paths."

"Not really," Magus said. "The other ones are going to disappear along with everyone and everything else in less than fourteen hours."

NATHANIEL LOOKED IN the direction of the frantic shout. The corridor was still lined with ESU personnel—those who had stood their ground while the others fled. Through the gaps created by the deserters he saw a small black object hurtle out of the target doorway. It hit the wall and bounced off onto the floor.

The bottom dropped out of his stomach.

A quick-thinking ESU officer threw his curved riot shield over the grenade and then threw himself belly down on top of it.

Three tightly spaced explosions ripped the air. The blast and flash made the officer and his riot shield jump from the floor, dark smoke billowed around them, then they both came down hard.

For his part, Nathaniel felt as if he had just been snap-kicked center chest. It left a dull ache under his breastbone.

The brave-as-hell ESU officer didn't get up off the

shield. He didn't move at all. It was impossible to tell how badly hurt he was or if he was dead. The concussion alone of a grenade detonating that close would be enough to knock a person unconscious.

Two had gone off inside the apartment, though.

They shouldn't have been thrown unless the men inside were already dead.

As Nathaniel was entertaining that grim thought, another officer primed a pair of grenades and two-handed them through the apartment doorway.

No warning shout this time.

The officer chucked and ran.

Instinctively Nathaniel counted down the fuse time in his head. Before he got to three, both grenades flew back into the hall. They had a low-to-high arc, as if they'd been drop kicked. They hit the ceiling, ricocheted off the wall and fell to the floor.

Too far away for the remaining ESU men to reach. A couple of them made it through the nearby doors to the other apartments; the rest sprinted for the building entrance.

Holmes grabbed Nathaniel by the arm and pulled him into a crouch just as a matched pair of deafening whacks shook the walls and sent sharp bits of steel slicing through the air. The pair of ESU men closest to the grenades were cut down in midstride, hit in the back by the spray of shrapnel and slammed onto their faces on the floor. Boiling clouds of dark gray smoke rolled over them.

Nathaniel heard a rumble of heavy footfalls, then the purple hoodies burst through the caustic smoke, apparently unharmed.

They moved remarkably fast for their size and

weight. Fast enough to catch up to the rear of the fleeing officers before they could reach the front door. Two
of the ESU men were pulled down from behind. Then
to Nathaniel's horror, it was tear-open-the-piñata time.
Thumb talons and raw power made short work of the
body armor and clothing, then the perps slung stripes
of gore across the ceiling. The speed with which they
killed was astonishing. It was as if they shifted into
another gear once they had hold of a victim.

As in the precincts earlier in the day, there was nothing anyone could do to stop the slaughter. Three more
officers were dragged down before the others made it
out the front door.

The operation's chain of command had been broken. There was no time to alert the snipers. No time
to regroup the troops. The remaining survivors were
fighting for their lives.

Holmes was below him as they backed up the stairs,
firing steadily with his Glock. Nathaniel could see his
slugs plucking at purple satin. Holmes was like a machine, a hit with every shot.

But the bullets had no visible effect.

Not so for the grenades.

When one of the creatures came up the staircase
after them, Nathaniel saw that half of its face had been
de-hided, stripped clean. The short snout was without
hide, as well. Shiny blue bone showed underneath. It
looked as though the grenade had gone off right under
its chin. The shrapnel wounds were devastating, but the
creature seemed to be in no pain. And there was no
sign of blood.

Holmes continued to fire as the monster mounted
the steps, and they moved backward, shooting it over

and over, full in the face. The bullets zinged off the
blue bone, taking loose chunks of hide with them.
When Holmes's slide locked back, Nathaniel tried to
pull him aside so they could switch positions and he
could hold the monster at bay with more close-range
gunfire. But the creature had already grabbed the ESU
leader by the front of the armor vest. A tug of war ensued as Holmes tried to reload from his combat harness. Nathaniel couldn't get off a shot because his
brother officer was smack-dab in the way.

The standoff ended when the purple bastard raised
Holmes with one hand, lifting his boot soles two feet
off the ground. Nathaniel hung on for all he was worth
while trying to bring his gun muzzle to bear, but he
lost his grip when the perp twisted away and slammed
Holmes face-first into the wall. The chinstrap on the
lieutenant's helmet broke, and it went flying over the
bannister railing. The impact punched a face-shaped
hole in the lathe and plaster.

The hoodie let the limp body slide down the stairs,
feet first.

Nathaniel put bullet after bullet into the side of the
bastard's head. The slugs ricocheted off, cutting holes
in the wall and ceiling.

Again they had no effect.

The creature didn't even look mad as it followed him
up the stairs. Nathaniel dropped to a knee on the edge
of the second-floor hallway and put five quick shots
dead center in its massively bulging groin.

Effect.

A pair of new expressions lit up the monster's ruined face. First surprise. Then pain. As much as the

bone structure would allow, it grimaced. The hoodie was stopped cold.

It was only a temporary reprieve, Nathaniel knew. The low-aimed bullets had zinged off without penetrating. He jumped up and dashed through the first open door, which led to the apartment of Veronica Currant, the place where it had all started.

The hallway behind him quaked from the footfalls of his pursuer. Because it was the closest cover, he considered diving into the strange machine and closing the door, but that looked too much like a dead end—what if the lock didn't work? What if the monster knew how to open it from the outside?

As the enforcer burst through the doorway, Nathaniel ran for the nearest, emptied front window. He didn't stop when he jumped onto the sill. He launched himself into space, legs churning.

When ESU sniper Matt Carter first looked down on the kill zone from a rooftop across the narrow street, he saw the mission ahead as a chance for Team Alpha's redemption. He knew his fellow sniper, Pete Balwan, and their spotter, Joe Gaspers, felt the same way. Their unit had been embarrassed earlier in the evening by a different group of perps who had managed to slip out from under their guns without taking so much as a scratch. Lieutenant Holmes had rubbed it in over the com link, too. That still stuck in Carter's craw.

Three minutes into the operation, after a frenzy of autofire inside the building, Carter still had no targets. No one had exited, and the standing order was to hold fire until suspects tried to leave. The limo that had brought them to the scene sat double-parked in the middle of the street with its doors wide open and courtesy lights on. There wouldn't be a quick getaway, not with him and Balwan behind a pair of Barretts. But shooting an engine block wasn't what he had in mind. They all had friends in the Eighteenth and the other precincts that had been hit.

He wanted some .50 caliber payback.

Carter pulled back from the night scope's eyepiece and blinked. An annoying flare of light was coming from the second-floor window of an apartment next door. The infrared sight magnified it. Gunfire continued to roll out of the target building and then a cluster of grenades detonated. He had seen the CCTV video from the precincts. That the shooting hadn't slowed down by now was starting to make him nervous. And nervous was the last thing he wanted to be.

When he tucked back into the rifle butt and scope, he saw some of Team Beta stumble out the front door, jump down the steps and hightail it down the street. A second cluster of grenades went off, and more ESU officers poured out onto the street. A moment later a man in an NYPD windbreaker jumped out a second-story window. He dropped behind a hedge, and Carter lost sight of him.

There were no hostile targets in pursuit of the officers. The shooting continued inside the building.

"What the hell's going on down there?" Balwan shouted at him.

"How should I know?"

"I've been trying to get a com link to command," Gaspers said. "Nothing back. No answer. I think the shit has hit the fan."

"We have to stay put until we get the call to stand down," Carter stated.

"The entrance!" Gaspers shouted.

Carter swung his sights to the left. Four purple-hooded suspects were running down the steps of the building. They filtered between the burned-out cars and started to cross the street in their direction.

"Shoot 'em! Shoot 'em!" Gaspers said.

Carter took a quick, settling breath, then squeezed off a round. The Barrett boomed and bucked. Balwan's gun and the other fifties along the line of rooftops joined in.

Through his scope Carter saw the impacts. The heavy slugs stopped their targets in midstep and drove them to the pavement on both knees, but they didn't go all the way down. There was no plume of blood and guts. And after a second, they hopped up and kept on coming.

He felt a flutter of panic in the pit of his stomach as he worked the bolt. No one got up after taking a fifty center mass. No one. It should have made a hole big enough to stick a fist through. He led his target and fired again.

And got the same nonresult, but with a ten-ring head shot this time.

On either side of him, the Barretts along the roof-tops were rapid firing.

"Bullshit," he said to himself. "Bullshit!"

He got a third shot off before his target reached the ground floor of their building. He saw the slug spark as it ricocheted off the hooded head, then spark again as it skipped off the pavement.

There was a loud crash from directly below as the

suspect broke through the entry door. And there was similar din from the buildings on either side.

"They're coming for us," Gaspers said, drawing his sidearm. "Fucking A, they're coming for us."

Balwan swung around his Barrett to cover the lone entrance to the rooftop. As Carter picked up his weapon and got to his feet, a flurry of gunshots erupted from the neighboring building, then a howling scream that ended abruptly. Through his nightscope he saw a hoodie throwing a sniper off the roof, in pieces.

EXPLOSIONS PUNCTUATED THE wall of gunshot clatter from next door. The end was near, Magus knew. Panic had set in. In this place and time, frag grens were the weapon of last resort.

"Pick me up," he told the driver. "Hurry!"

When the man took a step toward him with open arms and a pained expression Magus said, "No, you idiot, *that* me."

The driver squatted beside the corpse, slipped his hands under the shoulders and behind the knees, then straightened with his burden. The ruined head hung drooped over his forearm trailing long, swaying strands of congealed gore.

"Where do you want me to put it?" the driver asked as he looked around for a suitable resting place in the empty room.

"Out the damned front window. Step on it!"

Big bore blasters boomed from across the street. They sounded like Fourth of July cannons going off. The ricochets plowed through the brownstone facade, as if it was made of cardboard. A stray round zinged through the room, into the interior wall and kept on going. The near miss made the driver freeze. He looked back over his shoulder, pleading for a reprieve.

"I don't like giving orders twice," Magus said.

The man lowered his head and rushed up to one of the emptied window frames. After swinging the corpse back and forth a few times to gain momentum, he hurled the limp form feet first through the opening.

With a metallic clunk the body landed in a wrought-iron flower box bordering a tiny street-level courtyard.

"How rich was that?" Magus asked.

It was a rhetorical question.

"Get the captives in the unit," he told the enforcers. "Take your positions inside. We're out of here."

Magus always made sure he was the last to leave 2001.

He reached down and hit the on switch of the boom box on the floor. The CD started spinning, and between the booms of heavy caliber weapons outside, Frank Sinatra began the quavering strains of "New York, New York."

Magus cut a joyous, awkwardly veering, little dance turn, then limped into the unit and closed the door.

Chapter Twenty-Five

Ryan watched the fireball dissolve on the horizon behind the silhouetted park trees, like the last embers of the world's biggest campfire. As the light faded, the underside of the mushroom cloud became less and less distinct, until it blended into the overcast sky and disappeared.

Then silence closed in.

No traffic sounds. No sirens. No blasterfire. No screaming. In the wake of the unthinkable, the city had stopped breathing.

"Is it coming?" Ricky asked in a shaky voice.

No one had to ask him what *it* was; they all knew; overlapping Russian nuke strikes that would eat the city alive and turn everything in a ten-mile radius to ashes and slag.

It was the end of the world.

If that was the case, there was no reason for them to budge from this spot. Ryan had never put in much thought about where he was going to die. Or where he wanted to die. This seemed as good a place as any, and he was in as good a company as he could hope for.

Seconds passed as he waited for the barrage to begin. Seconds now were precious to him. He reached down into the front compartment and took Krysty by the hand. When she looked up at him, her emerald eyes were shining and there were tears streaming down her beautiful face.

"I love you more than anything," he said.

"I know, lover. And I love you."

Behind him in the compartment, the other companions were embracing. Slapping one another's backs and saying words that had never seemed appropriate until now. Not just "thank you for having my back."

To one another they said, "You are my brother."

"You are my sister."

"You are my steely fucking heart."

And when the words that needed to be said were all said, they moved apart and prepared to die.

A minute passed, then five, and they were still waiting.

"What's the bastard holdup?" J.B. finally asked in exasperation.

The remark was so off the wall that it made them all laugh.

"What's the matter, you got a hot date on the other side, J.B.?" Krysty asked.

"I thought this party was organized," J.B. said. "But it's the same old, same old clusterfuck. Hurry up and wait."

"Or 'Due to circumstances beyond our control the scheduled end of the world will be experiencing a slight delay. We thank you in advance for your patience,'" Mildred said.

More laughter rang out.

As time passed without incident, Ryan began to rethink their analysis of the situation. Maybe they'd jumped to the wrong conclusion. Maybe the explosion hadn't been Armageddon's first strike after all. He wasn't the only one with doubts.

"If it hasn't happened by now, folks, I don't think it's going to happen," Vee said. "An all-out missile launch is just that. The superpowers aren't going to wait around for the first one to hit before they fire some more. It's shoot until all the bullets are gone, then open your eyes."

"She's right," Mildred said. "This isn't the way it's supposed to happen."

On the horizon, the glow of the fireball had dwindled until it was barely visible behind the row of dark trees.

"If it isn't happening, what are we waiting for?" J.B. asked. "Let's get back to her apartment and make the chron jump."

"Indeed, let's," Doc said.

"Crank it up, Vee," Ryan instructed. He didn't have to remind her that time was an issue.

Once again she flattened the gas pedal and they shot off, engine wailing. Over her shoulder she said, "That blast is between us and my apartment. How wide a berth should I give it?"

"Streets might be blocked by debris," Ryan said. "Don't want to have to double back to get around it. Better swing wide as you can."

"Don't worry about the traffic signs," Mildred said. "There's no such thing as a one-way street anymore."

"Like minds," Vee replied.

In the dark, with the berth Vee gave it, they couldn't see the blast crater or its glow, but the haze of smoke pouring through the streets was triple thick. Vee had to slow down because, even with fog lights, they couldn't see more than twenty feet ahead.

With the engine's howl gone, they could hear the sounds of an intense firefight in the distance. As they drove on, the noise grew louder and louder.

When the smoke started to thin out, Vee stomped the gas again. "We're two minutes away!" she shouted over her shoulder.

In those two minutes the firefight peaked. There were tightly spaced explosions. To Ryan they sounded like grens popping off inside a building. By the time Vee turned the EMT truck onto her street, it was over.

Her headlights lit up the rear of a very long wag parked in the middle of the road. All its doors were open. And the light inside was on.

"Good grief," she said as she took in the ruin that surrounded them. "It's Mogadishu."

Ryan didn't know what that meant, but there were no police wags in sight. "Everybody out," he said after she pulled up behind the long wag. "Stay low. Watch for movement in the windows. We're on triple red."

On his signal they moved up on either side of the long wag. He poked his head in the rear compartment. The white leather upholstery was dazzling, but it had puddles on it. Stinking puddles.

"Magus beat us here," he told the others. "Could have already jumped back to Deathlands."

"I don't think so," Vee said with conviction. "Magus is still here." She aimed her blaster at the front of the apartment building next to hers. "Not going anywhere anytime soon, either."

Ryan turned and saw the body sprawled across a long flower box not thirty feet away. Keeping wary eyes on the windows above, and blasters ready, they all moved closer.

It looked like a cast-off meat puppet. The flesh-and-bone part of its head had been completely blown away, leaving the cirque of steel plate intact. The cavity had been virtually emptied of all its contents, right down to the brain pan. The guy wires on its cheeks had snapped, and the metal half of its jaw, complete with a row of metal teeth, drooped down the side of its neck.

"No way to mistake that unspeakable abomination," Doc said.

"Hard to believe it's over," Mildred added. "And that we weren't the ones to chill it."

"Yeah," Jak said, poking the corpse with the muzzle of his Python.

"Cops must have gotten lucky," Vee stated.

"It's the most recent version," Ryan said. "It's got two steel eyes."

A single gunshot roared from the roof across the street, ending the discussion and making them scatter and duck for cover. It wasn't aimed at them, though. There was no follow-up.

"That's a bastard fifty cal," J.B. said.

From the top of the building opposite, someone started screaming. Before the companions could react, the noise stopped. A few seconds later body parts started raining down into the street. An arm, then a head hit the roof of the long wag and bounced into the gutter.

"Magus might be gone, but the enforcers are still here," Krysty said.

"I think we'd best be on our way," Doc suggested.

"I've got to release the paramedic first," Mildred

said. "At least he'll have a chance to make a break for it."

"Go ahead, we'll cover you," Krysty told her.

Keeping low and moving fast, Mildred went to the rear of the EMT truck and slipped inside. A few seconds later she was helping the paramedic out of the vehicle. She pointed back the way they'd come. "Run that way and don't stop," she told him.

Without a word the man took off, high-kicking as if a stickie was biting at his heels.

Jak took the lead as they charged up the steps and into Vee's building. The carnage beyond the foyer hit Ryan like a punch in the face. He had seen a lot of death from a lot of battles, but this wasn't a battle. It was a meat grinder, just like what he'd seen at the police station. The floor in front of them was clogged with body parts. It looked as though someone had shaken up a big bag of heads, arms, legs, torsos and dumped them out. It reeked of burned cordite, blood and guts. There were huge black scorch marks on the walls and ceiling from the gren explosions.

A big operation had been set up here, either to catch Magus or them. Or both. Lots of men, lots of blasters, but the trap had backfired.

Ryan looked at the stairway leading up to Vee's apartment. It was the only place in sight free of detached body parts.

Jak started up. Ryan followed close behind. They were almost to the landing when a door in the hallway below banged back and something not human let out a deep bellow.

Ryan swung the Steyr around as an enforcer stormed down the hall toward the companions waiting at the foot of the stairs. They had their blasters up, a fat lot of good that would do them. He reached for a thermite gren. Even as his fingers closed on the red canister, he knew it was too late. The monster was already on top of them.

Vee stepped forward to greet it, putting her body directly in its path. Ryan couldn't see her face because her back was to him, but her stance said nothing short of death was going to move her aside.

The enforcer was four feet away when she touched off the Desert Eagle. It was three feet away when the gold handgun bucked in her double grip, emitting an earsplitting crack, two feet away when yellow flame a yard long and two feet high leaped from the muzzle. It engulfed the creature's head.

The heavy slug whined off its temple, a glancing impact that barely slowed it, but the flame didn't go away.

Vee shifted to the right and ducked under its arm. The companions fell back to let it pass.

The enforcer's head burned from the neck up, flames streaming out behind as it ran with outstretched arms for the front door. Ryan saw tendrils of fire shooting down its back, then with a whoosh, it was ablaze from head to foot. In a ball of fire that touched the ceiling, it crashed out the doorway and fell down the steps. By the time Ryan reached the doorway for a look, it was on the sidewalk, flames were leaping ten feet in the air and it was sizzling like bacon in a frying pan.

"Way to go, Vee!" Ricky exclaimed in pride and triumph.

"Amazing show of courage, dear girl," Doc said. "You stood like a matador facing down a charging bull."

"Did you know it would combust like that?" Mildred asked her.

"No," Vee said, "I just wanted to get one good lick in before it killed me. Not something I ever want to try again."

They walked single file up the stairs. The hall looked clear, but they took defensive positions against the opposing walls anyway. In a pale blur, Jak went through the open doorway to Vee's apartment, Python in two hands; everyone else followed in close formation.

The place she had called home was in even worse shape than when they'd left it. Debris was ankle deep and now evenly spread from wall to wall. Fragments of glass from the blown-out windows glittered like ice crystals. And there was blood, too, mixed in with the rubbish. The time unit's door stood half open.

Ryan watched the distress descend over Vee's face. Then it turned to despair. It looked as if she was going to break down in tears. It was a radical transformation from her mood seconds ago. Since he'd never owned a ten-thousandth of the material goods stored in the apartment, it was hard for him to understand her loss.

Doc had a different take on it.

"This," he told her, "is a preview of the devastation to come. You can't possibly think of staying here, my dear."

"That is for certain, Vee," Ricky said. "There is only death here."

"You and I could have a life in the future, Vee," Doc told her.

"But you could have a better one with me," Ricky said defiantly.

Ryan looked at Krysty and frowned. "Am I missing something? What the hell is going on?"

"You are guaranteed clueless, lover."

"Why does she have to choose either of you?" Mildred asked.

"She does not," Doc replied, then turned back to Vee. "Just come with us and *live*."

She smiled at Doc and Ricky. "Everyone dies and nothing lasts, boys," she said. "If the world is going to end tomorrow, I want to be around see it. It's as simple as that. I'm not leaving."

Doc's face turned red, and Ricky looked absolutely crushed by the news. Vee had delivered a harsh verdict: she'd rather be incinerated than go on living with either of them. Ryan had to turn his head away for fear he'd break out laughing.

Krysty shot him a glance that said, "You'd better not, mister!"

Vee left them and went into her bedroom. When she came back there were tears in her eyes. She said, "My cats have run away. Not that I suppose it matters, given the big picture."

Vee held out her arms to Doc and Ricky. "Come say goodbye, my friends. It's time for you to go."

First Ricky, then Doc gave her a hug and kissed her on the cheek. Ricky knuckled tears from his eyes while the others said their goodbyes.

Before Ryan closed the door to the time unit, Vee leaned in and said, "Thanks for the fun. I wouldn't have missed it for the world."

To everyone's surprise, she then unfastened her chest holster and handed the Bengal tiger–striped Desert Eagle and the extra mags to him. "Looks like I'm not going to need that baby where I'm going, but it might save your lives at the other end of the time hole. Chill a few of those knobby bastards for me, okay?"

"You can count on it, Vee," Ryan said as he lowered the weapon and harness to the floor. " We'll never forget you."

"I won't forget any of you, either," she said.

Ryan shut the door and spun the locking wheel. Then he turned to Doc, who was standing slumped at the far end of the unit. "Hit the LD button, Doc," he said. "I'm hoping it doesn't have a time limit."

"Honestly, my boy, I would prefer not doing the honors. It would make me feel like I am the one killing her."

"Vee knows where and when she wants to die," Mildred said. "And she's not afraid. You have to respect that."

"I do respect it," Doc said. "It seems such a terrible waste."

"She brave woman," Ricky said.

"And stubborn," Krysty added.

"Yeah," Ryan said, "she would've fit right in."

"I do it!" Jak said in exasperation. The albino reached behind Doc and punched the button.

Once started, there was no stopping the process.

The floorplates began to glow, and gray fog materialized in writhing tendrils near the chamber's ceiling. Ryan knew what was coming, and he steeled himself for it. First the stinging mist, then the vertigo. He tried to stay upright by supporting himself with a hand on the wall, but his legs gave out from under him, and he hit the floorplates on his back. His head smacked last with a whip-crack motion that made him see stars and groan.

It was worse than he remembered. Or maybe the problem was, everything was happening in reverse.

It started with violent compression when he was expecting the opposite. So when an impossibly powerful force began pancaking him end to end, he felt a rare moment of panic. That he was in the grip of something he couldn't fight made the panic worse.

Then it started to hurt. Really hurt.

Under the tremendous pressure, the long bones of his lower legs began to crack, then splinter and suddenly his ankles were grinding up against his kneecaps. His neck bones exploded, dropping his head between his shoulder blades. If the others were screaming, he couldn't hear them—he was screaming too loud, himself.

The pain didn't stop.

The compression continued at a faster and faster pace. Thigh bones gave way; ankles and kneecaps rammed into his hip joints. His rib cage disintegrated all at once, in an agonizing *poof!* With nothing to stop it, his head smashed into the top of his pelvis. In the middle of it all were his insides, and they and their contents were squashed flat. There was no rolling over this time: he projectile-vomited straight up in the air.

If it rained down on him, he never felt it. What he did feel was a powerful grip seizing his wrists and ankles and a force pulling him in opposing directions. Deep down he knew he was in the homestretch, but that didn't help while he was caught in the moment.

Every broken part of him was stretched out, all the jagged bits of bone, the ruptured vessels, the exposed nerve ends, drawn out thinner and thinner and then thinner still until he went blind, until his heart stopped, until he didn't exist.

Only the pain existed.

The pain inside his throat felt as if a tiny someone was trapped in there trying to hand saw his way out. Back and forth the blade went, ripping, ripping. The pain was from nonstop screaming.

Then there was a jolt and a sound like a siren winding down, from high pitch to low. Suddenly he was aware of the smooth surface beneath his back and something wet sliding down the sides of his face.

He coughed, sputtered, then opened his eye. He saw fog. Swirling gray fog.

They'd made it, he thought.

The floorplates under and around him were still glowing, but their brightness was fading. With an effort he raised up on an elbow and felt his skin crackle and pop with static. The others were all breathing.

He tried to rise and couldn't manage it. When he fell back, he hit his head again. He knew they had to prepare for the upcoming fight, but he couldn't summon a shout to rouse them. He lay there and watched the fog swirl near the ceiling. It had no pattern for the longest time—utterly random movement—then it began to spin counterclockwise, slowly at first, then faster, like water swirling down a drain. As it spun, it got smaller and smaller until it was gone.

It took a while longer for him to recover his strength. By that time the others were stirring. Ricky had puked himself dry again and was still heaving. His expression looked desperate. Mildred leaned over and patted him on the back, trying to calm him down.

Ryan rolled on his side, then struggled to his feet. To stop swaying, he leaned against the wall.

"You okay, lover?" Krysty asked.

"Yeah, yeah, I'm good," he lied.

He looked over at the porthole. The lights were on in the mat-trans anteroom, but from his angle of view, he couldn't see anything past the scratches the enforcers had made.

Using the wall for support, he edged over to the round window. As he pressed close to the glass, a dark, warty face appeared on the opposite side, two inches from the tip of his nose. Yellow eyes bored into him, and a ribbonlike tongue darted out over small, sharp teeth, flicking at the glass. It wasn't wearing a hoodie.

Chapter Twenty-Six

Magus relaxed in the executive chair of the redoubt's former commandant, a man dead over a century. The office suite was expansive and decorated to his personal taste—blank white walls, bare concrete floors, uncomfortable seating arrangements for guests. It was all about establishing dominance.

His reunion with Cawdor and friends had been in the planning stages for eight months. The do-over experience meant he could relive the parts of his life that were enjoyable and omit what wasn't. Or try something new.

The roboticist had completed work on his hand, but unfortunately for him, his was a very limited specialty. There were no correspondent tasks he could assume. Besides, Magus had tired of his constant whining. Their last conversation still stuck in his mind.

"I saved you from certain death, you ingrate," he had said.

"This place is worse than death," the man had replied. "You watch bugs fight for entertainment."

Magus had been tempted to punish him for his insolence, but fair was fair. He had done a fine job of rewiring the hand. His reward: instead of being given to the enforcers for a kick toy, he'd been shuffled off to the ruins of a predark nuke plant Magus had staked out for himself. Where, along with other slaves of Magus, he'd been set to work, mining the control rods from the reactor core. That had effectively quadrupled the scientist's life span, from zero to four months.

Had he said thank you? Of course not.

Dr. Nudelman's contribution had been a great disappointment, start to finish. All his attempts at miniaturizing the pee battery had failed. He had gotten it down to the size of a bread loaf, but to satisfy even the smallest power requirements, say operating his optical-servo motors, would have taken three of them. That meant they couldn't be carried inside his body. He'd have had to wear them strapped to his back or push them along in a cart. And their combined weight was prohibitive. The barrow that carried them would have needed to be motorized, as well. All this just to make his eyes blink.

The bioengineer had turned out to be something of a prima donna, too. He'd claimed he'd lacked the proper equipment to complete the task he had been given; he'd moaned about the unfairness of it. That had reminded Magus of the old saw about a poor workman blaming his tools.

He had left Nudelman hanging from a basketball hoop in a high school gymnasium, en route to the redoubt.

The only captive from his most recent trip to the past who had survived the full eight months was the wag driver, McCreedy. When pressed, he'd turned out to be a very resourceful fellow. Mechanic. Chiller. Carny master. The Deathlands' lifestyle agreed with him. And what was not to like? No traffic. No police. No laws. No wife. No mother-in-law. Plenty of jolt and joy juice and gaudy sluts. Two weeks into his stay, he had asked if he could carry a blaster. And when handed one, he'd promptly taken it and shot in the head a sec man who had been giving him grief. No one gave him grief after that.

Magus looked over at McCreedy, then at his head sec man, Kossow, both of whom sat on the hardest bench Magus could find. Neither of them was intelligent or educated enough to fully grasp the implications of what he had accomplished.

By taking the place of his former self and returning to Deathlands before he had in fact ever left, he had created a new parallel universe. One in which he hadn't yet caused the merging of timelines. Everything that had happened had to be repeated, only this time with a point in mind and a certain outcome: Cawdor's destruction.

The trail for Cawdor and his band to follow had been laid down as before, on purpose. His men were ordered to give away secrets in the gaudy, which led Cawdor and company to the redoubt. It would have been fine if the enforcers had chilled them before the jump, but that hadn't happened. He'd made the time jump, they'd followed, all according to plan.

Some people might find reliving their life boring. Not so with Magus. Killing never failed to amuse, and there were nuances missed in the first go-round. It all happened too quickly to capture every detail. And it gave him the opportunity to refine the story's unfolding and make the ending all the more satisfying.

Oh, what a surprise when the Cawdor crew arrived and saw what and who was waiting for them on the other side of the door.

They would have nowhere to go.

They would have no choice but to surrender to him.

The very thought of it made the human side of his face salivate.

Magus always considered himself a grand showman, if not a genius of spectacle. Having assured himself of the capture of Cawdor and his companions, he had spent much time and energy deciding what to do with them. A theatrical event centered around their torture and killing seemed most appropriate. Working out the details kept him up at night. He sketched scenery and elaborate torture devices. He sent out scouts to round up acts that would fill in the rest of the show: aerial acts, mutie fights, gladiatorial contests, a musical group or two. It would be a spectacle for the ages.

McCreedy had been a great help in the enterprise. He had a knack for knowing what Magus wanted in terms of entertainment and knowing how to find it. The wag driver had become his carny master. Magus saw him as a possible replacement for Silam, whose oversize head he had crushed after the Cawdor-induced disaster at gladiator island.

A carefully staged exercise in godlike power had turned out to be just the opposite. Magus's stranglehold on the hellscape was based on fear; that was the fiat by which he ruled. No one defeated him. No one crossed him and lived.

Cawdor had shown him to be vulnerable. The tales had spread far and wide.

That damage had to be undone.

By a public, not a private, show this time, with all the barons and their inbred families invited. Those who refused would be kidnapped and chained to their seats with their eyelids taped open.

"My men are nervous about all the enforcers on the loose," Kossow said. "They don't like running into them alone in the hallways."

Magus knew his sec men didn't trust the enforcers. And why would they? The reptilians were evil-tempered, foul-smelling bastards. The sec men had every right to feel threatened by creatures that couldn't be chilled. But Magus needed both types of soldier for his hellscape operations. The kind that killed until there was no one else to kill. And the kind that saw other routes to achieve a desired result. If the sec men had their way, the enforcers would all be locked in darkened cold storage, putting them and their primal urges into hibernation.

A knock on the door broke his train of thought. "Enter!" he said.

A sec man stepped into the bleak room. He seemed out of breath. "Sir, you asked to be warned when the time apparatus has been activated."

"That has happened?"

"Yes, sir. The sequence is underway."

"Excellent," Magus said. With a wave of his steel hand, he dismissed his carny master and sec man. They both had work to do.

McCREEDY TROTTED AT a brisk pace down the long corridor. He was a changed man. It never failed to amaze him how quickly he had cast off the trappings of civilization and embraced the mantle of savage. After eight months in the hellscape, he rarely thought of his previous life. There were too many exciting and interesting things to do. It was hard at first, because he had to learn the ropes, the chain of command, a language that was choked with new words and twisted meanings. Once he had a blaster in his hand, everything had fallen into place. Blowing off the head of that asshole sec man was the most satisfying experience of his life—up to that point. After being bullied and kicked, robbed, humiliated in front of Magus and the rest of the human crew, it was his coming-out party. After that the floodgates of plenty opened for him.

Magus was a big-time operator, the Donald Trump of Deathlands. And in the short span of eight months, McCreedy had become his right-hand man instead of an organ donor. It was a rags-to-riches story that could never have happened in New York City. Not even on a reality TV show. He was still servant to a greater master, but his service included being a rock promoter. A rock promoter in hell. It was a sink-or-swim proposition, but he had been raised on tabloids and gossip magazines, grown up watching big-league sports and action movies. He had the right credentials for the job.

Magus could be a generous employer, but working for him was like walking a tightrope. If something short-circuited in that cobbled-together brain of his, suddenly down was up and you were heading for the nuke power plant in shackles.

The threat of violent, horrible death no longer kept him up at night. Perhaps because he had seen so much of it in eight months.

The venue for Magus's big show had yet to be chosen. There were many options on the table, but he was looking for a natural amphitheater at a hellscape crossroads. An open-pit coal mine would do nicely. There was time to make the perfect choice. The actual per-

formance wasn't scheduled to take place for months. It
would take that long to construct all the stages, gather
the supporting acts and assemble the select group of
spectators.

He was going to promote it as the biggest event in
Deathlands since the nukecaust. The Second Coming
of Armageddon. Magus intended it to be a command
performance. From what McCreedy had gathered, most
of the hellscape royalty was going to be eager to at-
tend the festivities anyway. It seemed Ryan Cawdor
and his companions had made a lot more enemies than
just ol' Steel Eyes.

Chapter Twenty-Seven

Ryan held his ground in front of the porthole window. Warty faces fought for position on the other side, maws gaping, noses pressing, tongues flicking, their secretions smearing the view through the glass.

"How many are there?" Krysty said over his shoulder.

"I can't tell. The window is too small. Can't see into the room. And they all look alike."

"Does it matter how many?" J.B. said sourly. "One of those bastards can kill us all."

"We could always wait in here until we dehydrate to death or starve," Mildred said.

"Or go back to New York and be nuked," Doc added.

"Stop it!" Ryan said. "We got chased into this machine, thinking it was something else, not knowing what it really did. We figured it was a regular mat-trans unit because it looked like one from the outside. If we'd known what it was when we locked ourselves in here, we would have done something different. We had options we discarded."

"Such as?" Krysty asked.

"We didn't use thermite on the enforcers in the anteroom because we needed the system intact to get home."

"We home," Jak said.

"Exactly. We're never going down the time hole again. And never is anyone else. One thermite gren should do the trick in a room packed with enforcers. The floor has got to be slick with their sweat."

"Uh, Ryan, the gren could do us, too," J.B. said. "Those critters go up like napalm. A bunch of them jammed in a small room is a great big gren waiting to go boom."

"But they shouldn't explode," Mildred said. "They aren't violating some time paradox here. They should just burn."

"If we stay at the other end of the chamber, we should be okay," Ryan said.

"Sounds like a lot of *shoulds* to me," J.B. said.

"Look out the porthole, J.B.," Ryan told him. "You got a better plan?"

"Once we undog that door, they're going to be pulling it open," J.B. said. "They're ugly as shit and they stink like it, but they're not stupe. They'll get their big old hooks inside of it quick as a flash. You know how strong these bastards are, like bastard bulls. We'll never get it shut again, and its got to be shut tight before the thermite goes off or all our oxygen will burn up with them."

"Maybe Vee's hand cannon can help?" Mildred suggested.

"Shoot them and they don't die," J.B. reminded her.

"Sure, but shoot them and they catch fire," she said. "That would make them take a big step back."

"If we timed it right, that might just work," Ryan said.

"Okay," J.B. went on, "assuming we pull that off and don't burn up in here, what happens next? We have to get the plan together now. There's not going to be any time for a sit-down after we step out of this thing."

"Long way to surface," Jak said.

"Remember how many enforcers chased us in here?" J.B. asked. "We're not going to be able to burn them all. Not enough grens."

"Get out," Jak said. "Get bikes, get away."

"Excellent plan, but the first part is tricky," J.B. said.

"We have two weapons we know will work," Ryan stated.

"But the circumstances have to be just right to use them," J.B. countered. "And I doubt we can outrun them without a big head start."

"We followed the sweat trail to get in here," Mildred said. "Can we really follow it out?"

"I remember way," Jak told them. He tapped the top of his head. "All here."

"We don't know what else Magus left behind for us, either," J.B. said.

Ryan had had enough of the speculation. "I think we have enough to worry about. Mildred, can you handle the Desert Eagle?"

"My pleasure."

"Krysty will you chuck the gren?"

"What is that, *women's* work?"

"No, I just…"

She laughed at him. "I'm pulling your leg, Ryan. You know I like my lizard butt well-done."

"Yeah, nice and crispy," he said. "Mildred, after you take the shot, move to the back wall. Krysty, same for you. Drop the gren and get back. We need as many hands on the inside of the wheel in case they do hook their talons under it. We slam it closed and keep it closed while I dog the wheel. Then we dive for the rear wall, get as far from the fire as we can."

"Stay low," Mildred said. "Heat rises. And as long as we're talking about a lot of heat, maybe it could even melt the window glass."

"Don't say that," Ricky groaned.

"If this doesn't work out, I just want to say it's been nice knowing you," J.B. told them. He could hold a straight face for only a second before breaking into a wide grin.

"He's starting to sound like Vee," Krysty said.

"It's a big improvement," Mildred said.

Ryan handed her the Desert Eagle. She cracked back the action, checking the chamber for a live round.

"That puppy will buck some," he said.

"I'll try not to knock out my own teeth." Wrapping her hands around it in a double grip, Mildred stood with her right shoulder against the wall, next to the edge of the door.

"One other thing," she said, "when this thing goes off in an enclosed space, it's going to be loud. I'm not going to stick the whole weapon out the door, just the muzzle. I don't want one of them grabbing it before I can fire. I'm just saying we may lose our hearing temporarily, from the blast."

"We'll use hand signals, understood?" Ryan asked, looking from face to face for confirmation. Then he turned to Krysty. She knew what he wanted to hear.

"I'll yank the pin after Mildred pulls back," she said, "shove it out at the bottom of the door. Then hit the back wall. Low."

"I think we're ready, then," Ryan said.

Hideous faces were jostling at the porthole, trying to get a look inside.

"They're going to go crazy when they think we're opening up for them," Mildred said.

"Just do your job and we'll be all right."

Ryan started turning the wheel, rolling back the locking bolts. The enforcers didn't get excited until they heard the resounding click of the lock snapping open.

"Now, Mildred!" he said, pulling the door open two inches.

Mildred poked the Eagle out and fired once. The noise was earsplitting, the muzzle-flash lighting up the anteroom. She rode the recoil wave, raising the weapon up and out of the gap between door and frame.

The yard of flame fanned across two enforcer faces pressed to the glass. They went up like a pair of match heads. An amber talon hooked around the door for an instant, then it was beating on its owner's face, trying to put out the blaze.

Krysty let the safety clip pop off the red canister and tossed it out onto the anteroom floor.

"Shut it!" Ryan cried, throwing his weight against the inside of the door.

The others did the same and held it pinned while he dogged the lock.

The gren had a three-second fuse. They had only a second to reach the back wall. They were still a yard away when a roar like a blast furnace shook the little chamber. The far side of the porthole was solid flame.

Something heavy slammed into the unit's door. Then again. And again. The enforcers were whirling around, bashing into the front of the unit.

"Get down!" Mildred shouted.

The heat inside the chamber rose with incredible speed. In less than a minute their faces were dripping with sweat. Breathing became difficult because the air was so hot it burned noses and throats. The time-travel unit had turned into a bake oven.

The thumping from outside stopped.

"How long can they burn?" Ricky asked.

"How long before that wheel cools off enough for us to get out?" J.B. asked.

Ryan looked at it glowing red. If it started to melt, they were in deep shit.

McCreedy brought up the rear of Magus's welcoming committee. Ahead of him, the cyborg was borne along in the arms of one of his enforcers. Two more of the creatures bracketed them on either side. Behind them was Kossow and a phalanx of sec men. They marched with an absurd dignity, a pomp and circumstance that seemed entirely out of place.

The quintet of enforcers had started acting strangely the moment they'd reached the floor. Normally they were calm, now they were skittish, tongues darting; they seemed agitated.

"What is that smell, McCreedy?" Magus shouted back at him.

McCreedy had no immediate answer.

"I have half a nose, and even I can smell it. Something's burning. It smells like fish."

When they made a left turn at the intersection leading to the time unit, the burning smell became stronger and a haze of smoke was visible down the hall. At the sound of running feet, the sec men shouldered their weapons and the enforcers closed ranks around their master.

A fireball on two legs came running out of the smoke. It bounced off the wall and kept running, arms out in front like a sleepwalker. A hundred feet down the hall, it collapsed. A pillar of smoke rose from the body, spreading across the ceiling in a churning black fan.

Because of its size, McCreedy had no doubt it was an enforcer. It was one of the creatures Magus had assigned to guard the time unit. Something had gone very wrong.

"Get closer!" Magus shouted.

The enforcers reluctantly moved forward, as did the sec men. The heat from that end of hall was withering; it hit them full in the face.

"Uh, Magus," McCreedy said tentatively, "Maybe we should wait until it cools down a little and the smoke clears."

"Why?" Magus asked. "I'm not going down there; you are."

When thwarted, Magus made bad things happen. When he was double thwarted, the things he made happen were double bad.

"Okay," McCreedy replied, but without enthusiasm.

He set off at a trot, his mind racing. The closer he got to the time unit, the worse conditions got. He realized there was no way he could survive a peek inside. The heat was blinding, the smoke so thick he could barely breathe. If all the enforcers in the time unit were burning, he'd been sent on a suicide mission. He could do Magus's bidding and die in his service; he could die trying to run away from Magus's wrath—or he could simply lie.

He looked over his shoulder. It occurred to him that if he couldn't see Magus, then Magus couldn't see him. He sucked in as deep a breath as he could manage and plunged into the heart of the smoke. The heat stopped him after a couple yards. He counted to twenty, then threw in an extra five for good measure. The last numbers were very hard to hold out for. It felt as if he was going to burst into flames or melt.

Then he ran out of the smoke. He didn't take a breath until he could see Magus again. He coughed, he spit, he made a show of it. All the while, he was thinking through his story. He knew he was going to get only one chance to tell it.

After he regained his breath, he trotted back down the hallway. All he could smell was burned fish.

"Well?" Magus said as he stepped up.

"Looks like a malfunction in the time unit caused a fire that ignited the enforcers. Everything is burned up in there."

"What about Cawdor?"

"Never got out of the time unit."

"You saw him?"

"Couldn't open the door. Lock is fused. It's so hot everything in there is melted together."

"Is he dead?"

"If he isn't, then he's trapped inside the unit."

"Damn," Magus said. "This isn't how I planned it at all."

"At least you didn't send out the invitations yet."

McCreedy could have bitten his tongue. The remark just came out. He was thinking about Silam, about what Magus did to him after the failure on gladiator island. He decided he wasn't going to stick around for that kind of death. At the earliest opportunity, he was going to quietly slip away, disappear in the hellscape.

The enforcers were getting more and more stirred up. They had started making rhythmic grunting noises, the significance of which McCreedy had no clue.

Magus quickly settled them down.

Smoke continued to roll their way, obscuring more and more of the corridor.

"How could you see through that?" Magus asked him.

McCreedy was trying to think on his feet. He didn't want to give the wrong answer. The wrong answer would get him killed.

"Show me your hands," Magus said.

He didn't understand why he was being asked that.

"Your hands!"

Understanding was less important than obedience. McCreedy extended his palms.

"No burns on your fingers," Magus said.

"I'm sorry?"

"If you'd touched anything, your fingers would be blistered and red. You couldn't see through that smoke. You would have had to touch something to find the doorway. Ergo, you stopped short and are lying to me."

"No, really…"

McCreedy could feel his good fortune rapidly running out.

"If everything is as you say, there is no problem," Magus told him. "No harm done. If not, you will pay." To Kossow he said, "Put some manacles on his ankles so he can't run. Then have someone bring him to me. In the meantime I want your men to cordon off this hallway. Make sure nothing gets past you. Shoot to

wound, not to kill. If you bring me live captives, there
will be a bonus in it for you. After the smoke clears,
do a thorough search of the mat-trans chamber. I want
a full report. If there are bodies in the time unit, bring
them to me at once."

"The enforcers are really looking jumpy," Kossow
said. "They could turn on us."

Magus aimed steel eyes on the sec man. "Don't
worry about them," he said. "Worry about me."

Chapter Twenty-Eight

The heat inside the chamber had become unbearable. Ryan knew they had to get out soon or their ammo would start to spontaneously cook off. What a sad end that would be: shot to pieces by random bullets they could not escape. He got up from the floor and tried to turn the wheel on the door to their back, the one that had opened onto 2001. It wouldn't budge.

"That door leads nowhere," Doc said. "Don't waste your strength."

"He's right, Ryan," Mildred added. "In this time there is nothing on the other side."

"We've got to do something," Krysty said.

"Not wan die here," Jak agreed.

"The immediate enforcer threat is over," Doc said. "If we can get out of this death trap and through the anteroom, we have a chance."

"The smoke will hide us," Ricky said.

"It'll also smother us," Ryan told them. "If we open that door, it will pour in, and there will be no alternative. We'll have to press onward or suffocate in here."

"I'm game," Mildred said.

"We're all game," Krysty told him.

"Look how thick it is," Ryan said. "We'll be running blind. There's only so long we can last, breathing it. Then we'll lose consciousness."

"You're right about that," J.B. said. "And if we pass out, that's where we're going to die. We'd have to tie ourselves together. If someone goes down, the others can pick them up."

"I get us out," Jak said. His ruby eyes flashed.

"How?"

"Forget I know way?"

Ryan had never had reason to doubt the tracking skills of the albino. He'd proved that he could find his way blind on the deadly nukeglass road leading to the Slake City massif, Though the one-eyed man had no idea how he did it. Some questions had no answers.

Making the decision was not easy, but he had made similar ones many times before. At a certain point you just had to take your chances.

"Tear up some clothes for face masks," Ryan said. "We can stop some of the smoke from getting in our lungs that way."

"And like I said, we need to tie ourselves together," J.B. repeated. He produced a coil of thin rope from one of the pockets of his leather jacket. "This should do it."

"The heat and smoke aren't the only things we have to worry about," Ryan told them. "There could be more enforcers. Mebbe sec men. Keep your blasters ready. Use the thermite if an enforcer is bearing down on us. Mildred, you got point with the Eagle."

"What about the sec men?" Ricky asked.

"That's the easy part," Ryan said. "Shoot them down."

They set about tearing strips of cloth for masks. When they all were masked, J.B. slipped his line through their belt loops, tied it in front to Jak's waist and to the rear around his.

"We'll go through the door single file after Jak,"

Ryan said. "There will be bodies on the floor outside. They'll be hot. If you fall, the people in front and back will feel it, and someone will help you up. Now, let's see about that door."

The front wall of the unit was so hot it was painful to even step close to it. "We've got to wrap the wheel in something, or we won't be able to turn it," Ryan said.

Ricky took off his jacket and handed it to him.

After Ryan draped it over the wheel he said, "Everybody take slow deep breaths, get as much air in your lungs as you can. When the door opens, we go. No talking. Save your air. Don't breathe until we get clear of the thick smoke."

Ryan followed his own advice, pushing as much air out of his lungs as he could, then refilling them deeper. Air out, then in deeper. When he'd reached his limit, he said, "Jak, let's open her up."

The wheel was searing, even through the coat, and something inside the locking mechanism had stuck; the metal had probably expanded because of the heat. They couldn't budge it.

"Doc, Ricky, give us a hand," Ryan said. When they were in position, he said, "All together now…"

The wheel resisted their combined force for an instant, then rotated to the left. Ryan spun it as fast as he could. "Deep breath!" the one-eyed man said through his mask. Then he pulled the door open.

Smoke as black as ink boiled into the chamber.

Jak was already moving over the threshold. His white hair vanished into the cloud beyond. As visibility quickly dropped in the chamber, Ryan felt the tug at his waist and stepped out after him. Outside the chamber, he could see nothing. Absolutely nothing.

Footing was bad because the enforcers hadn't completely turned to ash. There were lumps, things that rolled underfoot. He stumbled but used the butt of the Steyr to right himself.

He had only thought that it was hot inside the chamber. Outside it was like walking on a bed of red-hot coals. It jolted his every nerve end. Maybe they were red-hot coals; the gloom was so dense he couldn't see past the end of his nose. He felt the tug of Krysty on the line behind him. She had cleared the unit's door.

They were moving steadily, but not fast enough.

He stumbled again, caught himself again, then his shoulder hit something hard. Jak had found the door to the control room. As Ryan slipped around it, he made the mistake of breathing in just a little. It felt as if he'd inhaled razor blades. He choked down the urge to cough.

Ryan felt himself being pulled away from the security of the wall. Jak was leading them into the redoubt proper. When the left-hand wall brushed his arm, he put his palm against it and let it slide along over it.

The smoke hadn't thinned at all. His chest began to ache. A deep throbbing ache. The reflex to inhale was getting harder and harder to fight. If someone fell, he thought, they were all going to die. Then he felt a reassuring tug from in front and behind. Everybody was moving.

At first it was almost imperceptible, but it was definitely getting lighter ahead of them. Black smoke was turning gray. He could see the line stretching out in front of him. Then he got a glimpse of Jak's white hair.

Hold it, hold it, don't breathe yet, he commanded himself. Another few steps. Just another few steps. The smoke had cleared, but it still swirled around him. He wasn't sure he could inhale without breaking out in a fit of coughing. If there was someone or something waiting for them on the other side of the dark haze, the sound would be a dead giveaway.

Then Jak reached back with a throwing knife and cut the tether between them. That told Ryan two things: the pall thinned out even more ahead and Jak thought they needed to be able to move quickly and independently. Something dangerous was just out of sight.

Ryan pulled out his panga and, with a swipe of the blade, cut the cord between him and Krysty. Her prehensile hair had pulled up close to her head in tight coils. The tightest coils he had ever seen it make. Although her hair showed fear, her eyes were bright and sharp. She nodded at him and reached for her own knife.

They kept on moving forward. After another ten steps Ryan could make out the sides of the corridor. He took a quick breath through the mask. The air rasped down his throat but didn't make him cough. Jak darted away from him to the other side of the passage.

Whatever lay ahead was close now.

Ryan turned and hand signaled for Krysty to go that way, too.

He didn't remember how many doors there were along the route; he'd been running for his life the last time he'd come this way. There was an intersecting corridor, though. He remembered that. From its corner, he and Jak had chucked thermite grens at the enforcers. The rest of the passageway they were walking down was a long, unprotected straightaway.

In other words, a shooting gallery.

KOSSOW'S MIND HAD long since drifted onto things other than waiting for the fire to burn down and the smoke to clear. He was reminiscing about a particularly favorite gaudy slut of his when one of his men jarred him with an elbow out of the reverie.

"Something moved down there."

He knew that was impossible. Nothing could survive the heat and smoke, not even an enforcer. The rest of his men were looking at him expectantly. It was comical how stupe they were. But for Deathlands they were the cream of crop, the best of litter. "You're seeing things, Reggie. You've been staring into the smoke too long. Take a break."

"No, there it…"

The sound of a longblaster shot cut him off in midsentence—a boom from the edge of the murk, then a thwack as the slug plowed into Reggie's head. It was a big bore slug. The back of the sec man's skull exploded in a wet whoosh of gore, and he toppled onto his back. His legs kicked once, then were still.

Kossow blinked in astonishment. It took a terrible, long second for him to fully realize what was happening. The impossible was happening. As he opened his mouth to give the order to fire, something slammed into the side of his head. It happened so fast, the impact barely registered; in the next instant his brains lay in a plume on the floor, alongside Reggie's.

RYAN TOOK THE second shot, watched his target fall, then shouted to the others. "Go! Leapfrog! Covering fire!"

Bursting out of the smoke, they laid down a bristling carpet of blasterfire. From the intersection, longblasters barked back. Bullets sang over Ryan's head and skipped off the floor. The one-eyed man aimed and fired, working the bolt like a machine. Downrange, men dropped on faces and on backs.

As more of them fell, the survivors seemed to lose heart. Then shooting from that direction stopped. The sec men had turned tail.

Ryan stared down his scope. The intersection was deserted. The shooters had fled in both directions. There was no way to get them all.

A second later, the warning Klaxon began to sound. It pulsed over and over, echoing down the long hallway.

They had to keep moving; they were several levels from the surface. Ryan remembered the traps they'd passed. Those were out of commission; there were probably others that could still bite.

"Jak!" he shouted. "Back the way we came. Exactly the way we came!"

Chapter Twenty-Nine

When the alarm started sounding, Magus knew something had gone seriously off the rails. Then a breathless sec man burst into his office suite and gave him the terrible news.

"Cawdor isn't dead," the man said between gasps for air. "He and the others shot the hell out of us, and they're coming this way!"

Magus knew what the one-eyed man was capable of when free to operate in an open field. With him and his cohorts running loose in the redoubt, anything could happen. All of his effort in revising the timeline, reliving the past, all his glorious plans for a return of status and respect had just gone out the window. There was only one safe option left: retreat. Another ignominious retreat. But losses had to be cut. Defeats swallowed. Wounds licked.

"Kill him!" Magus said, pointing a steely finger of doom at the bearer of bad tidings.

Such things were expected of him.

The enforcer seized the man by the neck and stabbed him in the chest with a talon. One slice ripped him open from sternum to pelvis. The creature then proceeded to yard out the contents of his torso while he squealed and thrashed.

McCreedy gave Magus a desperate look.

"No, you will live a bit longer," Magus said. "I need you to drive me. Toss him the keys. Let him free his legs."

McCreedy caught the keys the enforcer threw at him. He quickly unlocked the manacles around his ankles and got to his feet.

"Carry me!" Magus shouted at the enforcer.

Like a small child, he was scooped up, draped across the creature's brawny arms and rushed out of the room to the beat of its heavy feet. The up-and-down motion made his head loll wildly. Objects in his field of vision lurched and yawed.

There were obvious benefits in living one's life twice. This time he had had the foresight to plant another set of gassed-up escape vehicles in the next arroyo.

He kicked his legs at the knees to make the enforcer run faster.

Chapter Thirty

They heard the enforcers coming long before they saw
them. Even over the pulses of the alarm horn, the tramp
of bare feet on concrete was an audible rumble, which
grew louder and louder behind them. Ryan kept driving
his companions onward with shouts of encouragement.
He wasn't thinking about finding a place for them to
stop and make a stand. The only way to survive was
to put miles between them and the creatures who were
in hot pursuit. He wasn't thinking about how far they
had to go to reach safety, either. He was looking ahead
in short increments, distances of fifty, a hundred feet,
trying to remember the details he had seen only once.

They dashed past the burned-out elevator doors
where they had cooked the first enforcer.

Seconds later Jak led them through the half-open,
steel-barred and armaglass gate of the floor's guard post
and designated kill zone. Ryan remembered the sign
on the wall that read: NO UNAUTHORIZED PER-
SONNEL BEYOND THIS POINT. And the machine-
blaster posts staggered on either side of the hall.

Just beyond the kill zone's second gate, they picked
up a tail of enforcers. The creatures shot out of a side
corridor and fell right into step behind them.

Jak slammed through the stairwell door, and they
started up, taking the steps three at a time.

At the first landing Ryan looked back and down, letting the others pass him. Enforcers were pouring through the shaft's entrance. He didn't pull a thermite gren, though. There were precious few of them left. To maximize the body count, he had to wait until the stairwell was fully packed.

He was halfway up the next flight when he saw the door on the landing above swing open. As it banged back and an enforcer jumped out, Mildred was just passing. Instinctively she swung up the Desert Eagle. The creature stuck out its arms to grab her, closing the gap in a single stride. The gold handgun boomed in her hands, spitting a heavy slug and three feet of crackling fire. The slug knocked the enforcer's head to one side. As it snapped back, the blaze caught, first on its cheek, then shooting across the top of its head. It beat its face, but that only spread the flames to its hands.

As Ryan ducked past, fire engulfed it from the waist up. Blinded, it turned left, missed the first descending step and fell head over heels down the staircase like a burning tumbleweed.

The enforcers coming up from below were gaining ground until that moment. As he turned to go up the next flight, for a split second he could see below him. The creatures had needed to stop and flatten themselves against the opposite wall to keep from being hit and ignited by one of their own.

The breathing room didn't last long. At the next floor, the stairwell door banged back as he passed it. The enforcers were scenting them, like bloodhounds. He didn't pause as he turned for the next flight up, but he shouted over the alarm's wail. "Mildred!"

She spun around on the landing above, the Desert

Eagle in both hands. He took three steps in a single bound, then saw the expression on her face. Before he could flatten, she fired twice. The muzzle-blasts numbed the right side of his face and made that ear go dead.

As he scrambled up beside her, she took her first step down. The powerful handblaster roared again and again. Ryan looked back to see her shoot point-blank into an enforcer's face. Another of the creatures was already on fire from the chin up, whirling in panic. With a flash of light and heat, the second enforcer's head simultaneously jolted and ignited. When the two blind bastards collided, they locked arms around each other like long-lost friends. They maintained their balance and the embrace for a fraction of a second before toppling head first down the stairs in a double fireball.

Again they were granted precious time.

They still had a lead when they burst through the door to the redoubt's ground floor, but it was only about a hundred feet. There still weren't enough enforcers in the stairwell to merit using one the last thermite grens. Either most of them had died in the mat-trans anteroom or there weren't that many to begin with.

The question was, could they beat the enforcers to the redoubt entrance before the enforcers pulled them apart?

By the time they closed distance on the first trap, the one that blocked access to the redoubt proper just inside the vanadium door, the answer was no. On flat ground and a straightaway the enforcers could outrun them. And were doing so. One hundred feet had become seventy-five, and there was still another hundred to go. If they didn't do something, they'd be caught just inside the redoubt's entrance.

Ryan racked his brain to remember the details of what he'd seen in the automated machine-blaster post. The blasters were disconnected from the cams that automatically operated them, but that didn't mean the weapons themselves were decommissioned. He recalled seeing the belts of 7.62 mm ammo, because he had thought about scavenging some of it for his Steyr. Were the belts of linked ammo still hooked up to the feedway and ready to fire?

He made another hard decision. He decided it didn't matter because the result would be the same. The enforcers would be distracted long enough for the rest of the companions to get away. Trouble was, he couldn't do the job by himself—there were too many enforcers behind him.

"J.B.!" he shouted at his friend's back as they ran. "M-60 post coming up! You and me!"

He didn't need to say anything else. J.B. gave him a thumbs-up.

"Krysty!" he yelled. "I'm going to pin them down in the trap. You turn back and fry them! Everyone else, keep running!"

As J.B. fell back beside him, the others snaked through the steel-barred sec gate at the near end of the guard-post kill zone. He and J.B. didn't go that far. The access door to the bowed-out blaster turret stood open. They ducked inside the cramped space. There wasn't time for a discussion of who was supposed to do what. Ryan knelt behind the M-60 on the far left; J.B. took the one on the right. Ryan could feel the tramp of heavy feet through the concrete. He checked the feedway and found the belt correctly connected. Two flicks of the charging handle advanced a new but tarnished 7.62 mm round into firing position.

J.B. finished brief seconds before him. He just had time to thumb his glasses up the bridge of his nose before the enforcers appeared at the sec gate.

There was no way to aim through the horizontal firing slot—there wasn't enough room behind the blasters. But aiming was optional. The machine blasters were set up to cut human-size targets in two. All that mattered was Ryan timing his burst so the first one in line was hit before it cleared the maximum arc of fire.

Holding his head low, he tracked the movement in the corridor through the firing slot. Instead of leading his target, swinging the sights through it, he veered the blaster into the target with the trigger pinned. The M-60 roared, spewing lead at five hundred rounds a minute. Smoking hulls streamed from the ejection port. The first bastard was going nowhere. J.B. joined him in the onslaught, working on the other end of the line of enforcers, doubling the roar and the rounds per minute.

On the other side of the turret, Ryan visualized the enforcers, trapped between blazing blaster barrels, pinned against the backstop by an unbroken torrent of lead. They'd be unhurt but unable to move forward or back.

Dammit, hurry, Krysty! he thought.

Ryan didn't hear the soft whoosh of a thermite gren's ignition. He couldn't hear anything for the clatter of the machine blasters in the narrow space, not even the blaring Klaxon horn. Then a searing blast of heat and light shot through the firing port, and he knew Krysty had done her part. He let go of the M-60's pistol grip and shoved J.B. toward the access door.

They hit the deck as the fireball behind them bloomed larger and the stacked canisters of M-60 belted ammo began to cook off.

Ryan and J.B. lay on their bellies on the floor with their fingers in their ears until the ammo stopped exploding and the ricochets stopped flying.

"We did it," Ryan said as he sat up.

"Black dust, we sure did!"

The others were waiting for them outside. From the height of the sun and the heat, it appeared to be midafternoon. The loss or gain in time that had happened in transit seemed unimportant as the companions joyously reunited. It was as if they hadn't seen each other in years. The backslaps and congratulations were interrupted by the sound of wag engines starting up; everyone stopped what they were doing and dug for their blasters.

Ryan was looking over the scope of his Steyr as a big Winnie lurched into view above the rim of an arroyo and then sped toward the dirt access road they'd come in on. He didn't have a clear shot on the driver because of the sun reflecting off the windshield. It made a brilliant starburst right in front of the steering wheel. The Winnie was followed by two pickups.

As the wags sped past, Ryan saw a figure behind one of the rear windows. It motioned with a hand.

"Is that who I think it is?" Doc asked.

"No, that's *what* you think it is," Mildred said.

Ryan shouldered the Steyr and touched off a shot, but the already-falling, bulletproof window shutter blocked it at the last second. The round sparked on the steel and zinged off across the desert.

They watched helplessly as the Winnie and other wags zoomed away in a cloud of red dust.

"Did Magus just give us the finger?" Mildred asked.

"The steel finger," Doc corrected her.

"Nukin' hell," J.B. said.

SINCE MAGUS HAD left behind the camp of circled wags, Ryan suggested they spend the night in comfort instead of on the ground. They would pick up their dirt bikes early in the morning, when it was still cool outside. There were no objections to that, or to stealing Steel Eyes's wag fuel, or eating the food and drinking the water still in the wags. Before they settled in, he had Ricky rig a boobie inside the redoubt entrance using the remaining thermite grens. That was in case any surviving enforcers decided to come pay them a visit after dark.

As the sun dipped below the western mountain, they were all seated around the camp's fire pit, enjoying the dancing flames and full bellies. The desert air smelled sweet and clean. In the distance a coyote yipped; it was answered a few seconds later by another series of yips.

They were hunting something, Ryan knew, maybe a mated pair working in tandem, giving each other directions from either side of the arroyo. He found that thought deeply satisfying. And the sounds, too. He knew he was really home.

"So, how did Magus come back to life?" J.B. said. "Anybody care to speculate? I think we can all agree on the fact we saw that broken corpse in 2001."

"Guess what we saw was just one of the many," Mildred said.

"We're never going to figure it out," Krysty added.

"Not enough information. The important things are we all made it back safe and the time hole is closed. Magus won't ever be able to use it again."

There were grunts of agreement around the campfire.

Then Doc spoke up. "It is all over by now," he said disconsolately.

"What's over?" Mildred said.

"In 2001 it's already well past noon. Vee's gone."

"Doc, what are you talking about?" Mildred said. "'Well past noon'? That happened more than a hundred years ago."

"It does not seem that way to me," he said. "Seems like I just said goodbye to her."

"Me, too," Ricky chimed in. The youth looked as gut shot as Doc.

"But you didn't just say goodbye to her," Mildred told them. "You said it a century ago. We all did."

"You can't change what's past, Doc," Krysty said gently.

"That does not mean that it is painless," he said. "I still dream about Emily and the children." The old man sniffed.

Then he rose to his feet, walked over to Ricky and extended his open hand. "No hard feelings," he said. "We both lost something precious—whether it was today, a hundred years ago is immaterial."

Ricky got up and grabbed Doc's hand. As he shook it he said, "We'll never forget her, Doc."

"Never, my dear boy."

Epilogue

Vee slowed the Subaru station wagon as she approached the international-border crossing. A Mexican immigration officer in a gray-and-brown uniform, hat and mirrored sunglasses stood beside what looked like a miniature traffic light. Green. Yellow. Red. She slowed the Subaru to a crawl, keeping her eyes on the light. The light was green and it stayed green. There would be no spot check, no pulling over into the adjoining parking lot for a vehicle search and document inspection. A wave of relief passed over her. As she rolled by the officer, she smiled at him. His eyes were hidden behind the sunglasses, but the mouth below the pencil mustache smiled back.

The road ahead was open. Four lanes of freedom lay ahead.

Nukeday had never come to pass.

Not in her universe anyway.

After Doc had explained the Armageddon scenario that had created Deathlands, she had become more and more convinced that a different script was being written by the chaos of overlapping time lines, a script that didn't include an all-out missile exchange.

In the days after January 20, 2001, the media had broken an amazing story about a frantic, three-way, red-telephone conversation—Russian premier, one soon to be ex-President, one President to be—that had temporarily overridden all contingency plans for nuke first strikes and counterattacks. Clearly, outside forces, extra-governmental forces, were at work in Manhattan.

As nervous about terrorists as his American counterparts, the premier had offered whatever aid and assistance he and his nation could provide. Long story short, the worst disaster in the history of humankind had turned into a "Kumbaya" moment.

Vee understood, though, that in some alternative universe, she had died that day, that the world had been nuked, and that a one-eyed leader and his crew were caught in a future fighting to survive.

It was too terrible to imagine.

When her world didn't end as promised, Vee found herself left holding a big bag of brown. And there was no going back to her former life. Not unless she wanted to spend the next twenty years in prison first.

Vee had never thought of herself as a surrendering kind of person.

Luckily she had an option. She'd dyed her hair platinum blonde and got some blue contact lenses. She'd have to get used to a new name on her passport. Her freedom depended on it.

Turned out her cat-loving neighbor Mrs. Blair had taken in Talu, Petey and Lucy for safekeeping after the first terrorist attack.

The five of them—Vee, the three cats and a striped, replacement Desert Eagle—were en route to a little fishing village on Banderas Bay, north of Puerto Vallarta, where there were no high-rises and her savings would last them a good while.

And she had an idea for a new series of books.

* * * * *

COMING NEXT MONTH FROM

GOLD EAGLE®

Available April 7, 2015

THE EXECUTIONER® #437
ASSASSIN'S TRIPWIRE – *Don Pendleton*

American high-tech ordnance has gone missing en route to Syria. Determined to destroy the stolen weapons before they can be used, Mack Bolan discovers nothing is what it seems between the Syrian regime, the loyalists and the beautiful double agent working with him.

SUPERBOLAN™ #173
ARMED RESPONSE – *Don Pendleton*

A rogue general sets out to stage a coup in the drought-stricken Republic of Djibouti. Hunted by the police and the army and targeted by assassins, Mack Bolan won't stop until the general and his collaborators face their retribution.

STONY MAN® #136
DOUBLE BLINDSIDE – *Don Pendleton*

The killing of US operatives in Turkey threatens US–Turkish relations. While Able Team moves to neutralize the threat in the States, Phoenix Force heads overseas, where they discover the dead agents are just the beginning.

COMING SOON FROM

GOLD EAGLE ®

Available May 5, 2015

THE EXECUTIONER® #438
THE CARTEL HIT – *Don Pendleton*

Facing off against a Mexican cartel, the Executioner races to secure the lone witness to a brutal double murder.

DEATHLANDS® #122
FORBIDDEN TRESPASS – *James Axler*

While Ryan and the companions take on a horde of hungry cannibals, something far more sinister—and ravenous—lurks beneath their feet...

OUTLANDERS® #73
HELL'S MAW – *James Axler*

The Cerberus warriors must confront an alien goddess who can control men's minds. But are they strong enough to eliminate this evil interloper bent on global domination?

ROGUE ANGEL™ #54
DAY OF ATONEMENT – *Alex Archer*

A vengeful fanatic named Cauchon plans to single-handedly resurrect the violence of the Inquisition to put Annja and Roux on trial... and a guilty verdict could mean death.

Ryan wanted the enemy to run, and preferably not stop until he and his companions had escaped.

He saw J.B. coolly step into the road and fire a medium burst from his Uzi. A man to Ryan's left screamed and clutched his paunch as a line of red dots was stitched across it. He fell howling and kicking to the ground.

Ryan shifted targets and fired. Another man fell.

The chill joined at least a dozen others fallen in the roadway. At the rear of the mob, which had lost momentum and had begun to mill about, Ryan saw a tall woman, just visible before the bend. She had raven-black hair and creamy skin. She looked shocked, and her eyes were wide.

It was Wymie, the woman responsible for all their problems—including the fact they were now fighting for their lives against what seemed like half the population of the ville.

"Fireblast," he said, and lowered his aim to shoot a young man trying to point some kind of flintlock at them.

"Why didn't you chill her, lover?" Krysty called from the cover of the nettles across the road.

"She's the leader," he called back. "She's beat. She'll spread her exhaustion to the rest once we chill or drive off the hard core."

Even as he said that, he saw it start to happen. The initial volley of blasterfire from his team, crouched in cover to either side of the thoroughfare, had dropped so many of the attackers they formed a living roadblock. Those behind, mad-eyed and baying for blood a heartbeat before, now faltered. This mob had clearly let self-preservation reassert itself in the face of their waning bloodlust.

They were done. It was all over but for the fleeing.

Then, from the corner of his lone eye, Ryan saw a skinny old man, standing by the side of the road, leveling a single-action Peacemaker at Ryan's head.

He already knew he was nuked, even as his brain sent his body the impulse to dive aside.

The ancient blaster and its ancient shooter alike vanished in a giant yellow muzzle-flash. It instantly echoed in a blinding red flash inside Ryan's skull.

Then blackness. Then nothing.

Don't miss
FORBIDDEN TRESPASS by James Axler,
available May 2015 wherever
Gold Eagle® books and ebooks are sold.